# MYSTERY LOVER
## Vicki Lewis Thompson

D0053203

# *Do* you *have a midnight fantasy?*

### *Mystery Lover—Vicki Lewis Thompson*

B. J. Branscom has always fantasized about sexy
Jonas Garfield, but he's always only considered B.J.
a friend. Now she has a chance to seduce him
senseless—and she's going to do it incognito...

### *After Hours—Stephanie Bond*

Rebecca Valentine has given up on dating. Now she
uses her costume shop to indulge in her fantasies of
being someone else...*with* someone else. But when
Michael Pierce walks into her shop, she never dreams
he'll insist on joining in on her fantasy, too...

### *Show and Tell—Kimberly Raye*

The adopted daughter of a small-town judge,
Laney Merriweather has always had to be very,
very good. Only now, this *good girl* wants *bad boy*
Dallas Jericho. And the time has come to let him—
and everybody in town—see it...

# Midnight Fantasies

*Some daydreams last well into the night...*

Award-winning author *Vicki Lewis Thompson* hangs her hat in Arizona, where the sun's hot and the chili peppers are even hotter. And her more than fifty sizzling romances fit right into the landscape. If you enjoy *Mystery Lover,* don't miss the sequel, *Notorious,* the first book in the new Harlequin Blaze line. *Notorious* will hit the shelves in August and is guaranteed to send the mercury soaring.

*Stephanie Bond,* who lives in downtown Hot-Lanta, loves a chance to turn up the heat. Known for her outrageously sexy comedies, Stephanie enjoys writing about young women who are old enough to know what they want from a man, women who are strong and determined, yet have a weakness for red shoes and sexy, noble guys. Don't miss Stephanie's next book, *Two Sexy!,* the sequel to *After Hours,* also available in August.

*Kimberly Raye* has always been an incurable romantic, so romance writing is the perfect job! At the moment, she's hard at work on *The Pleasure Principle,* her upcoming September release for Harlequin Blaze, which is linked to her novella, *Show and Tell.* Both stories feature her favorite type of hero—a rough-and-tough cowboy with tight jeans and a killer smile! Kim lives in the Lone Star State with her very own cowboy and young son, Joshua.

# Midnight Fantasies

## Vicki Lewis Thompson

## Stephanie Bond
## Kimberly Raye

*Three sizzling love stories
by today's hottest writers...*

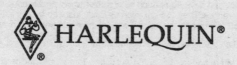

# HARLEQUIN®

TORONTO • NEW YORK • LONDON
AMSTERDAM • PARIS • SYDNEY • HAMBURG
STOCKHOLM • ATHENS • TOKYO • MILAN • MADRID
PRAGUE • WARSAW • BUDAPEST • AUCKLAND

ISBN 0-373-83464-0

MIDNIGHT FANTASIES

Copyright © 2001 by Harlequin Books S.A.

The publisher acknowledges the copyright holders of the individual works as follows:

MYSTERY LOVER
Copyright © 2001 by Vicki Lewis Thompson

AFTER HOURS
Copyright © 2001 by Stephanie Bond Hauck

SHOW AND TELL
Copyright © 2001 by Kimberly Raye Rangel

This edition published by arrangement with Harlequin Books S.A.

® and TM are trademarks of the publisher. Trademarks indicated with ® are registered in the United States Patent and Trademark Office, the Canadian Trade Marks Office and in other countries.

Visit us at www.eHarlequin.com

**Printed in U.S.A.**

# CONTENTS

# CHAPTER ONE

RAIN SLUICED DOWN to the desert floor, warm and heavy, soaking B.J.'s T-shirt in under ten seconds. She didn't care. A good summer downpour brought her almost as much satisfaction as a good orgasm. These days a downpour seemed a more likely source of satisfaction.

Unfortunately her horse, Hot Stuff, wasn't big on getting drenched. Some trauma from his childhood, no doubt. B.J. had all she could do to keep the gelding from bucking her off. She knotted the reins in case he succeeded, so he wouldn't step on them and cause more problems. Even if she stayed on this horse, the ride back to the ranch promised to be rough.

The storm had blown in suddenly, catching her coming back from a neighborly good deed for a newcomer to the area. Sarah was a sculptor, and she'd rented a little house about five miles away. She'd asked B.J. to pick up her mail and water her

plants for a week while she went to a gallery showing in New York.

Tightening her thigh muscles as Hot Stuff crow-
hopped another ten yards, B.J. estimated the distance to the barn. Then she estimated the distance
to a cozy cave where she and her sister had played
as kids. The cave was closer.

She wrestled Hot Stuff's head around and
pointed him in the direction of the cave. The rolling
hills in this particular part of Southern Arizona were
strewn with large granite outcroppings. Two particularly huge ones had sparked the name of the
ranch—Twin Boulders. Many jokes had been made
over the years about the phallic significance of
those jutting pieces of stone.

As if to balance out the maleness of such a prominent formation, another cluster of rocks closer to
the mountains contained a cave about the size of a
three-person dome tent. Assuming the flashlight in
her saddlebag revealed no snakes, she'd wait inside.
Hot Stuff could cool his heels outside until he was
ready to become civilized again and then they could
mosey on home.

Soon the cave appeared in front of her, the boulders shellacked with rain. The deluge kept coming,
running off her hat in a steady stream. Keeping a

tight rein on Hot Stuff, she spoke soothingly to him and kept an eye on the tilt of his ears while she reached behind her to dig the flashlight out of the water-slicked saddlebag.

As her hand closed around the barrel of the flashlight, the wind gusted, throwing water in Hot Stuff's face. He laid his ears back and leaped into the air with such force that she lost her stirrups. Then he launched into another twisting maneuver creative enough to land her in the mud on her butt.

Still clutching the flashlight, she scrambled to her feet. Before she could grab the reins, Hot Stuff took off in the direction of the ranch.

B.J. sighed, more angry than alarmed. The horse should be okay. The reins were still looped over the saddle horn and he knew his way back. As long as no one noticed him coming in riderless, which might cause a panic, there would be no harm done except for the long walk ahead of her.

Fortunately her dad and Noah had driven into town to run some errands so they wouldn't be there to notice Hot Stuff had dumped her. That left Noah's brother Jonas, and she didn't think he'd be hanging around when her father and Noah weren't on hand to suggest he spend a rainy afternoon cleaning tack. Given the choice, Jonas much pre-

ferred whiling away the hours in the arms of which-
ever girlfriend was currently in favor.

As she debated whether to follow her horse home
since she was already wet and muddy, the rain
turned to hail that ricocheted off her hat and bit the
exposed skin of her arms. She was willing to walk
in the rain and the mud, but being pelted with hail
was a whole other thing. Flashlight in hand, she
turned toward the cave.

Passing the beam over the entrance, she took off
her hat, stooped and went in. As a kid she hadn't
had to stoop, and about the time she'd grown too
tall to walk in without crouching, she'd decided to
abandon the cave. Yet for years it had been the
perfect hideout.

She and her sister Keely had spent hours in here
planning battle strategies against Noah and Jonas.
For some reason the girls had been allowed to keep
the cave to themselves, probably because the boys
had built a tree house they thought was more stra-
tegic and far more cool because they could pull up
the rope ladder and be isolated.

Funny how the dank smell of the cave instantly
brought back those days. She ran the flashlight
beam over the dirt floor and the smooth rock ledge
that had served as table, chair or bed, depending on

what adventure she and Keely had been cooking up at the time. Except for some leaves that had blown in, the cave was empty and dry.

Brushing the leaves off the rock ledge, she sat down. Then she hung her hat on an outcropping they'd once used to suspend an electric lantern. But she wasn't drawing treasure maps or decoding messages today, so she didn't need to see. She switched off the flashlight.

Outside the hail continued to fall, bouncing up from the ground like popcorn. She leaned back against the cave wall and watched. Despite her wet clothes, she felt snug and protected, the way she always had inside this place.

But all the memories swirling around in her head made her miss Keely terribly. She'd never known their mother, who'd died when B.J. was born, so her older sister had been doubly important to her. In the beginning they'd had an ideal childhood. Their dad, Arch Branscom, was the head wrangler for Twin Boulders, owned originally by George Garfield, a widower and father of Noah and Jonas.

The four kids had grown up almost like brothers and sisters. But then Keely had hit puberty with a vengeance and nobody on the ranch had seemed to know what to do about that. Keely's rebellion had escalated until she'd posed nude for the centerfold of *Macho* magazine at the age of nineteen. After a huge fight with Arch, she'd left and had never come back.

That had been ten years ago. Most of the time B.J. tried not to think about her sister, but in this musty cave, she couldn't help it. Nothing had turned out the way she'd dreamed it would as a kid. She'd imagined Keely would marry Noah and she would marry Jonas.

Now Keely was who-knew-where, and Noah seemed too busy for romance now that his father had died and he was responsible for the ranch. As for Jonas, he more than made up for Noah's lack of interest in female companionship. Jonas had turned into the Romeo of Saguaro Junction. He seemed to have the hots for every eligible woman in the county, with the exception of B.J.

She could only think of two possible reasons for that. Number one, he considered both her and Keely as sisters, so they were off-limits. Number two, he'd never seen her in anything other than dusty jeans, never watched her do anything but ride and rope like a good ranch hand was supposed to. That hardly contributed to her sex appeal. Even her nickname, B.J., made her sound like one of the guys.

No doubt Jonas had forgotten it stood for Belinda June.

A few times she'd thought of putting on something sexy to see if she could change his perception of her, but she never had. For one thing, she didn't want to risk the humiliation if he failed to react. For another, she couldn't bear to be nothing more than one of his many conquests. If she couldn't get rid of her secret yearning for him, at least she had a dose of pride to go with it.

The hail had let up some, but the rain seemed even heavier. B.J. decided to wait it out. Just for something to do, she pulled her long braid over her shoulder, took off the elastic holding the end and unbraided her hair. Ah, that felt better. She massaged her scalp and finger-combed her long hair, made wavy by the braid. And that was another thing—Jonas hadn't seen her with her hair down in years.

The sound of hoofbeats from outside the cave surprised her. Surely Hot Stuff hadn't circled back. Trigger he definitely wasn't.

"Easy, son, easy. Sonofabitch. It's really coming down."

*Jonas.* That was sort of weird, considering she'd just been thinking about him. She started to call out and warn him that she was in here. With no horse outside, he wouldn't expect to find her waiting for him and it might scare the stuffing out of him.

Then she closed her mouth again. Maybe it was her rekindled memories of all the pranks the boys had pulled, and all the times she and her sister had plotted revenge, or maybe it was her general dissatisfaction with Jonas's lifestyle these days, but she had the childish urge to make him yelp in fear.

She heard him sloshing through the mud toward the cave, and her heart beat faster. This would be fun. Of course, if he had a flashlight, then he'd see her right away, but he still might yell when the beam hit her. Maybe she'd make a face at him, to unnerve him even more.

As he approached, he uttered a colorful curse. "Dead batteries. Perfect. I have a choice of getting drowned or snakebit. Okay, snakes, look out! I'm coming in!"

While B.J. held her breath, he took off his hat and ducked into the cave. Then he paused, as if listening for a telltale rattle. "So far, so good," he muttered.

She stayed very still.

"All right, snakes! If you're here, make yourself

known!'' He crept slowly over to the ledge where she sat.

With the light from the cave's entrance at his back, she could make out his movements, but obviously he couldn't see her.

He reached toward the ledge and his hand closed over her thigh. *"Jesus!"* He leaped backward, bumping his head on the top of the cave. "Who's there?''

She clapped a hand over her mouth to hold back her laughter, because in that split second she decided not to tell him who she was. Maybe he wouldn't guess right away, and she could pretend to be meeting him for the first time. It could be interesting. "My...my name's...Sarah,'' she said in a voice made husky by the laughter she'd swallowed.

He crouched, rubbing his head. "Well, you scared the hell out of me, Sarah.''

Amazing. He hadn't recognized her voice. She'd need to keep it lowered when she talked, though, or he'd know it was her. "Sorry,'' she said.

"How come you didn't say anything when I started in?''

"You scared me, too.'' She discovered it wasn't

as hard to disguise her voice as she'd expected. "When I get scared my throat closes up."

"Oh. Well, I'm sorry, then. I guess you came in to get out of the rain, too, huh?"

"Yes." She breathed in the scent of damp male and the spicy aftershave that was Jonas's trademark. This was more exciting than she'd imagined it would be, sort of like a masquerade ball. The cave was growing darker, she noticed, as the afternoon light grew weaker. That would keep him guessing for a little longer, anyway.

"Are you from around here?" he asked. "I don't think I know anybody named Sarah."

*Good. He hadn't met Sarah yet.* "I just moved in."

"That explains it. Come to think of it, I did hear about a woman who was renting the old Hawthorne place. An artist."

"That would be me. I sculpt." B.J. decided she might as well milk this for all it was worth. Then she'd confess the charade to Sarah when she came back. From what B.J. knew of Sarah, she'd probably get a kick out of the whole thing.

"Really? I don't think I've ever known a sculptor. So you carve statues and stuff?"

B.J. thought of Sarah's work created from discarded pieces of machinery. Fascinating, but not particularly sexy. "I love the human body," she said, "so I sculpt mostly nudes." She swallowed another bubble of laughter. Nude statues. That should flick his Bic.

"Really? Men or women?"

"Both, but I'm especially fond of the male physique. I'd have to say that's my favorite subject."

"Now that's interesting." He sounded plenty interested, too. His voice had become a little rougher, a little deeper.

A thrill of awareness shot through her. He'd never spoken to her in that tone of voice. No wonder women flocked to him. That voice was a killer.

She realized he couldn't be particularly comfortable standing hunched over like that, and the polite thing would be to suggest he share the ledge with her. If he'd known who she was, that would have been no big deal. But he thought she was someone else, a new and potentially uninhibited person who sculpted nudes, mostly male nudes. She wondered what he'd do in close proximity to such a woman.

Only one way to find out. She slid over toward the wall and quietly put her flashlight on the ground at her feet. "If you'd like to sit down, there's room for two on this ledge," she said.

"Thank you. I'd appreciate that." He started toward her.

Her skin flushed and her heart beat so fast she was afraid he might sense her agitation. She almost lost her nerve and told him who she was. Then she thought of her sister Keely. In this same situation, Keely would play this situation to the hilt.

"Sure is dark in here," he said. "I can barely see you."

"I'm right here." She took a deep breath for courage and reached out for him. "Give me your hand. I'll guide you over."

In the dim light his hand found hers. Contact. And what contact. She tried to imagine why it felt so different, so electric.

She'd certainly touched Jonas before. As kids they'd thought nothing of grabbing each other in the course of a game or a fight. As adults they occasionally had to touch as part of working together on the ranch, but it had always been efficient and impersonal.

Yet here in the cave, when he thought she was an exotic stranger, his skin seemed warmer, his grasp tighter. This must be how he touched women he was attracted to.

''Come a little closer.'' She drew him toward the ledge. ''Okay, now turn around and sit.''

He followed her instructions, settling next to her, his thigh against hers, his shoulder brushing hers. Damn, but he smelled sexy. What's more, he hadn't let go of her hand.

''There's not a lot of extra room,'' he said.

Sitting this close to Jonas and pretending to be someone else was really turning her on. Things she'd never have said otherwise came easily to her. ''I don't mind the tight fit if you don't.'' She gave his hand a gentle, encouraging squeeze.

''You won't hear me complaining.'' He squeezed back. ''Your fingers feel good,'' he said, rubbing his thumb across hers in a subtle caress. ''Soft, yet strong.''

Her breath caught. He was coming on to her. Maybe once he'd decided she was a stranger, he'd stopped looking for clues that would have told him she was his old pal B.J.

Obviously she could do almost anything she wanted and he wouldn't guess now. So she needed to decide how far to take this little charade. Truth or dare? *Dare.* ''My hands are strong from molding the clay,'' she said. ''I love how it feels when I work it, so moist…so…pliable. I find the process very stimulating.''

''I'll bet you do.'' He cradled her hand in both of his and began a gentle massage. ''I'd love to watch you work with that clay sometime.''

''Oh, I don't think so. I need my space when I create.'' The devil had got hold of her tongue. ''And in this heat, I've been known to work without any clothes on.''

''You shouldn't have told me that,'' he murmured, bringing her hand to his lips. ''Now I really want to watch you work. Watch you get…stimulated.'' He brushed her knuckles with a gentle kiss.

She nearly passed out from the pleasure of it. Years ago, she used to imagine scenes like this with Jonas, and then she'd given up all hope that they'd ever get past their brother/sister relationship. Yet here he was, pressing his mouth to the back of her hand. Of course, he thought it was the hand of a sculptor named Sarah, a woman who molded clay into nudes while she waltzed around her studio in her birthday suit feeling sexy.

''Maybe I could make an exception and let you watch,'' she said. ''Although I have a feeling you would distract me.''

"I'd be very quiet." He opened her palm and circled his tongue there.

She tried to steady her breathing. A woman of the world wouldn't fall apart because a man was kissing her hand. "What's...what's your name?" she asked.

"Jonas." His breath whispered over the inside of her wrist. "You smell like rain," he said, just before he placed his warm mouth against her pulse.

"Jonas." She murmured his name, rolling it over her tongue as if she'd never heard it before, as if she'd never yelled it across the yard or muttered it under her breath in total frustration. "Do you believe in Fate, Jonas?"

"Maybe." He cupped her elbow and lazily made his way from her wrist to the inside of her elbow. "Do you?"

"Maybe." Her heart thundered in her ears. Surely the more he touched her, the better his chance of figuring out who was in this cave with him. But until he did figure it out, she might as well enjoy the fantasy. Chances like this didn't come along every day.

"I sure never expected to find someone like you here today." He caressed the tender inside of her elbow with slow strokes of his finger.

"Someone like me?" The breathy laugh didn't sound like her. It sounded like a daring woman who created nudes for a living. "You know almost nothing about me."

"I know more than you think." He shifted his weight, bending one knee so he could turn toward her on the ledge. "I know you're very creative. I know you spend your days exploring the wonders of the human body, and as a sculptor, you'd have to be very sensitive."

"I am."

"I knew it. I could tell from the way you shivered when I kissed the inside of your arm." His hand brushed her cheek in a seeking gesture. Then he caressed the line of her jaw. "And while it's true I can't see you very well, all my other senses are wide-awake. I know you have smooth, soft skin, that you smell like rain, that your voice is low and makes me think of sex."

She swallowed and tried to keep her voice steady. "Really?" He definitely didn't know who she was. Jonas had never, ever thought of sex when she was around.

"You shouldn't be surprised." He brought his other hand up and combed it through her hair. "You're obviously a very sensual woman, a woman who likes to let her hair down. You have beautiful hair. What color is it?''

She thought quickly. No use giving him any clues by telling him the right hair color. Once he started thinking of her as a blonde, he might put two and two together. ''Chocolate-brown,'' she said.

''Perfect. I love chocolate.'' He drew a section over her shoulder and combed it down over her breast, although he seemed to take care not to touch her there...yet. ''And your eyes?''

''Jade-green.'' She'd always wished they were, at any rate. Keely had green eyes, but B.J. had ended up with blue.

''Jade-green.'' He ran his thumb gently over her lower lip. ''Most women would say they had brown hair and green eyes, but you added the chocolate and the jade part. I have a feeling you're a very unusual woman, Sarah. I'd like to get to know you better.''

She'd begun to tremble with anticipation. He was going to kiss her. She would finally find out what it was like to kiss Jonas. But if she expected to keep him mystified, she had to treat this moment the way a sophisticated woman would. In other words, she had to act, instead of being acted upon.

"We seem to have some time on our hands." She tried to think what Keely would do under these circumstances. Summoning all her courage, she reached over and began toying with a button on his shirt. "Maybe we should make use of it to…get to know each other." She unfastened the button.

He drew in a breath. "I couldn't have said it better."

The more she dared, the bolder she became. She undid the next button, and the next, while his breath quickened. She was exciting him, exciting this man who'd made love to more women than she cared to think about. "Your shirt's wet. That can't be very comfortable." Using both hands, she pulled it from the waistband of his jeans. "Let's take it off."

"What an incredible woman you are."

"Ah, but you're quite incredible, yourself." She pushed the shirt off his shoulders, lingering over the process, caressing him. "Such muscles. I would love to sculpt you."

"Anytime." His voice quivered slightly.

That quiver brought a dizzying rush of power. So this was what it felt like to have a man totally under her spell. What a delicious experience.

She leaned forward slowly, breathing in his scent. Although she recognized it as belonging to

Jonas, she'd never experienced the underlying note of arousal that spiced his skin now. She moistened her lips and pressed them against the curve of his shoulder.

His skin was cool from the dampness of his shirt, but it warmed quickly under her mouth. He tasted forbidden. Forbidden and sweet. Heart pounding, she ran her tongue along his collarbone and nuzzled his throat.

"Oh, *Sarah*." He combed trembling fingers through her hair. "Sarah, you're driving me crazy."

"I intend to." She outlined his jaw with teasing, nibbling kisses. "Just relax and let it happen."

"Oh, Lord." He began to shake.

She'd made him want her so much he was *shaking*. She couldn't get over it. She'd never seduced a man before. Who knew it was so simple? Only one little problem. She was shaking, too.

To steady herself, she cupped the back of his head with both hands. "I want you to kiss me, now," she murmured, lifting her mouth to his. "Kiss me, Jonas."

With a soft groan he settled his lips over hers. With that first meeting, mouth-to-mouth, tongue-to-tongue, she forgot to play the role of the experienced woman of the world. She whimpered with delight.

Apparently that only inflamed him more, because he groaned again and took the kiss even deeper.

She'd never been kissed like this—full-out, no holds barred—and she wallowed in it. Slackening her jaw, she gave him all the access he wanted. They kissed, shifted angles and kissed again, came up for air and went back to kissing again.

They were both gasping when Jonas finally drew back a fraction. "Your clothes...are wet...too," he said as he struggled for breath.

She gulped for air. "Yes."

"Sarah...let me...touch you."

## CHAPTER TWO

EVER SINCE HE'D LOST HIS virginity at fifteen, Jonas had dedicated a good part of his time to loving women, and he'd had some amazing experiences. But nothing like this. He'd never come across a free-spirited temptress by accident and found her ready and willing to play.

And Sarah was more than willing. Sarah. He didn't even know her last name, and he probably wouldn't recognize her if he passed her on the street. That made this escapade even more exciting. He'd never made love to a complete stranger before.

And yet, she didn't feel like a stranger. Something about her seemed familiar and right. That made no sense, because he was positive he'd never known anybody named Sarah. He'd been involved with a lot of women, but he could recite each of their names and phone numbers. Still. If he closed his eyes, he could also remember the shape of their breasts and the color of the soft curls between their thighs.

He'd given some thought to marriage over the years, but he required two qualities in a wife—a good heart and a wild imagination. So far he'd never found both in the same woman. He already knew Sarah possessed one of them.

Her breath tickled his mouth. "Take off whatever you like," she said in a voice richer than fine whiskey.

He wanted to shout *everything,* but this was a classy woman. She probably expected finesse and a gradual undressing. So he'd oblige her. "Let's start with this." Slowly he drew the hem of her T-shirt out of her jeans.

"All right." She leaned back, a shadowy creature out of his dearest wet dreams. "Go ahead." Then she raised her arms.

He pulled the shirt off mostly by feel. He really couldn't see what he was doing, but he was discovering that operating only by feel provided its own special reward. He dropped her shirt to the floor of the cave.

Then, before he could reach for her, she took hold of his wrists and guided his hands to her lace-covered breasts. "I believe this is what you wanted," she said.

His moan of agreement sounded as if someone had him by the throat. His hands trembled, and he couldn't remember ever feeling such promising sweetness in his life. His mouth watered.

"Let me undo the hooks," she murmured. She reached both hands behind her back and arched toward him.

He couldn't wait. With another moan he cupped the breasts she'd thrust toward him and leaned down to close his mouth over one lace-covered nipple.

"Impatient, are you?"

Her teasing words doubled his hunger. With a soft growl he nipped at the lace until it went slack in his hands. Then he pulled it away and dropped it to the floor of the cave. As he reached for her again, she drew back.

"Wait."

He couldn't wait. Not for a second. "Sarah—"

"Let me make this easier."

*Easier.* As he listened to the sound of her boots being tossed to the floor of the cave, he decided a wise man wouldn't question her statement.

"Hold still," she whispered. Resting her hands

on his shoulders, she got to her knees on the rock ledge. "Now close your eyes."

He closed them. He could barely see her, anyway. As he waited, heart pounding and groin tight, her nipple grazed his cheek and stroked deliberately across his lips. The scent of her skin filled his nostrils as she eased her other nipple over his mouth. He groaned and lifted his hands to touch her.

"Don't do anything. Leave your hands at your sides. Let me do it. Just relax."

Out of the question. No man could be expected to relax while a woman rubbed against his face with her breasts—velvety, plump playthings that carried the scent of rainwater and desire. Yet he stopped touching her, somehow. "Sarah, let me—"

"Soon." With slow, yet constant movements she teased him, sliding back and forth, never letting a nipple rest very long against his parted lips.

He loved it. He hated it. He wanted her so much he was afraid he'd start drooling. With every gentle motion, his penis grew harder, pressing painfully against the zipper of his fly.

At last she paused, one erect nipple touching his mouth. "Now you may."

With a sigh of pleasure he sucked in and thought he might come right there. She tasted incredible and her little gasps of delight made him light-headed with desire. Then she offered her other breast, and he lifted a hand to caress the one he'd so recently enjoyed.

She grasped his hand and guided it to her belt buckle. "Here," she said softly.

Lord, she was bold. Wonderfully bold. He'd always dreamed of an encounter like this, but never imagined he'd be lucky enough to have one. His heart beating hard and fast, he unfastened her belt, undid the top button of her jeans and pulled down her zipper.

"Yes." The word came out as a sigh.

He needed no more encouragement. Her jeans and panties slipped easily over her slim hips. She lifted each knee in turn, and then, just like that, he was alone in this cave with a naked woman.

A naked woman who was guiding his mouth lower. Lord in heaven, he'd hit the lottery today. Sometimes his lovers would turn shy on him and he'd have to coax them into this maneuver he loved. But there was nothing shy about this woman if she'd take such a caress from a man she'd just met. He should have made the acquaintance of more female artists.

Or perhaps the darkness of the cave made all the

difference for her. In any case, she'd invited him to explore her most intimate treasure, which made him a happy man. He pressed his lips against her warm, salty skin, gliding down the valley between her ribs as he braced his hands on the ledge and slid to his knees on the cave floor.

Once there, he started to cup her bottom in both hands.

"No," she murmured. "No hands."

"Why?" he asked, his lips brushing her skin.

"I want...to be in charge."

He had no quarrel with that. She could direct him as long as she liked, if this was his reward. He gripped the ledge so he wouldn't forget her conditions as he continued his journey to paradise.

When he reached her belly and dipped his tongue into her naval, she quivered. Ticklish or very aroused. He'd bet on the latter. As for him, he was in agony, his penis straining to be free, to be stroked, to be brought to climax. But he would endure a little while longer.

He began to blaze a deliberate trail through her curls and her breathing quickened even more. Because he was a man who'd learned how to interpret every subtle signal a woman gave him, he listened carefully to the tempo of her breath. He knew when she paused that she was having second thoughts.

Even though she obviously longed for the intimate touch of his mouth, they were strangers. Poised on the brink of this daring adventure, she could be losing her nerve.

He didn't want that to happen. But she'd said she wanted to be in charge. Maybe she knew he could press his advantage and take the control away from her. He could. Perhaps she'd thank him for it later.

If he knew her better, he might take that chance. But he didn't really know her at all, and this moment of decision rightly belonged to her. He hesitated, the womanly scent of her beckoning him, while he let her choose.

With a moan that sounded like surrender, she leaned back on her braced hands and lifted her hips.

"Oh, Sarah. My sweet Sarah." Then he touched his tongue to that precious cleft. Ambrosia. He grew dizzy from excitement as he tasted and teased, nibbled and licked, explored new territory. Then he settled in with a more steady rhythm, coaxing her, reveling in the way she opened to him. Gradually her needy cries filled the cave and blended with the steady beat of the rain.

He'd been told he did this well, but all thought

of technique deserted him in the midst of this incredible, mysterious moment. Instinct was his only guide, instinct and the changing patterns of her breathing. Now he would always associate the scent of the rain with the scent of this woman, the sound of the raindrops with her soft pleas begging for release.

When he gave it, he nearly tumbled over the brink himself. But he didn't. He maintained enough sanity to wait and see what this woman had in mind for an encore.

Her words of gratitude spilled out between labored breaths as she sank back on her heels and leaned against the rock wall.

He ran his tongue over his lips. Delicious. He was ready to do it all again. Or maybe...maybe she would suggest that turnabout was fair play. He could deal with that.

Her breathing slowed, and the cave grew silent and thick with the passion they'd shared, the passion that still existed between them. Gradually he became aware that the rain had stopped.

She swallowed. "I need to leave, now."

"Leave?" Surely she wasn't planning to *abandon* him at a time like this, when he was full, pulsing, desperate?

"Yes, I have to go." She cleared her throat. "The rain's stopped, so there's no reason to stay in the cave anymore."

"But..." He found he couldn't ask her for what he needed. He didn't know her well enough, and for the first time in years, he was afraid of being rejected.

"Ah. Would you like some relief, yourself?"

*Well, duh.* He snorted in frustration. "It crossed my mind."

"I wish I could help you, but I really must go. I'll need my clothes. I think you're kneeling on them."

He rose to a crouch and fumbled with the tangled clothes on the cave floor. He had his pride, and he'd be damned if he'd beg her to help him out. No, ma'am. If she couldn't freely give, as he had, then to hell with—

"I'd like to repay your generosity," she said. "Would you like to meet again?"

*Oh, God, yes.* "Maybe." He handed over her clothes.

"I thought this was exciting, not being able to see each other, yet becoming very intimate. Did you think so, too?"

"It had its moments." Moments he would never, ever forget.

"I have an idea how we can keep the excitement going."

"Is that right?" He could barely make out her shadowy figure in the gloom as she pulled her T-shirt over her head. How he ached. He would ache for a week if she didn't—

"You could come over tomorrow night after dark," she said.

"Possibly." Tomorrow night was an eternity away. But he wouldn't ask for tonight, instead. He had his standards.

"I'll leave a blindfold hanging on the doorknob for you."

"Hmm." *A blindfold.* Hot damn. More fun and games. That could be worth waiting for. And he'd thought he couldn't be more aroused. Whew. The woman knew what buttons to push on this ol' boy.

"I realize you didn't get everything you might have wanted this time," she said in that low, sexy voice of hers. "But if you'll come by and put on the blindfold before you walk in, I'll even the score."

"I'd like that." Then he had an unwelcome

thought. "Listen, you're not plug-ugly, are you? Or horribly scarred from some accident?"

"What do you think?"

Then he remembered cradling her face in his hands, kissing her breasts and belly. His mouth and hands had recorded nothing but gorgeous. "I think you're beautiful. As perfect as one of your nude sculptures."

"I've been blessed with the basics," she said.

"Then why not let me look at you next time?"

"Think about it, Jonas. Didn't you find that making love to a woman you'd never seen before was a wild experience?"

"Yeah. Yeah, I did."

"Then let's explore that idea some more."

"Couldn't we just leave the lights off?"

"We could, but then I wouldn't be able to treat you to some special effects."

His voice grew husky with anticipation. "Special effects? Like what?"

"That will be my secret. Here's the absolute truth of it, Jonas. I've never been totally in charge of a lovemaking session with a man. After what happened between us this afternoon, I've discovered I really like it."

"I kind of liked it, myself." Understatement of

the year. "I've never let a woman be in charge, either." But he'd dreamed about it, he now realized. Not many women were willing to take the initiative, and he hadn't found any who seemed willing to direct the whole scenario.

"Then this is uncharted territory for both of us, a true adventure."

"How do I know you're not crazy as a bedbug?"

"Well, I guess you don't have any way of knowing that." She reached out and stroked his bare chest. "But I'm not crazy. I only want to have a little fun. Discreet fun. What do you say?"

Wild horses wouldn't keep him away from her door tomorrow night. "I might drop by."

"You have to promise to put on the blindfold. If you don't, then it's over."

"Okay."

"Tie it good and tight. No peeking. I'll get to be in charge, and I suspect that not being able to see will make the experience that much more thrilling for you."

He could imagine it would, so long as she wasn't certifiable. And even then, he was inclined to take his chances. "I'll tie it tight."

"Good. And now I have a suggestion, to help you relax."

"Which is?"

She pulled on her boots. "I suggest you take matters into your own hands."

"Aw, Sarah—"

"I'd help, but I really am late. Of course, if you want to build your anticipation for tomorrow night, you could forget my suggestion and go grab a beer at the Roundup Saloon instead. I'll bet denying yourself satisfaction will give you a really awesome orgasm when you finally get to that point."

His chest was tight with desire, his vocal cords barely working. "And will I get to that point?"

"Oh, yes." She trailed a finger down his chest. "I promise. See you tomorrow. Or rather, I'll see you, but you won't see me." She started out of the cave and turned back. "I'd go for the beer if I were you."

"Wait. Are you walking all the way home?"

"I'm not going home. After that rain, a little pool I know about will be full enough for me to go skinny-dipping."

"Oh." There was no end to this woman's sensuality. He wanted to go with her, but he knew without asking that she wouldn't allow it. And she was making the rules. He could play by them and have the sexual adventure of his life, or he could break them and possibly lose her completely.

"Until tomorrow night, then. Goodbye, Jonas."
She slipped out of the cave and walked away.

After she left he considered his options. Painful
though his erection was, he didn't relish taking care
of the problem alone in this cave. He hadn't had
much practice with denying himself, though.
Women tended to gravitate to him often enough
that satisfaction was fairly easy to obtain.

Matter of fact, he could ride over to Cathy's
house right now and expect to be asked inside. Before this cave incident, that would have seemed like
a terrific option. But a mysterious woman had captured his imagination, and he didn't think an average roll in the hay would measure up tonight.

With a sigh he picked up his shirt, shook it out,
and ducked out of the cave into the fragrant, rain-
drenched desert. He'd go for a beer.

B.J. HURRIED HOME, praying all the way that Jonas
didn't take a third option and head back to the
ranch. If he made it there ahead of her, he'd find
Hot Stuff hanging around the corral. He might not
figure out the cave thing immediately, but he'd be
worried sick about her, and she didn't want that.

But if he *did* beat her home and came out looking
for her, she'd dream up some story of getting
thrown off her horse and knocked unconscious.

Yeah, that was it. She'd been knocked out cold for the past hour.

Yet he still might wonder when he noticed that she was wearing a T-shirt that had to remind him of the woman in the cave. Oh God, what had she gotten herself into? She still couldn't believe what had happened in that cave.

Once she'd decided to adopt a different persona, she'd changed from timid B.J. to daring Sarah almost instantly. Apparently all those urges had lived within her for years waiting for a chance to be turned loose. One bold move had led to another, until she was naked and asking for... Goodness! Asking for everything. Had she really done that? Her cheeks warmed at the memory of how wantonly she'd behaved. And how powerful she'd felt.

She'd brought Jonas to heel. As Sarah the sculptor, she'd wrapped him around her little finger. And she'd loved it!

A grin teased her lips, followed by a chuckle, and finally a bubble of laughter. Lifting her arms over her head she danced a little boogie step of triumph. For the time being, the Romeo of Saguaro Junction belonged entirely to her.

## CHAPTER THREE

B.J. MADE IT HOME AHEAD of everybody. She had time to put her horse away, shower, change clothes and braid her hair before her father and Noah came back from town. Fortunately she and her dad lived in a little cottage separate from the main ranch house. She pretended exhaustion and turned in early so there was no chance she'd have to face Jonas again that night.

She'd expected to toss and turn for hours, but instead she fell into a deep, dreamless sleep and awoke feeling fantastic. As she stretched and climbed out of bed in the pale light of dawn, she decided that her bold alter ego must be good for her health. Lusty sex must be good for her, too. She'd never felt more alive.

It was early, not yet six, but Arch was already up and gone. He'd have fed the horses by now and was probably working with Noah to unload the hay they'd bought the day before. B.J. grabbed a banana and poured a cup of coffee into her favorite no-spill mug before she went out to help them.

Even this early, the rising sun had a bite to it. Today would be hot and steamy as the moisture from yesterday's rain saturated the air. B.J. glanced at a bank of clouds forming close to the mountains. Maybe it would rain again this afternoon, or maybe even tonight. *Tonight.* Despite the growing heat of the day, she felt goose bumps on her arms at the thought of making love to Jonas.

And speak of the devil. She paused when she noticed that Jonas was in the round pen putting a filly through her paces. The young horse's russet coat gleamed in the sunlight as she circled the enclosure on a long-line.

Before six in the morning was early for Jonas to be out of bed. He never had taken this ranching business as seriously as his brother. Of course Noah worked harder than he had to—everybody agreed about that. Jonas, on the other hand, did no more than was absolutely necessary, preferring to spend his spare time socializing.

Yet here he was, up and working this morning. Interesting. Despite being a football field's distance away, she knew immediately it was Jonas and not his brother. Noah was about an inch taller than

Jonas, and his hair was a lighter shade of brown. But it was the way the two men moved that identified them for B.J. Noah's motions were deliberate and sure, inspiring confidence and trust in both people and animals. Noah was steady.

On the other hand, Jonas had the innate grace of a large jungle cat. A cat on the prowl. He wore his jeans a little snugger than most men and seemed a little quicker to shed his shirt in the heat of an August day. While Noah leaned toward the cattle side of the ranch operation, Jonas liked working with the horses, and the more high-spirited, the better.

Some of the neighbors thought Jonas was lazy, but B.J. knew better. When he was interested in a project he was tireless, but tedium bored him. He rated every activity by its pleasure quotient.

Because of that, B.J. was sure that making love ranked very high on the scale. From the jut of his pelvis to the twinkle in his eye, he was obviously a man who enjoyed his own sexuality and looked for that quality in the women he met. Jonas wasn't what you'd call steady, but he sure was exciting.

Until yesterday afternoon, B.J. hadn't thought she could ever interest a man like Jonas. A flush spread through her as she recalled how completely she'd caught his interest. She wondered if she'd be able to meet his gaze today without blushing. How could she answer his smile of greeting without staring at that sensuous mouth? She knew where that mouth had been, knew what it could do.

She had plans for that mouth tonight. She had plans for the rest of him, too. And if she expected those plans to work out, she'd have to act totally nonchalant today.

That meant she had to stop staring at him and get on with her chores. She cleared her throat. "Hey, Jonas," she called as she walked past the round pen. "You're up kind of early. Did Noah drag you out of bed?"

"I wish I could blame Noah. But I got my own self up early, for some stupid reason. Couldn't sleep."

*Because he was excited about what would happen tonight.* Her stomach flip-flopped. Staying nonchalant wouldn't be easy. "How's it going with Imelda?" They'd named the filly Imelda because she seemed to need shoes more often than any of the other horses.

"Oh, like a typical girl she's teasing me." He flashed her a grin. "But I have her number. She'll come around."

"One of these days you're going to run up

against a female who'll beat you at your own game, Jonas.''

He winked at her. ''Maybe so. But it hasn't happened yet.''

''Pride goes before a fall, and all that.'' B.J. had always found Jonas's cocky attitude maddening, but sexy. Now that she'd literally brought him to his knees, she loved the challenge of baiting him, knowing she would make him quiver with desire later on. She wanted to believe that she was doing it for all the women he'd loved and left, but in her heart she knew that wasn't true. She was playing this game for herself.

''I'm not proud,'' Jonas said. ''Just good. Are the banana and coffee for me?''

She'd forgotten she was holding them. ''Nope. It's my breakfast.'' She set her coffee mug on the fence post and peeled the banana. Maybe her experience from yesterday had started coloring her world, because the banana suddenly took on sexual significance.

A banana was a very sexy fruit, come to think of it. She closed her lips and tongue over it and savored the sensation of holding it in her mouth.

''Hey, we're not making X-rated movies today!'' Jonas said with a laugh. ''Cut that out.''

She glanced at him. Although he was smiling, there was a spark of awareness in his eyes. Well, that was natural. He was anticipating his evening with Sarah, so ordinary things were sexually charged for him, too. Still, it was the first time he'd ever worn that expression while looking at her.

She bit off a chunk of her banana, chewed and swallowed it. "I have no idea what you're talking about," she said. Then she picked up her coffee mug and walked toward the barn. If there was an extra sway to her hips, well, she couldn't help that, now could she? And if Jonas happened to notice, she couldn't be held responsible for that, either.

On the far side of the barn, her father and Noah were stacking fresh bales of hay under the open-sided hay shed. They both worked with the economical movements of men who'd been doing such chores all their lives. And they might complain about the hard labor, but neither of them would trade it for the world. Ranching was in their blood, as it was in hers.

It hadn't been in her mother's, unfortunately. From what her father had said, her mother hadn't been very happy here. Arch thought B.J.'s sister Keely had inherited their mother's high-strung, adventurous spirit, which is why she'd needed to leave. B.J. had always thought of herself as conventional, like her father, but after yesterday, she'd begun to wonder if there wasn't some of her mother lurking in her, too.

Arch hadn't remarried after his wife died, although B.J. had watched several local women try to snag him. He was a good catch, still slim and athletic. The gray in his red hair and mustache only added to his appeal, in B.J.'s opinion. But she suspected that Arch's memory of his creative, sensual wife had spoiled him for women who colored inside the lines, and that described most of the female population of Saguaro Junction.

Her father heaved another bale up to Noah and turned toward her. "Well, if it isn't Sleeping Beauty," he said with a smile. "You feeling okay?"

"Great," she said.

"That's good. With you going to bed so early I was afraid you might be coming down with something."

"Fortunately I'm not. Hey there, Noah."

"Hey, yourself." Noah smiled down at her from the stack of hay bales. "If you were getting sick, I'd say you sent that bug packing. You look totally healthy. Extremely healthy."

"Good." Apparently the glow she felt showed. "Is that your way of telling me to take this healthy body, hitch up the tractor and rake the corral?"

Noah laughed. "Couldn't hurt."

"I'll get right on it." But first she had to come up with a reason to spend the evening at Sarah's house, a reason that would sound logical to her father and Noah. Jonas would have no trouble getting away tonight. He was expected to gallivant around the countryside without accounting for himself. But she'd established a pattern of letting her father know where she was going.

Probably in order to differentiate herself from Keely, she'd taken pains not to flaunt her sexual activities in front of Arch. A couple of years ago she'd become involved with a guy she'd wanted to spend the night with, and she'd paired their dates with trips to Phoenix for country-western concerts. She'd been vague about the sleeping arrangements, but her father had known the name of her hotel. That romance had fizzled, and she'd had no sleep-over urges with anyone since.

She started toward the barn, where the tractor was parked. Then she paused, as if suddenly remembering something. "By the way, I need to spend a few hours over at Sarah's tonight."

"A few hours?" her dad said. "She must have a damned greenhouse over there if it takes you a whole evening to water her plants."

"The indoor plants are no problem, but the vegetable garden needs a good soaking, so I thought I'd take a book and do that tonight." B.J. was amazed at herself. Keely had been the one who could spin tall tales at a moment's notice, but B.J. had never considered herself good at it.

Arch snorted. "You can soak all you want, but it'll be a waste of water. I guess since she's from back East, she doesn't know that it's useless to try and grow vegetables in August unless you tend them constantly."

"You're right, but I told her I'd do what I could," B.J. said. "I'm not sure when I'll be back, but I didn't want you to worry."

"I never worry about you," Arch said. "I just hate to see a waste of good water."

"After one summer I'm sure she'll figure it out. Well, I'd better go start cleaning the corral before the steering wheel gets too hot to hold."

"We picked up a new thermostat for the tractor yesterday," Noah called down from the top of the hay. "I set it on the shelf by the door, in case you need to put it in."

"Okay." As she walked toward the barn she thought of how casually Noah had mentioned the thermostat to her. He knew she could handle the situation. But she doubted if Sarah had ever replaced a thermostat, and Keely definitely hadn't. It would play hell with her manicure. But good old B.J. could put a new thermostat in a tractor. That B.J. was just like one of the guys.

She sighed. No wonder Jonas had never thought of her as a femme fatale girl.

JONAS CLUCKED HIS TONGUE and coaxed Imelda into reversing her direction in the round pen. She had a smooth gait and lots of spunk. He was looking forward to the day he could ride her, but working with Imelda hadn't been the reason he'd climbed out of bed so early this morning.

His blood was already running hot, his body humming with eagerness, and he had more than twelve hours to go. He wasn't sure how he'd make it through the day. Of course, there was always a fence to be repaired and post holes to be dug. Both activities would take the edge off, but he didn't want to take the edge off. He didn't want to exhaust himself and be unable to enjoy every single minute with Sarah.

He was already worried that he hadn't racked up enough z's to be fresh and alert come eight o'clock. But the possibilities of what Sarah planned to do with him had kept him awake a good part of the night. He'd had an erection most of that time, too.

After a night of fantasizing, everything this morning had made him think of sex—the shower nozzle, the vibration of his electric razor, the yeasty smell of pancake batter, the butter oozing over his pancakes, the syrup. The syrup bottle, for God's sake.

That probably explained why he'd looked at B.J. with the banana this morning and had such X-rated thoughts. As if B.J. would ever in her life go down on a guy. When she'd acted like she didn't know what he was talking about, he'd believed her.

He knew she wasn't a virgin, though. At least he assumed that when she'd been attending all those concerts in Phoenix with Jeff Cheney, something had been going on postconcert in the hotel.

But with B.J. it was probably missionary position all the way.

Funny that in all these years he'd never noticed what a cute butt she had, though. As she'd walked away from him, he hadn't been able to take his attention off of her behind. Those faded back pockets shifted in a real sweet rhythm when she walked, and the back seam of her jeans was pretty damn snug against her crotch. She had a nice package there.

She probably didn't realize how sexy her butt was in those tight jeans. B.J. didn't think in those terms. For the first time he wondered how a nice girl like B.J. would react to someone who had the skill to break through that reserve of hers and tap into her more primitive instincts. Jeff Cheney wouldn't have had the combination. Jonas would bet his last dollar on that.

Then he felt guilty for even having such thoughts about a girl who was like a sister to him. All this business with Sarah had him going crazy. Next he'd imagine himself lusting after their middle-aged housekeeper, Lupita. He was a sorry case, all right. B.J. would laugh her head off if she knew what he'd been thinking. She'd call him a sex maniac. Today he probably was.

At any rate, he'd run Imelda around enough, considering how the day was heating up. He gave her the carrots in his pocket, stroked her all over so she'd get used to the feel of his hands, then scratched behind her ears as he took off her bridle and turned her loose in the corral.

When he carried the tack into the barn, he was met with the sight of B.J. folded over the fender of the tractor, her butt pointed in his direction. Damn, but her fanny was inviting today. His hands tingled with the urge to cup those round cheeks and give them a friendly squeeze. She would have a heart attack if he did, though.

As he approached, he could hear her swearing. She was also breathing hard while she wrestled with whatever was wrong with the tractor's innards. Once again, his preoccupation with sex got the best of him and he imagined B.J. breathing like that in the midst of a wild bout of lovemaking. She sounded a lot like Sarah, come to think of it. That wasn't surprising. Heavy breathing was heavy breathing, after all.

But this was a woman fixing a tractor, not one approaching orgasm. He needed to get his mind back on track. "Need some help?" he asked.

She lifted her head quickly and cracked it on the tractor's raised hood. "Damn it!"

"I'm sorry." He looped the long-lines and bridle over a nearby hook and started toward her. He knew what a bump on the back of the head felt like. His head was still sore from whacking it on the roof of the cave yesterday. "Here, let me rub it to keep it from swelling."

"That's okay. I've got it." She scrambled off the milking stool she'd been standing on and lifted a hand to the back of her head.

"Wait, you'll get grease in your hair."

She lowered her hand. "It doesn't really hurt, anyway."

"Still, let me rub it." He cupped the back of her head and stroked gently with his fingers. "There?"

"Yeah."

Her hair was silky against his massaging fingers. Sarah's hair felt like this, but it was chocolate-brown, she'd said. B.J.'s hair reminded him of sunshine. This morning it was curling in little wisps around her face and even her braid didn't look very solid, as if she'd fixed it in a hurry. He couldn't remember the last time he'd seen her hair down. Ten years, at least.

She had a smudge of grease on her cheek and he had to stop himself from rubbing it off with his thumb. Or maybe he liked her better with the grease. Typical B.J.—freckles sprinkled over the bridge of her nose, her eyes fringed with pale, thick lashes, her mouth naturally pink, and engine grease on her cheek.

She looked up at him warily. "I thought you were outside."

"I finished. But I'm sorry I didn't sing out when I came in the barn." He'd been too preoccupied by her backside to remember to do that.

"I'll live."

He grinned at her as he continued to massage her head. "I sure hope so. Otherwise I'll have to fix that tractor." Something seemed different about B.J. today, but he couldn't figure out what it was. He'd looked into those blue eyes at least a million times over the years, but he didn't remember ever truly *looking* into them. This morning he was surprised to be doing that. And enjoying it.

At the very moment he admitted to himself there was something going on between them that never had before, she broke the connection and stepped away. "I'm fine. Thanks." She climbed back on her stool. "Guess I'd better finish up. The day's not getting any younger."

What was that he'd seen in her eyes? It was almost as if she...no, that was ridiculous. B.J. wouldn't think such thoughts about him, any more than he should be thinking that way about her. They'd grown up together, for crying out loud.

He ought to leave her alone and start fixing the fence. "What's wrong with the tractor?"

"Busted thermostat." She leaned over the fender again and reached down into the guts of the tractor.

Jonas had never been big on engine repair. He could do it if necessary, but he'd rather fiddle with things that had a pulse. Still, watching B.J. positioned like that was very intriguing. He'd never leaned a woman facedown over the fender of a car, but B.J. was giving him ideas. She'd probably never done it doggy style, either. She had the perfect buns for it, not too skinny and not too plump.

"If you're gonna stand there, you can hand me the wrench."

He picked up the wrench from where she'd laid it on the far end of the fender, took hold of her outstretched hand and put the wrench into it. The minute he touched her hand he felt a jolt of recognition. God, he was losing it if the warmth and texture of B.J.'s skin reminded him of Sarah. The two women couldn't be any more different.

"Thanks," B.J. muttered. "Listen, you don't have to baby-sit me. I can do this."

Well, maybe they were alike in one way, he thought with a wry smile. They both liked to be in charge. With B.J., though, he felt irritated that she stubbornly wouldn't accept his help repairing the tractor. He could be of some use. Leaning over this fender with her and wrestling with the greasy engine had a certain amount of appeal this morning, strange as it might seem. But she wasn't having any of that.

On the other hand, he would be more than happy to let Sarah take charge of their lovemaking tonight. That promised to be one of the most thrilling experiences of his life. Only eleven and a half hours to go.

# CHAPTER FOUR

BY THE TIME B.J. OPENED the door of Sarah's rented cottage at seven that night, she felt like a secret agent. If she could really pull off this caper, she might want to consider a career in undercover work. She hadn't had this much fun in years, although keeping Jonas literally in the dark was turning out to be quite a challenge.

Secrecy was especially difficult in her case, because until now, her life had been an open book. In a way, though, that played to her advantage. She'd be the last person in the world anyone would expect to set up a mysterious sexual rendezvous under an assumed name. That was more like Keely's style.

Although, if Keely were here, she might not be so surprised at her little sister's antics. The two of them had relished hiding in that cave to plot and scheme when they were kids. Then again, Keely might have been impressed with B.J.'s inventive-

ness. As the big sister, Keely has been so quick to
come up with ideas that B.J. had always let her
lead.

She'd always let *everybody* lead, she thought,
closing the door and setting down her bag full of
props. But not tonight. Tonight she was running the
show, and what a show it would be.

Her pickup truck was hidden behind the reno-
vated garage that Sarah used for a studio. Sarah
liked having a separate building to work in, which
was why this place had appealed to her. That and
the relative isolation. The house sat on twenty acres
of unimproved, cactus and sagebrush-studded land
that might become a housing development someday, but served as a perfect artist's retreat until
then. One side of the property bordered Twin Boulders land, which made Sarah and B.J. neighbors.

They'd met in the hardware store at the beginning of the summer when they'd both gone shopping for welding equipment. B.J. had been fascinated to discover that Sarah used a welder for
creating sculptures instead of mending broken machinery, and she'd asked to see Sarah's work. After
her first visit, she'd dropped by for coffee a few
times, but they'd both been too busy to spend much
time with each other.

B.J. had never mentioned Sarah to Jonas, which was turning out to be a good thing. This charade could be her one and only chance to make love to Jonas without risking her heart or her pride. She intended to make the most of it.

Thunder rolled overhead as she turned on the air conditioning. Luckily the house was small and would cool off quickly. It hadn't rained all day, although dark clouds had threatened a storm most of the afternoon. She'd hoped it would hold off until after Jonas arrived. The little house had a tin roof. Rain on that roof would add to the sensual atmosphere she was going for.

Sarah had rented the cottage completely furnished, which made B.J. feel a little more comfortable about this escapade. At least she wasn't making free with Sarah's stuff. Besides, the only thing she intended to use was the sturdy four-poster in the bedroom, and she'd brought all her own linens.

A quick glance at her watch told her that she had less than an hour before dark, and she had no doubt Jonas would be right on time. Reaching into her bag she pulled out a silk scarf, opened the front door and tied the scarf loosely around the brass knob. A rush of adrenaline left her shaky. This would be so scary. And so incredibly cool.

IT HAD BEEN THE LONGEST DAY of Jonas's life. Several times he could have sworn that the sun had stopped moving entirely. Other times he shook his watch, certain that the battery had died. By six he'd showered and shaved and changed clothes three times. Then he discovered he couldn't eat the perfectly good meal Lupita put in front of him and Noah.

"This must be a helluva date," Noah commented as he forked up another mouthful of enchiladas. "I've never seen you go off your feed on account of a woman before."

Jonas was so distracted, he hadn't realized his lack of appetite might alert his brother. "Oh, we'll probably grab a bite to eat, so I didn't want to stuff myself before seeing her."

"Gonna tell me who she is?"

"I don't think she wants me to."

Noah leveled a stern look at him. "You know I try not to butt in—"

"Oh, yeah, right." Jonas grinned.

"I said I *try*. I don't always succeed. And in this instance, I have one thing to say. If this woman is married—"

"Not married." Jonas was hurt that Noah would

even bring that into the conversation. "You ought to know me better than that."

"You're right." Noah looked apologetic. "Sorry, bro. It's just that you don't usually keep me in the dark, especially when the lady in question is important enough to change clothes five times."

"Three. And it was only on account of the weather. I couldn't decide if it would rain or not."

Noah eyed his brother over the rim of his coffee mug. "Can't wear a blue shirt in the rain, that's for sure."

"Do you think the blue shirt looks better?" Jason glanced down at the black one he'd finally settled on. "I still have time to change back to the blue."

Noah stared at him. "You're kidding, right?"

Jonas met his brother's gaze and warmth crept up from beneath his collar. He was behaving like an idiot. Tonight wasn't such a big deal, especially for a guy as experienced as he was. "Of course I'm kidding." He flashed Noah a confident smile. "Doesn't matter what color it is. What matters is how easy the snaps work. Can't have her ripping one of my best shirts."

Noah chuckled and shook his head. "Well, I'm glad one of us is getting some action."

"If you'd stop working so hard and take an evening or two off, I could fix you up with one of several very nice women.''

''Thanks, but no thanks.'' Noah sipped his coffee, his gaze amused. ''I doubt I could live up to your reputation.''

''I'm serious, man. It's not healthy for a guy to go without sex as long as you have.'' Jonas pushed back his chair.

''How do you know how long it's been? Are you keeping track?''

Jonas stood and picked up his plate to carry it to the kitchen. ''Don't have to, in a town this size. If you took up with somebody, it would get out sooner or later.''

''You might want to keep that in mind with your mystery lady. People will find out eventually. So why not tell me now?''

''Nobody will find out if tonight is all there is to it.'' Jonas didn't like to think about that, but he had to admit the possibility that he was about to become a one-night stand.

''Oh, *sure*. You can't tell me that you fussed with your wardrobe for an hour for a woman you're gonna see once. You want this one bad, bro. You're not gonna be satisfied with one night of fun and games, and you know it.''

Jonas did know it. He thought about that steamy episode in the cave and the blindfolded experience ahead of him. He would want a rematch, all right, but would she? For the first time in his life, he felt out of his depth with a woman.

"Then again, maybe you won't want to see her again," Noah said quietly. "I need to mind my own business."

Jonas blinked. He couldn't remember the last time Noah had eased up on him like that. His eager nervousness must be written all over his face. Damn. Any more of this and his rep as a cool guy would be shot.

He shrugged. "Easy come, easy go."

Noah rose and clapped him on the shoulder. "Right. But good luck tonight, anyway. I have a feeling this one's special."

Jonas started to argue and knew it was hopeless. After all, Sarah was special. He couldn't remember when a woman had excited him so much.

Once he left the dinner table, he had nothing more to occupy his time so he decided to drive around until it was dark enough to use his headlights. Usually driving his truck with the radio tuned to a country station calmed him down, but not this evening. He hadn't felt this vulnerable since his first junior high dance. No, check that. The junior high dance had been a cakewalk compared to what he was feeling now.

At last he switched on his headlights and started toward the Hawthorne place. In order to get there, he had to drive down a dirt road. Luckily the road had good drainage and had dried completely from yesterday's rain. He drove it slowly, partly because he wasn't sure it was dark enough yet, and partly because he'd washed his truck today and didn't want to get dust on it. Maybe he wouldn't be allowed to see Sarah, but he figured she'd be watching for him.

Even if his heart was beating as fast as a rabbit's, he didn't want her to see him sweat. He wanted to make an entrance, his black truck gleaming, the engine purring the way only a V-8 could, and his sound system delivering the sweet vocalizations of Faith Hill. He wanted Sarah to know she was dealing with a class act.

A powdery film of dust settled over the truck, because it was impossible to drive on a dry dirt road and not have that happen. Oh well. His custom paint job would show through a light layer of dust so long as nobody wrote their name in it. He'd still drive up lookin' good. Not much farther now.

He spied the house up ahead. A porch lamp cast a circle of light, but otherwise the house seemed completely dark. His stomach pitched as he realized she might have changed her mind. Instead of standing by a window waiting for his truck to appear, she might not even be home.

Then a few drops of rain fell. Only a few, but enough to create a polka-dotted, blotchy effect in the layer of dust. As he parked in front of the little cottage, the porch light reflected off the grimy-looking surface of his truck's hood.

At least his excellent sound system held up, the rich tones floating out the truck's open windows. But before he could shut off the engine, the Faith Hill song gave way to a loud commercial concerning jock itch.

So much for his entrance. But his entrance wouldn't matter if she wasn't even home. Then the breeze picked up and something fluttered at the doorknob. He looked closer. A red scarf was tied loosely around it.

*His blindfold.*

He grew light-headed and dry-mouthed with excitement. Oh God. This was really going to happen. His movements were jerky as he shut off the truck's engine and rolled up the windows. It was a wonder he even remembered to do that.

He started to get out when a gust of wind lifted the brim of his hat. Taking it off, he laid it on the seat before climbing out of the truck. If there was one thing he wouldn't need tonight, it was a hat. This was the wildest thing he'd ever done, and maybe he was crazy for agreeing to it, but he had to find out what awaited him on the other side of the door.

Mounting the steps to the small front porch, he glanced at the two cane-bottomed rockers and the mat in front of the door. It had Welcome carved into the short pile of the rug, and he'd seen several like it at the hardware store. Everything looked so ordinary, so like the front porches of other women he'd called on—everything except that red scarf tied around the doorknob.

Now he could see why no light showed from the house. The curtains in the living room were closed, and he'd guess all the other windows were covered, too. She'd turned the house into a cave.

With trembling hands, he untied the scarf from the doorknob and discovered his blindfold was made of silk. As he put it over his eyes, he imagined he could already feel her soft hands on him, her full lips, her tongue… By the time the blindfold was secure, he had a raging erection.

He turned his head to make sure he couldn't see. If this was the way she wanted the game played, he'd follow her rules—for now. He hadn't been blindfolded since the days when he'd played kissing games at boy-girl parties, and he'd forgotten that taking away the ability to see made all his other senses sharper.

A wind chime tinkled nearby. He hadn't noticed the sound before, or the steady chirp of crickets, or the smell of the light rain falling. It pinged overhead on the porch roof, and he remembered that the house was roofed with corrugated tin.

Taking an unsteady breath, he raised his fist and rapped gently on the door.

The knob squeaked, and cool air surrounded him. He smelled something heady and sensual and heard the soft wail of a saxophone.

"Hello, Jonas."

Her husky voice sent shivers of anticipation down his spine. "Hello, Sarah."

She took his hand and drew him inside. "Come."

"Be careful, or I just might."

She laughed. "See if you can hold off for a little while, or this will be a very short evening."

"Believe me, I'm working on staying in control." Her laugh sounded nice—familiar, too, as if he'd heard it before.

But that couldn't be right. She hadn't laughed while they were in the cave, at least not that he remembered. Of course, maybe they'd happened to be in the Roundup Saloon on the same night but sitting in different booths, or they'd been in the Mini-Mart some afternoon shopping on separate aisles.

Yeah, that explained it.

She held his hand in both of hers. "Are you happy to be here?"

He trembled. "You have no idea."

"I'm happy, too." She brushed her lips over his knuckles.

The gesture reminded him of how he'd kissed her hand in the cave, and his heart thudded rapidly at the thought that she might be planning a complete reversal tonight. And that would mean...that his dreams would come true.

"I appreciate your trusting me to be in control." She ran her tongue into the crevice between each finger.

He shuddered. Obviously she had some sexy moves all her own. "No problem."

"I'd like you to be passive tonight, but if at any time you feel uncomfortable with the situation, let me know and we'll make adjustments." She took his little finger into her mouth and sucked gently.

That worked him up but good. She probably had twice as much experience as he did. "All—" He cleared the tightness from his throat. "All right."

"First of all, I want you to let your hand go limp, as if you were a puppet, and I'm the puppeteer."

He nodded. Allowing his hand to go limp was one thing, but he didn't think his penis would ever be limp again. He relaxed the muscles of his hand.

"Good. Now, through touch, I'll let you 'see' me, so to speak." She held his hand against her throat.

He could feel her pulse beating a quick tattoo against his fingertips. Maybe she wasn't as in control as she sounded. "Do you…want me to undress you?"

"That won't be necessary." She drew his hand down over her collarbone to her bare breast.

His breath caught. *She was already naked.* His fingers flexed automatically, wanting to caress her.

"No," she murmured. "Remember, you're only

a puppet.'' She drew his hand to her other breast.
Then she placed her hand over his and closed his
fingers over her ripe warmth. ''Mmm. Very nice.''

Her taut nipple pressed into his palm, driving him
crazy. He loved the shape of her breasts, remembered the taste of them and her whimpers of delight
when she'd allowed him to suck…. ''Sarah, let
me—''

''Be the puppet,'' she whispered, easing his hand
down between her breasts, turning it so his fingers
led the way over her flat belly.

He groaned when he encountered soft curls. He
wanted—

''I'm the puppeteer,'' she reminded him softly.

When she guided his hand lower, he had to
clench his teeth to keep from curving his fingers
and seeking her moisture. The seductive scent of
her arousal rose to taunt him and his groin throbbed
relentlessly. The rain fell harder, drumming rhyth-
mically on the roof.

She flattened her hand over his and pushed
against his middle finger, settling it into the groove
that held her pleasure point. The delicate protrusion
pulsed against his finger as she pressed him in
tighter and gasped in reaction.

He trembled with the desperate need to do something. "Sarah."

"Be…still." Her breath came more quickly as she rubbed his finger back and forth.

"Let me hold you."

"No. This is…how…I want it. You are my boy…toy."

He should be insulted. Instead he was turned on beyond belief. He wanted her to use him, torment him, draw out the pleasure. His head spun and he clenched his free hand at his side to keep from reaching for her and spoiling her fantasy of a man totally at her beck and call.

She gripped his shoulder. "Soon," she whispered, increasing the friction. The rain played a faster tattoo on the roof. "Oh…yes…*yes.*" Squeezing his hand against her drenched curls, she slumped forward, panting wildly as she leaned her head against his chest.

He could barely breath. "Good?" he said hoarsely. As if in league with her response, the rain eased up.

"*Oh,* yeah." She drew in a long, trembling breath and lifted her head from his chest. Then she slipped his hand out from between her legs.

He wanted to bury his face down there. "God, but you smell terrific right now."

"You mean my cologne?"

"No, I don't mean your cologne." He was so hot for her, it was a wonder he didn't spontaneously combust.

"Ah." She lifted his hand and waved it beneath his nose. "You mean this?"

He groaned. "Let me taste you."

"Not now. Maybe later I'll let you," she said in her low, sultry voice. "If you're a good boy."

"You'll be amazed at how good I can be."

"I hope so. Because now I'm going to take you back in the bedroom and have my way with you."

He nearly lost it right then and there.

# CHAPTER FIVE

B.J. HADN'T PLANNED THAT first maneuver. She'd always had a practical streak, and she'd decided to greet Jonas naked because she didn't want to fool with undressing once he was there. She'd be far too busy for that. Originally she'd intended to lead him straight back to the candlelit bedroom and gradually let him realize that she wasn't wearing anything but a smile.

Then she'd opened the door to find him standing there blindfolded and eager. Sensual images had bombarded her, jolting her with an awareness of her own power. Leading him inside by the hand, into the love nest she'd prepared for him, had been an erotic experience in itself. The puppet and puppeteer thing had popped into her mind, and her imagination and libido had directed the action from there. The rhythm of the rain on the roof hadn't hurt, either.

All day she'd worried about being nervous, but

the blindfold took care of that—the blindfold and his belief that she was someone else. She could never have dared any of this as herself, although now she realized a sexual adventurer lived within her soul. At least for tonight, she would let that adventurer out to explore.

She guided him down the short hallway to the bedroom where scented votive candles would allow her to see, and Jonas to breathe in the aroma of vanilla. Keely had once told her that vanilla was a sexually stimulating scent, and lo and behold, the hardware store sold vanilla candles in tall glass containers. They must have stocked them for the tourists, because B.J. couldn't imagine any of the ranchers buying them.

She'd bought ten. Her old friend Henry had been working the cash register this afternoon, and she'd told him she was getting an early start on Christmas. The feather duster had caused no comment, fortunately.

At Millie's Crafts she'd used the same starting-early-on-Christmas story to explain the five yards of red velvet cord and two red silk scarves. Nobody at the Mini-Mart had asked her about the can of whipped cream or the bottle of cooking oil. The whipped cream was in a bucket of ice next to the bed, and the oil, flavored with a dash of cherry syrup, sat on the nightstand.

She'd also brought her portable CD player after finding a disk Keely had left behind that was specifically labeled *Seduction*. The mellow saxophone was the final touch.

Well, up until now. Having Jonas standing in the middle of the bedroom, his breathing ragged and an erection pushing at the crotch of his jeans was the absolutely final touch. She had caused that erection to appear and she loved knowing that.

She led him over to a straight-backed chair in the corner of the room. "Here's a chair. I want you to sit down and take off your boots and socks, so we don't have to fool with them later."

He edged down to the chair cautiously, but once he was sure of his position he took off his boots quickly and dropped them to the floor. Then he stripped off his socks and tossed them aside. "Now what?"

She made a mental note to suck those sexy toes before he left tonight. "Stand up and undress for me."

He swallowed. "You don't want to…help?"

"No. I want to lie on the bed and watch."

"You're just going to lie there and watch me?"

She stretched out on the bed, sliding her flushed body over the cool sheet. "Maybe not. Maybe I'll touch myself while I watch." She had no idea where these outrageous statements were coming from. She'd never talked that way, but she loved the effect it had on Jonas.

He began to quiver. "I guess you know what it does to me, when I imagine something like that."

This bad girl behavior came more naturally than she ever would have believed. "I can see what it does to you," she said in a husky murmur. "But I want to be able to see better. I want to see how hard you are, how much you want me."

His hand went to his belt buckle.

"Shirt first."

He paused and reached for the snaps at his wrists. After popping them open, he quickly undid the top snap on his shirt.

"Go slower. Make it last a while." She wanted him naked *now* but exercising her power over him was its own kind of aphrodisiac.

He took a deep breath and slowed down, unfastening the snaps in a lazy rhythm. "Better?"

"Much." She began to tremble with anticipation. And as she'd hoped, the rain began to pelt the roof again, heightening the mood.

"What are you doing now?" he asked in a voice roughened by desire.

She moistened her finger and drew it around her sensitive aureole. "Playing with my nipple."

He sucked in a breath. "Are you going to let me do that?"

"We'll see."

"You're driving me insane, you know." He dragged the tails of his shirt from the waistband of his jeans.

"Do you want to change anything that's happening?"

"No. But I've never...I've never had a woman direct me. It's..."

"Wildly sexy?"

"Yeah. Yeah, it is."

"I want you to remember tonight." Being the mystery lover he'd never forget would be some sort of compensation, she thought.

"I'll remember." He shrugged out of his shirt and dropped it to the floor.

She'd seen him shirtless hundreds of times. Whenever she'd been certain he wouldn't notice, she'd admired the powerful breadth of his shoulders, the dark hair sprinkled in a triangular pattern on his broad chest, his sepia-colored nipples hidden beneath.

She'd seen him grimy, sweaty, even bruised from a fall. But she'd never seen him like this, his chest heaving with excitement, a fine sheen of perspiration making his skin glow in the candlelight. The rain beat harder on the tin roof.

Her glance moved down to his flat belly ridged with muscle, and lower, to the belt buckle he'd unhooked and the metal button of his jeans that he'd already slipped through the buttonhole. Her breathing slowed and a bead of moisture slid between her breasts.

"What are you doing now?" His voice quivered.

*Watching you.* But she wanted to continue taunting him with what he couldn't see. "I just put my hand between my thighs."

He moaned.

"It feels good." And it did. Incredible. She stroked lightly, following the rhythm of the rain, going for pleasure and not orgasm while she waited for him to pull that zipper down.

The zipper rasped and the denim parted.

*Oh Lord.* Even her most erotic fantasies hadn't prepared her for the sight of his unzipped jeans and the skimpy black briefs straining to hold him. She cleared her throat. "Nice."

"Do you want me to…take off the briefs…when I take off the jeans?"

"No. Just the jeans. I'll take off the briefs. When I'm ready." She was totally ready now. But she'd wanted to draw this out in ways he'd never experienced before. This night would be burned into his memory forever.

He shoved the jeans down and stepped out of them.

She took it all in—the ripple of his thigh muscles, the firm perfection of his calves, and, most of all, the bulge between his thighs that she'd need both hands to cradle.

He stood before her, a blindfolded Greek god who had surrendered himself to whatever she had in mind. Maybe she'd never find a man who measured up to Jonas. Maybe she'd settle for less, or maybe she'd never marry at all, but at least she would have this night with the man of her dreams. She doubted many women could claim that.

She slid off the bed and came to stand in front of him. "Take my hand and I'll lead you." She put her hand in his.

He gripped her hand tightly. "I don't know how long I can hold out. I'm right on the edge now."

Her pulse raced as she realized that the slender thread of control she was using to command him could snap at any time. All he had to do was whip off the blindfold and end the game. Then she would be revealed.

"What I'm thinking," he continued as he struggled to speak normally, "is that if I can spend the whole night, then it won't matter, because I'll have more time to—"

"I'm afraid you can't spend the whole night." She'd tried not to panic. The longer he stayed, the greater the chance he'd find out who she was. Besides, she'd never be able to concoct a story that would explain her being gone that long.

"When do I have to leave?"

"I can let you stay another hour."

"That's *all?*"

"Yes."

A muscle worked in his jaw. "Then I'll just have to hold out as long as I can."

"I'll help you. When you think you're about to come, tell me. I'll back off."

"Sarah, I've been about to come ever since yesterday in the cave."

"Then I guess we'll test your stamina, won't we?" She tugged on his hand and drew him over to the bed. "And Jonas, you understand the blindfold must stay in place at all times."

"Even afterward?"

"Especially afterward."

"I'll bet you have a birthmark. I can live with that. I can't imagine that anything about you would be a problem."

"No, I don't have a birthmark." She searched for a workable explanation. "I'm usually very shy." There. It was even the truth.

"I don't believe you."

"Oh, but I am. Your blindfold works like magic for me, setting free the sensuous person inside." Amazing how well the truth served her cause. "If you took it off, that person who excites you so much would disappear. I love letting her out to play." She ran the tip of her finger over his lower lip. "Please don't ruin this for either of us." His mouth was like velvet. She wanted him so.

He took a shaky breath and his tone gentled. "I get it. You're an artist, and you put all your sexual feelings into your work. But I could teach you to be that sexual person with me, even when I'm not wearing a blindfold. Just knowing that side of you exists and comes out in your work should give you courage. Please. Let's try.''

"No. If you push me, I'll send you back out the door now.''

"You fascinate me.'' A note of desperation crept into his voice. "I want to know you better. I want to teach you how to—''

"I'll send you home this minute, Jonas. I will. And I'm warning you, if you try to contact me later, I'll call the sheriff.''

"The *sheriff*? Listen, I only want to—''

She lowered her voice to a sensuous murmur. "But if you'll be a good boy and lie down on the bed, I'll give you more pleasure than you dreamed possible, as long as you leave that blindfold on.''

He groaned. "Okay. I'll play this your way. I have to. Just don't send me home. I need you so much.''

"Then let me give you what you need,'' she whispered, urging him down to the bed as the rain pounded on the roof. "That's it. Stretch out. Like that. Oh, yes, just like that.'' She ran her hand down his chest and stopped at the waistband of his briefs. "Would you like me to take these off?''

"Yes. Lord, yes.''

"Soon.'' She leaned down and placed a kiss on

his navel while inhaling the musky scent of his arousal. They'd had a close call, but now she was back in control.

JONAS LAY THERE in an agony of anticipation. He'd been thinking of loosening the blindfold, of letting it slip. He wanted to see her face, wanted to look into her eyes. He was beginning to long for a greater connection between them than just the mating of bodies.

But she'd confessed how shy she was, and after his first disbelief, he knew it was true. He could tell by the ring of sincerity in her voice, and besides, it was the only explanation that made sense.

Here he'd imagined her to be far more experienced than he was, and she was far less. That excited him even more. She was playing out fantasies that had only existed in her mind, which meant he was probably the first man she'd ever done this sort of thing with.

Maybe, at long last, he'd found his dream girl. And she wouldn't allow him to really know her. Still, there had to be a way. He wouldn't let her detour him forever, and he didn't believe she'd call the sheriff on him. Besides, he knew the sheriff, whereas she was a stranger in town.

"I want you to enjoy all sorts of different sensations tonight," she said. Then she brushed something feathery over his mouth and down his throat.

His nerve endings began to sing in response. She trailed the softness over his nipples and they tingled in a way he never remembered before. As he breathed in the scent that he would always associate with her, she brushed lightly over his rib cage, drawing ever closer to his primary focus. The sound of the rain blended with the sensuous notes of the saxophone.

When she drew the feathers over his briefs he gripped a handful of sheet in both hands. She teased the inside of his thighs, and he'd never realized how sensitive he was there. Maybe it was the prolonged foreplay that had caused every square inch of his body to become an erogenous zone.

"Don't tickle my feet," he warned. "I can't take that."

"I know," she murmured.

"You do? How did you know that?"

"Uh…I guessed. Most people—"

"Wait. You said you knew. Have you been asking questions about me?"

She paused. "You have a lot of former girl-friends around here."

"You talked to them? What did they say?"

"Well—"

"No, don't tell me. Sarah, listen. Maybe I haven't been into commitment before, but I've never met anyone like you. If you talked to my girlfriends you probably think you could never trust me with your shy nature. You think I'd hurt you in the end. But I—" He felt her fingers at the waistband of his briefs and his brain stalled. He tried to remember what he'd been saying. "You can trust me, because—"

"Lift your hips, Jonas."

Whatever he'd meant to say lodged in his throat. The moment was here. He did as she asked and she pulled the briefs down over his knees, over his ankles, over his feet.

She drew in a quick breath. "Will you look at that bad boy," she murmured.

He was gratified by her response. Typical man that he was, he loved her admiration. But more than that, he wanted her trust, and that was new for him. He'd never worried about gaining a woman's trust. It hadn't mattered before.

Then she used that feathery thing, stroking him until he was gasping from breath.

"You're beautiful," she said softly.

"I'm desperate."

"Want me to stop?"

"Just…give me a moment." He clenched his jaw and fought the urge to come. The rain pouring down outside didn't help matters.

The mattress shifted and she left the bed. Rustling sounds drifted to him, and then she was back, looping something soft around his wrist. She snugged it up.

He wasn't so sure about this. "What are you doing?"

"Tell me you've never imagined this." In seconds she'd immobilized his arm.

His heartbeat thudded in his ears. He tested the velvet rope and decided if necessary he could break it. And he *had* fantasized about something like this, although he'd never acted it out with anyone.

When his other wrist was tied, his throat grew dry with excitement. "How do I know that I can trust you?"

"Use your instincts." She leaned over him, her breasts swaying against his chest as she dropped a kiss on his mouth.

"I dare you to do that again."

"Later." She moved away and circled his ankle

with another velvet rope. "Do your instincts tell you to be afraid?"

"No. My instincts tell me…this is crazy…they tell me I've known you all my life."

She grew still. "But you haven't."

"Maybe I have, in my mind. Maybe you're the woman I've been looking for. I've been surrounded by cowgirls, ranching women. None of them captured my imagination like you have, Sarah. Maybe I just needed to meet this sensuous artist, a shy woman who molds nude statues and lives an unbelievable fantasy life."

She tied his other ankle. "I'm not the one for you." Her voice sounded funny, sort of choked up.

"Don't say that. Don't give up so quick. Don't—oh, Lord." He lost his train of thought as she began to rub his leg with a slippery piece of material. Silk, he decided, just like his blindfold, and it created the most amazingly erotic friction. And as she rubbed, she began to suck his toes. One by one. And the rain kept coming down.

"Sarah…Sarah, stop."

She paused. "Too much?"

"Oh, yeah." He pulled against his restraints while he struggled not to erupt. "It's almost as if you're sucking on my…"

"That's the idea." She dragged the scarf gently up his thigh and looped it around his penis. "Would you like the real thing?"

It was all he could think about. And yet she might finish him off in no time, and this wonderful event would be over.

"You're afraid you won't last." She drew the silk back and forth slowly.

He clenched his fists and squeezed his eyes shut behind the blindfold as the lazy movement of the silk teased him right to the brink. "Yep."

"Maybe I can cool you down a little."

He couldn't imagine an ice-water bath would work on an erection this determined. Then with a whoosh of sound, something soft and cool nestled over the tip of his penis. He cried out in surprise.

Then he recognized the sweet aroma of whipped cream and nearly passed out from eagerness. But he'd never make it through that. "You're going to…lick it off?"

"Mmm-hmm."

"Sarah, it'll be over then."

"Mmm-hmm." Her wet, warm tongue swiped away a layer of the whipped cream.

The rain came down harder as he felt his orgasm building. "Stop, please…stop. I brought…a condom. I want to make love to…'' He gasped as her tongue lapped away at his straining penis. ''Please…let me…''

''Tomorrow night,'' she murmured. Then she stopped licking and took his penis smoothly into her mouth. The rain nearly drowned out the sound of the saxophone.

She sucked once, and he had the climax of a lifetime, a climax that lifted him off the bed and ran like wildfire through his whole body, a climax that made him pull against the velvet ropes and yell like a man gone crazy. Which he had. Completely. He would do anything for this mystery woman. Anything in the world. He would wear a blindfold forever, as long as she allowed him to return to her mind-shattering world of sexual fantasy.

## CHAPTER SIX

B.J. UNTIED JONAS'S restraints as he lay panting and glistening with sweat. His reaction told her all she needed to know. She'd given him an experience he would never forget.

As she gazed at him sprawled on the flowered sheets looking totally wiped out, a rush of tenderness took her by surprise. Maybe it was wrong of her to fool him this way. From the way he was acting, he was getting emotionally involved with the woman he thought her to be.

Then she remembered his remark about "cowgirls who didn't hold his interest," and her sympathy vanished. Her desire for him, however, did not. She knew she was taking quite a chance stretching this fantasy to another night, but she couldn't bear to think of ending it now. She had more ideas to try, and before this was over she wanted to know what it would be like to have Jonas deep inside her.

When his breathing slowed she handed him his clothes. "I need you to leave now," she murmured.

"I wish…" His chest heaved. "I wish you'd let me stay."

"I can't do that. The longer you stay, the more you're going to be tempted to take off that blindfold."

"Yeah." He took another shaky breath. "Are you sure you couldn't do without it?"

"I'm sure. If you can't deal with the blindfold, then we can forget—"

"No! I'll wear the blindfold." He cleared his throat. "I'll wear it."

"And you have to promise not to bug me about this blindfold business."

"I promise." He sat up and began putting on his clothes. "Sarah, that was…spectacular."

"I'm glad."

"But I don't feel as if you had your share." He stood and pulled up his jeans.

"We can worry about that tomorrow night."

He nodded as he buckled his belt. "Tomorrow night. Yeah." He hesitated. "Thank you for giving me that."

Once again his vulnerability tugged at her heart. "I want another night, too," she said softly.

"You do?" He glanced in her direction, even though he couldn't see her. "That's nice to hear."

"You turn me on, Jonas." *You always have.*

"I think it's obvious that you turn me on, too, Sarah. In fact, if I could stay a little longer, I'd probably recover enough to—"

"It's better if you go now." She handed him his socks and his boots.

"Maybe so." He sat down on the bed to put on his socks. "You're right. The longer I'm with you, the more I want to see your face. Is it that you don't think you're attractive?"

"I'm passable. My face wouldn't frighten little children."

"I'm sure you're pretty." He put on his boots. "In fact, I'm very sure of it. But even if you weren't, I'd think you were beautiful because of the way you made love to me tonight. A man doesn't need conventional beauty when a woman gives of herself the way you did."

"Time for you to leave, anyway, Jonas." She took his hand. "I'll lead you to the front door."

He stood and followed her, but at the door to the bedroom he stopped and inhaled deeply. "I love the way this room smells."

"It's vanilla."

"It's more than vanilla. It's you, it's me, it's the smell of good, healthy sex."

Much more of that kind of talk and she'd lead him right back into that bedroom. "Let's go."

He sighed and followed her down the hall.

The closer they came to the door, the less she wanted him to leave, but she had a lot to take care of before she could go home. "What will you do now?" she asked.

"You mean after I leave here?"

"Yes." She needed to know, so that she could avoid him if at all possible.

"I'll probably drive around a while. The rain's stopped, and I love the desert after a rain. Want to come with me?"

More than he knew. She'd love to ride through the warm, rain-drenched night with Jonas. They could find a secluded place to park and pick up where they'd left off. "Thanks, but no thanks."

"I thought it was worth a try."

She placed his hand on the doorknob. "Go on out to the porch, now. Leave the blindfold where you found it."

He rested his hand on the doorknob. "Just one thing before I go."

"What?"

His other arm slipped quickly around her. "This." He brought her in tight and unerringly found her mouth with his. The kiss was deep, hot and wet. But more than that, it was possessive. Extremely possessive. It left her gasping. "See you tomorrow night," he murmured, releasing her. Then he opened the door and stepped outside.

In seconds, she was alone.

She stood with her hand to her mouth long after the sound of his truck died away. For the entire evening she'd convinced herself that she was in control, that she'd stay in control. Jonas had seemed so eager to continue their relationship that she hadn't expected any aggressive behavior on his part.

Then he'd kissed her the way a man kisses a woman when he's staked a claim. And suddenly she wasn't so sure that she could control Jonas, after all.

NORMALLY JONAS WASN'T MUCH for gossip. Too often the stories were about him, anyway. But he hadn't lived in Saguaro Junction all his life for nothing, and when he needed to find out something, he knew where to go.

The next morning he told Lupita he needed to

put gas in his truck and he'd pick up breakfast at the Cactus Café before he came home. Less than a half hour later, he was sitting on a stool at the only eating spot in Saguaro Junction, a mug of coffee in front of him and his order for steak and eggs on the griddle. The morning waitress, Sue Ellen, was usually good for some information, but his luck was running today because Henry from the hardware store was having his breakfast at the café this morning, too. Henry knew everyone and everything that went on in this town.

"How's it going, Henry?" Jonas asked after he took his first sip of coffee.

"Can't complain." Henry poured a generous amount of syrup on his pancakes. "How about you?"

"Glad to get the rain." Jonas had grown up learning the rhythm of these conversations. The weather had to come first, to establish that comfortable common ground.

"Yeah, we really needed that rain," Henry said.

"Is the family doing okay?"

"Oh, Shirley still has that problem with her back, but I'm sure it doesn't help that she's always carrying those grandchildren of ours around when they come to visit."

Jonas knew that was his cue to ask to see current pictures, which he did. And they were cute little tykes, two boys and a girl. Jonas felt sorry that his own father hadn't lived long enough to have grandchildren, because they were obviously the highlight of Henry's life.

Sue Ellen had delivered Jonas's steak and eggs and topped off his coffee before he finally got around to the main reason for his visit to the café. "Say, Henry, do you think old man Hawthorne ever plans to sell that little place he owns?"

Henry swallowed another bite of his pancakes. "Last I heard he didn't think the market was right, yet. Why, you interested?"

"Maybe."

"Well, he's got a renter in there, so I doubt he'd sell it out from under her. Real nice woman. A sculptor."

Jonas concentrated on cutting off a piece of steak so he wouldn't give anything away by his expression. "I think I heard something about that. Do you know her?"

Henry started to laugh. "Okay, I know what this is about. You heard there was a new single woman in town, didn't you?"

Jonas managed a sly grin. "You caught me, Henry."

"I swear, boy, you're going to wear yourself out before your thirtieth birthday. But somehow I don't see you dating Sarah. She doesn't seem at all your type."

*That's what you know.* "Really? Why's that?"

"Well, first off, she's…well, let's just say she has a very generous figure."

"Are you saying she's overweight?" Jonas tried to reconcile what Henry was saying with the woman he'd kissed the night before. Sarah had felt sensual, soft and willing in his arms. Had he been so delirious that he hadn't noticed she was on the chubby side?

Henry took a swallow of his coffee. "Technically, I guess so. But she's such a nice lady that I don't like slapping that label on her. But her weight isn't the only thing that doesn't seem to go with your taste in women."

"Oh?" Jonas had completely abandoned his meal as he turned to stare at Henry. "What else?"

"I've never known you to take up with older women."

Jonas thought about that. Sarah might be older than he was. Her skin was smooth, but some women maintained that kind of skin well into their forties. Maybe that was her hang-up. He wasn't sure how he felt about that. If she was past childbearing age, that would be significant.

*Significant?* Had he really started thinking in terms of marriage and kids? He didn't even know the woman's last name. Oh, but he knew her fantasies, and that seemed more important than a last name that he'd probably try to convince her to change, anyway.

He might as well get what information he could from Henry. If age was a stumbling block, he'd find a way around it. Maybe they could adopt. And modern science was doing some amazing things these days which allowed older women to have children, if they wanted to.

Jonas picked up his mug of coffee. "How old do you think she is?" he asked in as casual a tone as he could manage, considering.

"Hard to say exactly."

"Take a guess."

"Late fifties, early sixties."

Jonas spewed coffee all over his plate. No way he'd been making love to a grandmother. No way.

"Goodness, boy." Henry clapped him on the

back. "Sorry to break it to you like that. Didn't know you had your heart set on taking her out."

Jonas mopped the coffee from his face and cleaned up around his plate. "For some reason I thought she was...younger."

"Well, maybe I have it wrong." Henry eyed his plate. "You sure did make a mess, there. Maybe you should order yourself a new breakfast."

"That's okay. I'm not really that hungry." He gazed at Henry. "Late fifties, you say?"

"Why don't you ask B.J.? She knows her."

"Maybe I'll do that." Like hell he would. He didn't want B.J. to get even the slightest whiff of this. If Henry was right about the age thing and B.J. found out he'd been fooling around with someone old enough to be his mother, he'd never hear the end of it.

Henry had to be wrong. Or maybe Sarah was on some special hormone program. Maybe she'd had cosmetic surgery all over. He needed some time to think about this. Age aside, it had been the best sex he'd ever had. He didn't want to jump to any hasty conclusions just because of some silly prejudices he might be able to get rid of in no time.

"Yeah, ask B.J.," Henry said. "I think Sarah mentioned that B.J. was going to watch her place this week while she went back to New York for some gallery showing. And while you're at it, ask B.J. what the heck she's planning to do with all those vanilla candles she bought yesterday.''

Jonas froze in place. Then his head began to buzz. He shook it, certain he'd misunderstood Henry.

Henry's voice seemed to be coming from far, far away. ''Hey, are you okay? You must be getting sick. You look awful.''

Jonas swallowed and slowly turned to look at Henry. The buzzing in his ears wouldn't go away, but he had to straighten this out. ''Did you say Sarah's out of town?''

''Yeah, but that's not important right now. I'm worried about you. Sue Ellen, get this boy some water and a cold cloth. I think he's fixing to pass out on us.''

Jonas coughed and shook his head. ''I'm fine. Really.''

''I don't think so.'' Henry took the damp dish-cloth Sue Ellen handed over the counter. ''Here, put this at the back of your neck.''

Jonas did as he was told, and the coolness helped. ''Thanks.''

Sue Ellen leaned over the counter to peer at him. "Want me to call Noah?"

"No!" Jonas's mind edged around the information he'd received but wasn't in any shape to process. Vanilla candles. It could be a coincidence. It had to be.

"I know," Sue Ellen said. "Let me call B.J. A woman's better in a situation like this."

*"No!"* B.J. He couldn't escape logic. If Sarah was gone, and B.J. had been watching the house this week... No. He didn't even want to go there.

Sue Ellen drew back. "Okay, I won't call her. But B.J.'s good in an emergency. I'm sure she could—"

"I'm fine." Although his head was still buzzing, Jonas managed a weak smile. "Just the flu, I guess. I'd better get out of here before I expose you all." Laying the cloth next to his plate, he reached in his back pocket for his wallet.

"On the house," Sue Ellen said. "You didn't eat it, anyway."

"That's okay. I want to pay." Jonas laid some bills on the table. "That should cover it. I'll head on home." Home was the last place he wanted to go, but he'd figure out how he'd deal with that later.

"Are you sure you can drive?" Henry asked.

"Oh, yeah. I've been worse off than this before." Jonas slid off the stool and walked out of
the café on rubbery legs. Once back in his truck,
he started the engine and drove aimlessly.

Or so he thought. Apparently he had a destination
in mind, after all. Soon he was sitting in front of
Sarah's house. Or the house rented by Sarah, which
was presently being watched by B.J. He gripped the
steering wheel. *B.J.*

Closing his eyes, he leaned against the headrest
and tried to piece it all together, starting with the
cave. He'd stumbled in and been thrown completely
off guard by finding a woman there. She'd told him
her name was Sarah, and she was a sculptor. He'd
wanted it to be true.

He still did. He didn't want to face the fact that
his mystery lover, the fantasy woman he'd been ob-
sessed with for the past two days, didn't exist. He
couldn't deal with knowing that all the things he'd
done with and to Sarah, all the things she'd let him
do to her, had involved a girl he'd known all his
life.

*I feel as if I've known you all my life.* He'd said
that, but he sure as hell hadn't meant it literally. As
the shock began to wear off, anger moved in to take
its place. She had no business engaging in such

behavior! She wasn't like that! Never had been, never would be! *Then how had she managed to give him the time of his life?*

And *why?* Was this part of some diabolical plot to blackmail him later? That didn't make sense. He'd have as much blackmail material as she would.

If she'd meant it as the practical joke of the millennium, he had to hand it to her. She'd come up with a beauty. But practical jokes weren't any fun if only the jokester and the victim knew about it. And he couldn't believe she would ever want anyone to know what they'd done in the cave, what they'd done in Sarah's bedroom.

And oh, what they'd done. He opened his eyes and gazed at the little cottage. The doorknob was bare now, but unless he changed things, it would have a red silk scarf tied on it by dusk tonight. In spite of everything, he was becoming aroused again thinking about it. In spite of everything, he wanted more. But he wanted his mystery woman back. He couldn't play those kinds of games with B.J.

Or could he? A picture of her mouthing that banana flickered into his mind. He'd noticed her butt yesterday, too, for the first time. And truth be told, he'd rather have his mystery woman turn out to be B.J. than someone pushing sixty.

But he never would have believed that B.J. could have such ideas in her head. With all those years of growing up together, working side by side as adults, he never would have guessed what was going on behind those innocent blue eyes.

Come to think of it, knowing that she wasn't what she seemed was kind of exciting. *Extremely* exciting. If he kept their date tonight, he would know who she was, but she wouldn't know he knew. He could egg her on to be wilder and wilder, and she'd probably do it because she'd think her identity was safe. She deserved some payback for the way she'd tricked him.

Funny, but the anger was gone now. He felt sort of warm all over, as if things were falling into place the way they were supposed to. When he'd first found out that he'd been making love to B.J., he'd been totally freaked. But now…now there was a rightness to it all that he couldn't ignore. B.J. Who would have thought?

He wondered if she'd ever planned to tell him. And once again, he was back to the question of why she'd pulled this elaborate charade in the first place.

Once he knew that, he could decide what to do about it.

Of course he could go back to the ranch right now, confront her with his information and get the whole thing out in the open. He could do that, but then there would be no secret rendezvous tonight. The decision boiled down to whether he wanted to satisfy his curiosity now, or satisfy his lust tonight and his curiosity another time.

Oh well. He could live with being curious.

## CHAPTER SEVEN

HAVING COME TO THE DOOR naked the first night, B.J. decided she needed to do something different this time, wearing seductive clothing that would add to the tactile enjoyment when Jonas touched her. Something erotic and naughty. Yet she'd never owned sexy lingerie and she didn't have time to go shopping.

Then inspiration hit. She'd taken part in a fancy riding demonstration in Phoenix a few years ago, and the event had been televised. For that occasion she'd bought an incredibly soft vest and chaps in red suede, an outfit that was way too beautiful for regular ranch work. She'd never worn it again.

At first her practical side rebelled at the idea of sacrificing such an expensive outfit to the cause. Once she'd made love to Jonas while wearing it, she'd never be able to put it on without thinking of what they'd shared. But she could keep it in the bottom of her closet for a souvenir. It might be the only one she'd ever have. If she wore the vest open and nothing else but the chaps, she'd definitely be X-rated.

And after all, she was building memories to last her a lifetime. She decided to sacrifice the outfit to her fantasy.

She was leery of using the garden-watering excuse a second time with her father. Instead she told him that Sarah had offered her use of a DVD player and she'd just discovered that Sarah owned a bunch of good movies.

The excuse could be expanded to include more hours in Sarah's house the following night, in case she decided to risk it. To continue these meetings would really be pushing her luck, but how she loved her intimate encounters with Jonas. She couldn't bear to have them end.

By seven-thirty she was in Sarah's bedroom putting on her vest and chaps. She discovered that the vest rubbed erotically against her nipples when she moved, and the chaps stimulated her inner thighs. When she glanced in a full-length mirror, she could hardly believe she was the woman reflected in it. Her unbound hair rippled over her shoulders, her breasts peeked from under the red suede and the golden triangle between her legs was blatantly emphasized by the cut of the chaps. From the rear, with nothing covering her bottom, she looked even more provocative.

Now for the bed. She stripped it down to the mattress and put a protective cover over it. Then she made it up with a fresh sheet. Tonight they would experiment with the flavored oil, and she didn't want to ruin Sarah's mattress. Fortunately she knew that none of this would shock Sarah. The older woman had a liberated sex life and hadn't been shy about sharing a few of her more colorful stories. Some of their conversations might have helped B.J. shed her inhibitions with Jonas, now that she thought about it.

Heart beating with anticipation, she lit the candles. They'd only burned about a third of their length the previous night, so they were good for tonight and maybe one more session. After that…well, after the candles were gone she really should play it safe and stop before the situation got out of hand. She was crazy to imagine the charade could go on much longer. Jonas wouldn't agree to wear a blindfold forever.

But he'd agreed to wear one tonight. She turned on the CD player just as a soft knock came at the front door. *He was here.* Her skin warmed and her body moistened.

Tonight they would play as before, but when the playing was done, she would finally make that magical, elemental connection with him. He wouldn't understand the significance of that, because he would still be thinking of her as Sarah, his mystery woman. But she would know. And she would carry that memory with her always.

Her suede chaps rustled as she walked to the door and opened it. There stood Jonas, the red scarf tied firmly over his eyes. A shiver of delight passed through her as she looked him over. Tonight he had on a wear-softened T-shirt and snug jeans with no belt. The faded denim molded to his body and revealed exactly how excited he was. His feet were bare.

He lifted the boots he held in one hand. "Thought I'd save some time."

"Excellent." She trembled as she reached for his hand and drew him inside. Then she started to lead him toward the hall.

He paused, bringing her hand to his lips. "How have you been?" he murmured as he kissed her knuckles.

"I...um...I've been fine."

"Been working in your studio today?"

"Uh…yes."

He ran his tongue in the crevice between each knuckle. "Did you think about me while you worked on a nude statue?"

"Of course I did." She wasn't sure all this talking was a good idea. She might stumble and say something that would give her away. "And it made me really, really want you." She tugged on his hand.

He resisted. Gently, but still he wasn't moving. "Then you were working on a statue of a man?"

"Yes."

"I've thought about your work, and I wonder if you get…excited…when you're making the penis."

She swallowed. "I…I like doing that."

"I'll bet you do, Sarah." He caressed her fingers. "I get really hot imagining these soft hands squeezing the clay, shaping it, molding your very own—"

"Well, it's all about art, of course."

"Of course. But, Sarah, will this statue look anything like me?"

"Yes. No. I mean…I wouldn't want anyone to recognize…"

"My penis? I don't think that's likely. It's not *that* well-known."

"I meant your face." She tugged harder. "Jonas, please. I need you so."

"That's good to hear." At last he followed her toward the hallway. "Because I've been thinking about you, about this, all day. I spent most of my time alone, riding the fence, checking for breaks in the wire. I just didn't feel like being with people when all I wanted to do was think about you."

She'd wondered where the heck he'd gone today. But not having him around had made her life easier. At least she hadn't needed to put up a false front. But he was sounding way too interested in her sculpting career and also kind of lovesick. That wasn't good. A lovesick man might do something stupid, like drive over here sometime, hoping to find the object of his affections working on her nude statues.

Okay, tonight would be the end. She couldn't chance another meeting, no matter how much she wanted it. Just this afternoon, she'd figured out how she'd make sure he never found out what had happened.

She'd send him a letter explaining that she wasn't Sarah, but Sarah's younger cousin, who had spent these three days in Arizona while Sarah was gone. The "cousin" would then simply disappear, and B.J. could verify that Sarah's cousin, who was mentally unbalanced, had paid a surprise visit and stayed at the house. B.J. would fill Sarah in on the whole thing, too, so she'd back up the story.

The plan wasn't perfect, but B.J. was counting on the fact that Jonas wouldn't want to spread the word that he'd indulged in erotic activities with a woman he didn't even know. When the woman vanished, he might be embarrassed that she hadn't wanted him enough to stick around.

At the bedroom doorway he took a deep breath. "I'm glad you didn't change the candles. Or the music."

"I was hoping they would trigger your response." The scent and the music certainly had an effect on her. The tops of her inner thighs were already damp.

"Consider my response triggered." His voice dropped to a low murmur. "But you're not naked tonight."

She whirled in a panic. "Are you peeking?"

"No. I promised I wouldn't. But I heard something rustle. It sounds like...like something I've heard before."

Then she realized that Jonas had seen the chaps and vest when she'd worn them on the television program. She didn't want him to make the connection. "I went shopping today and found this outfit."

"It doesn't sound like silk and satin."

"No, it's leather."

He stopped dead in the middle of the hall. "*Leather?* Maybe we need to talk. The bondage thing last night was great, but I'm really not into whips and chains."

She smiled and tugged on his hand. "Don't worry. This is about pleasure, not pain."

"Good. You had me going for a minute."

"Well, just relax and enjoy it." She led him over to the bed and gazed at the T-shirt. Taking it off could dislodge his blindfold. She wondered if he'd done that on purpose.

"I want to touch you." He reached for her.

"Soon." She stepped back, still thinking about his T-shirt. He might be planning to arouse her so thoroughly that she'd forget about everything but getting him naked. And if she pulled off his blindfold while yanking off his shirt, then he couldn't be blamed for that.

"Take off your jeans," she murmured.

"What about my shirt?"

"I think that shirt is a trap, so I want to leave it on for now."

His laugh was low and sexy. "It's not a trap, Sarah. I was hoping this time you'd undress me."

"And when I pulled your shirt over your head, the blindfold would accidentally come with it?"

"You're more clever than I am. I didn't think of that. No, I didn't want you to pull it over my head. It's an old shirt. I want you to rip it off me."

The idea hit her with a jolt of excitement. "One of your fantasies?"

"Yes."

She approached him. "I can do that."

"But first let me touch you," he begged. "I'm going crazy not being able to touch your body."

"All right." She took his hands and placed them on her shoulders. "See if you can discover what I'm wearing."

Breathing faster, he caressed the material with a light touch. "A suede vest."

"That's right."

"What color?"

"Black." She eased his shirt from the waistband of his jeans.

He slid both hands under the vest. "Oh, Lord.

And nothing underneath.'' He cupped her breasts. ''I wish I could see how you look.''

''Imagine.''

''I'm imagining. I can't believe how you fill my hands. I never thought—I never thought I'd find such a perfect fit, as if my hands were made to hold you this way.''

She moaned as he kneaded her breasts. His caress was the only one she'd ever want, and after tonight she'd never feel it again.

''Does it make you wet when I do this?'' He stroked her nipples with his thumbs.

Being bold came so easily when she was in disguise. She tipped her pelvis forward. ''Why don't you find out for yourself?''

His breath caught. Sliding one hand down to her belly, he touched the fringed belt that held up the chaps. Then he explored lower. ''Chaps,'' he whispered. ''Perfect access. Damn, but I want you. Heaven help me, I want you more than I've ever wanted a woman before.'' He slipped his fingers into her heat. ''I want those suede-covered thighs to spread for me.''

It took all her willpower to ease away from him. His talented fingers worked far too well and far too fast. This time she wanted her orgasm to blend with his. "That will happen," she said in a husky voice. "But not quite yet. Stand still as a statue now. No touching."

"You're torturing me."

"And you love it."

"Yeah. I do."

"Hold still." She stood on tiptoe and kissed him, using her tongue to lick and probe his mouth until he was panting. All the while she searched out a small rip in his shirt.

"I want you naked," she murmured against his mouth. "I want you stripped the way you were last night, writhing on the bed, begging, pleading."

He groaned.

She bit his lip softly. "I'm so hot for you that I could come just thinking of you naked. I'm going to rip the clothes from your body and then I'm going to lick every inch of you." She pulled hard on the T-shirt. The sound of tearing material fired her up even more, and soon she'd shredded the shirt and tossed it to the floor.

Then she pressed her mouth to his heaving chest while she nipped and licked her way over his salty skin.

"Let me…hold you," he said, gasping.

"Not yet." She fumbled with the button and the

zipper of his jeans while she licked her way down to his waistband. By the time she set him free, she was right there, ready to take his penis into her mouth. He tasted sinful and so very, very delicious.

"Don't..." he moaned. "Don't or I'll—"

Reluctantly she lifted her mouth. "I know. And I have more...more planned."

"Oh, Lord, Sarah."

"The longer you can hold out—"

"I know. I'm trying."

"Good." She finished taking off his jeans and briefs before guiding him to the bed. If this was to be her last time with Jonas, she planned to make it count.

Before he'd arrived, she'd placed the bottle of oil on the nightstand. The cap was already off. Right next to that was the condom she planned to use when the time was right. She poured a quarter-size puddle of oil into the palm of her hand.

"The thing is, I don't know...how much more I can..."

She stroked his penis with her oil-lubricated hand.

"Oh, dear God. You have oil."

"Yes." She massaged some over his chest and down his flat stomach. He was breathing harder than a charging bull by the time she finished massaging his thighs, calves and feet. "It's flavored oil. Guess what that means?"

"It means you'll drive me insane."

"I hope so." She moved back up to his chest and began to lick the cherry-laced oil from his nipples.

He quivered with every flick of her tongue. "Be…careful," he warned. "I'm so close. Ahh… Sarah…that's good."

Like a mother cat grooming a kitten, she lapped at every bit of him except his groin. And finally that was all that was left. She started on her final project.

"No," he said. "No."

"But I want—"

"Get the condom out of my jeans pocket." His voice was tight with desperation. "Or hand them to me and let me do it. If you put your tongue there again, I'll never make it. Please."

Now that the moment had come, a whisper of fear held her back. Until now she'd been able to treat this as a game. It was the most erotic, exciting, passionate game she'd ever played, but still a game. Instinct told her that once she joined her body with his, the game would change.

"Please, Sarah. I want to be inside you."

She wanted that, too. But she was afraid of the price she'd pay. Yet without that, her memory of these days would be incomplete. She reached for the condom packet on the nightstand and ripped it open.

"Ah, you found it."

"No, I had my own."

"Do it quick. Don't tease me with this, or we'll both lose."

Taking a deep breath, she unrolled the condom over his penis. "There. It's—" She gasped as his fingers tightened over her wrist. "Jonas?"

He sat up. "I don't have to see for this part."

Before she could react, he pushed her down and slid on top of her.

"Jonas, wait." He was taking over, and that could mean he'd force the issue of her identity. He'd been so docile that she'd never expected this.

"It's my turn." He grasped her other wrist and held both hands flat against the mattress. "Finally." He nuzzled her breasts, her throat, the tender place behind her ear.

And she was losing the fight to resist. Her protest sounded feeble. "You were supposed to stay on your back."

He nibbled her earlobe. "If you wanted to guarantee that, you should have tied me up again. Now kiss me, you wild, crazy woman." And with that he plundered her mouth.

She surrendered. She couldn't do anything else, wanting him the way she did. Oh, how she ached.

He lifted his mouth a fraction from hers and edged a knee between her thighs. "Open up for me."

As if she could help it. He was running the show now.

He moved between her thighs. "Now arch your hips and invite me in."

Gripping his firm bottom in both hands, she lifted toward him.

"Ah, that's good." He probed her slick entrance with the tip of his penis. "Do you want me?"

*"Yes."* She would die if he didn't plunge deep within her.

"Then tell me. Say it. I want to hear you."

She struggled for breath. "I want you."

"Say *I want you, Jonas.*"

Her heartbeat thundered in her ears. "I want you, Jonas."

"Have you always wanted me?"

She was delirious with need, barely making sense

of what he was saying, only knowing that she would agree to anything if only he'd fill her. "Yes," she said, panting.

"That's all I needed to know." He slid forward, slowly and deliberately, until they were locked tight.

Tears filled her eyes. This was so perfect, so completely and utterly perfect. She'd known it would be.

"It's good," he said.

She nodded, forgetting that he couldn't see.

"And it's going to get better." There was a tenderness in his voice, a gentleness in his rhythm.

She'd never imagined, after all the wildness they'd shared, that he would take this final step so slow and easy. The tears poured down her cheeks as Jonas made love to her, really made love to her. This didn't feel like a game anymore.

With each sure stroke Jonas took her closer to the brink. And all the while he murmured words of endearment, making her feel cherished. Making her feel loved.

"Now," he said, increasing the rhythm. "Come for me."

She rode on the crest, propelled by his movements, his whispered words of encouragement. And then, she was there, coming apart in his arms, quaking and sobbing at the beauty of it.

While she continued to tremble in the aftermath, he surged forward with his own release. Poised on his braced forearms, he clenched his jaw and groaned. Then he slowly collapsed against her. His voice was husky, his breath warm against her ear. "Ah, B.J. That was so great."

## CHAPTER EIGHT

HER NAME HAD SLIPPED right out while Jonas was basking in the glow of their togetherness. Making love to B.J. had been so wonderful, so right, that he'd totally forgotten to play the game. Hell and damnation, he hadn't meant to let her know at this delicate moment that he knew who she was. But it was done now.

She went rigid beneath him. Then she began to struggle to get away.

"Wait a minute, B.J." He pulled off the blindfold with one hand while he tried to grab her with the other. His movements were slow, weighed down with that lazy pleasure following great lovemaking. "Don't go getting all upset."

"You *knew!* You knew all along! Let me go!"

"I didn't know at first." Some of the slippery oil from his body had transferred itself to her and that made holding onto her more difficult. "I found out this morning."

''And you came here anyway!'' She managed to push him away long enough to scramble out of the bed.

''Yeah, I sure did.'' At last he had a good look at her in the red suede outfit, with her hair down, her skin flushed, her breasts heaving. He swallowed. She was something, all right. He'd seriously misjudged B.J. Branscom. ''And not a man alive would blame me for it. You started this whole thing, and I would have been a fool not to take advantage of the opportunity!''

She snatched up his jeans and held them over her crotch. ''Why, so you could laugh at me for the rest of your life?''

''*Laugh* at you? Are you crazy? In case you haven't noticed, I've been your slave for three solid days. If anyone planned to have a good laugh over this, it would be you, sweetheart!''

She was quivering, her eyes wild. ''I never meant for you to know.''

A cold fist gripped his heart. ''Never?''

She shook her head.

''And why would that be?'' he asked quietly.

At first it seemed she wouldn't answer him. Then she lifted her chin and met his gaze. ''I would think that would be obvious.''

As he lay there staring at her, his heart aching as it never had in his life, only one thing was obvious to him. She didn't want him for anything more than an anonymous roll in the hay. Maybe she'd been curious after all the talk and wanted a chance to find out how good he was in bed. But beyond that, he wasn't what she was looking for.

"Give me my clothes," he said. "I'm going home."

B.J. THREW HER SUEDE outfit in the Dumpster on the way home. She thought about not going home at all, of driving instead to Los Angeles and trying to locate her sister Keely. But she couldn't do that to her father. He'd mourned the loss of contact with Keely so much. If B.J. left, he'd have no family at all.

But she couldn't imagine how she'd be able to work on the ranch after this. Technically Jonas was her boss, although she seldom thought about that considering the way they all worked together like equals. Or had. That easy camaraderie was over now.

What a fool she'd been to think that she could keep her identity a secret. He'd probably gone to town that morning and asked a few questions about the woman renting the Hawthorne place. Saguaro Junction was a small place. Information wasn't hard to come by.

So now she was exactly what she'd never wanted to be—another one of Jonas's conquests. No point in thinking otherwise. If he'd meant to turn this thing around, to take the relationship seriously, he would have told her the minute he showed up tonight. He would have whipped off the blindfold right away.

Instead he'd let her continue the game and probably would have let her go on indefinitely. Except, in the aftermath of lovemaking, he'd forgotten to call her Sarah. She should probably be grateful for his slipup. Otherwise she might have been tempted to let him come back the following night.

She automatically looked for Jonas's shiny black truck when she drove toward the ranch house on her way to her father's little bungalow. The truck wasn't there.

A chill went down her spine as she pictured him downing beers at the Roundup Saloon. Would he tell anyone what had happened? If he did, if even one word of this got around town, she'd have to leave, no matter how much it hurt her father. In fact, her father might prefer that she left.

She had to hope Jonas wasn't blabbing everything to his buddies at the bar tonight. He probably wasn't. Rumors flew about Jonas's exploits, but B.J. had never known Jonas to say anything about the women he was involved with.

Still, it wouldn't hurt to get his word that he wouldn't reveal their secret, ever. Once Jonas promised something like that, he wouldn't break his promise. She'd grown up knowing that about both the Garfield brothers. Teasing and playing pranks had been part of everyday life, but when it came to serious things like keeping a confidence, both Jonas and Noah were men of their word.

She let herself into the darkened house where all was silent except the ticking of the grandfather clock and the snoring coming from her father's bedroom. Going into her own room, she undressed and crawled into bed. If only she could think of some excuse to go away.

There was Sarah's mail to be considered if she left, but Arch would be willing to take care of that for the last three days if B.J. told him she desperately needed a break. Even a short getaway would help put some distance between tonight and a future of working side by side with Jonas.

Although many women expected to marry and

move away from home, B.J. had always assumed she'd live on this ranch forever. She'd figured that if she married, her husband would live and work here, too. She loved everything about Twin Boulders—riding the gentle hills, working with the animals, even driving the balky old tractor.

Well, she'd certainly mucked up her happy little existence with this stunt. And tomorrow she'd have to face Jonas.

JONAS AWOKE WITH THE WORST hangover he'd had in years, a condition made even more painful by someone pounding on the roof over his head. No doubt his brother was trying to kill two birds with one stone—fixing some loose shingles while the sun was shining and getting Jonas's sorry ass out of bed.

He glanced at the clock. Nearly ten. Unfortunately the Roundup didn't open until noon or he'd be off to drown his sorrows all over again. Yet he knew he couldn't stay drunk because Noah needed his help on the ranch. Eventually he'd have to figure out how to handle this disaster.

Maybe Noah could spare him for a few days, though, so he could get away and figure out how in hell he'd be able to stay on this ranch and work side by side with B.J. And that's what he'd have to do, because he couldn't imagine living anywhere else, and he couldn't very well kick her off the premises.

Oh, technically he might be able to fire her, especially if he told Noah what she'd done. But of course, he wouldn't tell Noah. He wouldn't tell anyone. Besides, if he fired B.J., then Arch would leave with her, and that would make an even bigger mess.

He couldn't believe she'd done this to him. Sure, when they were kids he'd put a baby gopher snake in her bed once, and he'd booby-trapped her lunch box a few times, and then there was the crank call where he'd pretended to be that guy from *Dirty Dancing,* Patrick Swayze, singing "I Had the Time of My Life."

But she'd pulled her share on him, too. She'd dumped red food coloring in the washing machine, staining all his white briefs pink, and she'd lined up beer bottles on his bedroom windowsill so his dad had thought he'd been in his room drinking like a fish. Then she'd stolen the centerfold out of one of his magazines and made him buy it back with three sacks of Gummy Bears.

He'd thought they were about even. But they

were far from even now, and he had no clue how to settle the score, other than tattling on her. And he wasn't about to do that.

The fact was, he hurt. He hurt really bad. At some point during last night's escapade he'd realized that he was in love with B.J., probably always had been. He figured it out when he discovered she was wearing the red suede vest and chaps from that televised riding gig she'd done a few years back.

He remembered that riding demonstration perfectly—how proud she'd been of the show, how excited about the beautiful outfit she'd bought. And she'd looked fantastic in that arena. He might have asked her out after seeing that production if he hadn't still been hung up on the sister-brother relationship they'd always had.

She'd blown that illusion all to hell in the cave. Once he'd learned that she'd sacrificed her beautiful suede outfit to give him a sexual thrill, he'd decided that the two of them had something pretty special going on. He'd let himself name the emotion that filled his heart whenever he thought of B.J.

Then she'd squashed all hope that his tender feelings would ever be returned when she confessed she'd never planned to tell him who she was. The reason should be obvious, she'd said. God, how that hurt.

He had to ask Noah for a few days off, so he could slap some mental bandages over his gaping wounds. Noah had been wanting someone to drive up to Payson and look at a stud they were considering breeding to Imelda next year. A trip like that could be good for three days if he worked it right. Dragging himself out of bed, he took his pounding head and broken heart into the shower.

BY MIDMORNING B.J. hadn't seen hide-nor-hair of Jonas, which was fine with her. She'd also come up with a reason to leave the ranch for a few days, so she sought out Noah, who was taking advantage of the sunshine to fix some broken shingles on the main house.

Climbing the ladder, she called over to him.

He paused and glanced at her, tilting his hat to the back of his head. "What's up?"

"You know how you've been saying someone should take a look at that stud in Payson?"

"Yeah."

"If you think you can spare me for two or three days, I thought I'd drive up there and check him out. I can take some pictures and get an idea of his temperament."

Noah grinned. "Great minds must think alike. Jonas suggested going up there not ten minutes ago. You two wanna flip for it?"

At his casual mention of Jonas's plans, B.J.'s stomach clenched. If she had this kind of reaction when someone happened to say his name, she was in big trouble. But she'd known that.

She cleared her throat. "If Jonas is planning on going, that's fine. I don't have to go." It didn't really matter which one of them took off, so long as they didn't have to see each other for a while. "When's he leaving?"

"Pretty soon, I think. Listen, B.J., you've been working harder than Jonas. It's a hell of a lot cooler up in the pine country, so if you want a break I'll tell him to stay home."

"No!" That was the last thing she wanted. But she needed to talk to him before he left to make sure he wouldn't reveal their secret. "I wouldn't mind having him bring back some pine cones, though, so I can make wreaths again this Christmas. I'll go ask him about it."

"I imagine he's in the house throwing some clothes into a suitcase."

"Thanks. I'll go check." She was shaking so badly she nearly fell off the ladder as she climbed back down. She paused at the bottom and took several deep breaths. All she needed to ask was that he not tell anyone. Then she could leave. No big discussion required. Just her request and his answer. That was it. She could do this.

As usual, she went in the kitchen door. On her way through she gave a smile and a cheery greeting to Lupita, who was making tortillas. "I need to talk to Jonas," she said by way of explanation. She hoped Lupita hadn't noticed the tremor in her voice.

"He's down the hall, packing to leave," Lupita said. "Wish we could all go up to the mountains."

"Yeah, it would be nice." B.J. started for the hallway before she lost her nerve. "Jonas!" she called on her way to his bedroom. "I need to ask you something."

He appeared in the doorway of his bedroom, his dark eyes heavy-lidded, his expression grim. "What?"

She couldn't understand why he had to look so sexy right at this moment, or why her throat had to close up when she'd been perfectly capable of speech when she'd passed through the kitchen.

"What do you want, B.J.?" he asked quietly, his gaze neutral.

She would have thought he was calm, except that

his knuckles were white where he was gripping the doorjamb. Her one-sentence speech left her mind. "I'm sorry," she whispered.

He shrugged. "Easy come, easy go."

She struggled to remember what she'd come to say. "I wanted to ask that you…not say anything. To anybody."

Neutrality slipped away and anger flared in his brown eyes. His response was thick with fury. "How could you even think I would?"

She stepped back a pace. "I didn't. Not really. I just wanted to make sure, because—"

"Because you don't want anyone to know you stooped so low?"

She gasped. "I would never think that."

He glanced down the hall toward the kitchen and lowered his voice. "Seems like it to me. You were never planning to tell me, or anyone. I figure that's because you're ashamed of having had sex with me."

*Having had sex.* "You make it sound so cold."

"Wasn't it? Two strangers in the night seems pretty cold to me."

She clenched her hands in front of her. "It wasn't like that."

"Then tell me what it was like."

Her heart beat like crazy. He was pinning her to the wall, and she didn't know how to get away. "Don't make me humiliate myself even more."

His lips thinned. "Just as I thought. You're humiliated that you let yourself get so carried away. You're better than that, right? You're not like me, a real sex maniac. Sure, you had your fling, but now you're going to put it behind you."

As she gazed at him, his tone of voice finally penetrated her anguish. He sounded angry, sure, but underneath that anger was something else, something more vulnerable. He was hurt. She looked past him to the duffle open on his bed, clothes hanging out of it as if he'd stuffed them inside without caring what he took.

*He was trying to get away.* Slowly she went back over their heated exchange from the night before. She'd told him she'd never meant for him to know she was his mystery lover. Apparently he'd interpreted that to mean that she was ashamed of their time together.

She could let him continue to think that and save her pride, or she could admit her feelings and take away his pain. In the end, it was no contest. She loved him, and she didn't want him to hurt.

"Jonas, I wasn't going to tell you because I

didn't want to be another one of your discarded girlfriends.''

He stared at her for a long time, a muscle working in his jaw. ''Is that how you think of me?'' he said at last. ''An insensitive guy who loves 'em and leaves 'em?''

''You have to admit there have been quite a few—''

''Did it ever occur to you that I was extremely choosy, and although I kept trying, I could never find exactly the right woman for me?''

''Well, yeah.''

''And let me assure you, I agonize over the breakups each and every time.''

''Maybe you do, but you still manage to break up with them. And I didn't want to be part of that scene.''

He paused and his gaze flicked over her. ''Who says you would be?''

''Are you kidding? Look at me. I'm a cowgirl, just like the ones you said never could hold your interest. There's nothing unusual about me.'' She noticed his expression change as a smile tugged at his mouth.

''Well, there isn't! I'm good old B.J., who can fix the thermostat on the tractor—''

"Yeah, and you sure fixed mine."

"Jonas, pay attention. I'm trying to tell you that while I may be able to throw a decent rope—"

"You tie a mean velvet rope, too."

"—and ride a cutting horse without falling off—"

"You can ride me anytime, sweetheart."

"Listen, don't get me confused with that woman at Sarah's house, because I'm not that woman."

His eyebrows lifted. "You're not?"

"No."

"I could have sworn you were. Come here and let me get a better look." He took her arm and pulled her inside his bedroom.

"Wait a minute. You have the wrong idea."

"You don't even know what my idea is yet." He closed his bedroom door and twisted the lock.

Her pulse raced at the look in his eyes. "Listen, Jonas, this isn't the time or the place. In fact, we should probably get that straight. What happened between us can't happen again."

"Oh?" He walked her backward toward the bed. "Why not?"

"I've told you. I won't be toyed with." The backs of her knees came in contact with the edge of the bed.

"Damn. That's exactly what I had in mind."

"See, now that you know I'm not ashamed of what happened between us, you think you can make it go on some more, but it won't, because—oh!" She lost her balance and fell across the bed.

He followed her down. "Yes, it will." He slid his body over hers. "It'll go on constantly. It might go on right now."

"Jonas, no." She had to protect herself, even though her body was warming up beneath his. In salvaging his feelings, she had set the stage for sacrificing hers.

He looked into her eyes, and his tone was gentle. "I guess you're going to be one of those women who holds out for a wedding ring."

"I suppose you think that's funny, considering what we did together." Her breathing quickened. God, how she wanted him, but she had to be strong. "Yes, I've decided the next time I get involved with a man, that's what I want. A ring, marriage, kids, the whole works."

"I can handle that."

She figured he still didn't understand. He wanted to continue the fun and games until that potential husband came along. "The thing is, until then, I'm not having any more flings, no matter how much fun I had this time.''

"No more flings? That would be a crying shame, Belinda June. That feather-duster routine needs an encore, and I'll bet you have more of that flavored oil, too.''

She wasn't going to make love to him again, but knowing he remembered her whole name made her feel all mushy inside. Okay, so she was also getting hot, and wet, and achy. Once she escaped from this bedroom those feelings would ease up a bit.

"Have a fling with me, Belinda,'' he murmured. "It'll pass the time until the wedding.''

"What wedding? I'm not even dating anybody.''

"Our wedding.''

She lay very still, afraid to move, afraid to breathe. Surely she hadn't heard him right.

He brushed his forefinger over her mouth. "I can see from the total disbelief in your expression that you're either horrified by my proposal or you don't believe me.''

"I don't believe you.''

"But if you did believe me, you'd accept?''

"If I did believe you, I would, but I don't, so I can't.''

He chuckled softly. "Let's see if I can say the

right things to convince you." He cupped her face
in both hands and gazed at her earnestly. "I feel
like an idiot, because if you hadn't seduced me in
that cave, we might still be stumbling around this
ranch, so close and yet so far from each other. I'll
always be grateful to that rainstorm for showing me
what's been right in front of me. I guess I had to
be blindfolded to really see you for the first time."
He rubbed his thumbs caressingly over her cheekbones. "Oh, and by the way, I've decided I love
the Hawthorne place. Maybe we'll buy it and live
there."

Oh, God. He was serious. He was proposing. Little white specks flashed in front of her eyes. "You
have to let me up," she said, gasping. "I think I'm
going to faint."

Immediately he rolled off of her. Then he sat her
up and pushed her head down between her knees.
"Deep breaths. That's it. Deep breaths. Better
now?"

Gradually her head stopped spinning, but she still
couldn't seem to breathe normally. She looked at
him, sure he'd vanish in a puff of smoke.

"You *still* don't believe me, do you?" he said,
concern etched on his face. "Honey, what I'm trying to say is, I love you!"

The room began to spin again and she ducked her head between her knees while he rubbed her back.

"Look, you'll have to get used to hearing it, because we can't have you passing out every time I tell you I love you. That would be very inconvenient. Besides, I'm not into making love to an unconscious woman."

For some reason that struck her as funny, and she began to giggle. She wasn't a giggler, but that's exactly what she was doing.

"Lord, now you're hysterical. I hope the shock wears off soon, because I really, really want to start the kissing part."

So did she. Still grinning, she lifted her head and gazed at him. "Okay, I believe you."

"Glory be." He guided her back down to the mattress. "So the fling's on?"

"It's on." Her heart swelled with more happiness than she'd known it could hold.

"Followed by the wedding?"

"Yep."

"Hot damn." He eased over on top of her again. "How are you feeling? Dizzy again?"

"A little, but it'll pass." She gazed up into his

eyes. Next time they made love, she'd be able to see them. She could hardly wait.

"How come you feel like fainting when I tell you I love you and I want to marry you?"

"Because I've wanted that since I was four years old."

His eyes widened. "Get outta here."

"It's true. I've loved you ever since I can remember, Jonas."

His gaze warmed. "I think the same goes for me. Only I didn't have sense enough to know it." He shook his head. "Which makes me a real fool, but I plan to spend a lifetime making up for that, starting now." Propped himself on one elbow, he started unbuttoning her blouse. "It's fling time."

"Jonas! Right here?"

"Why not? Don't start in on that *I'm not the woman you think I am* routine. It won't wash, not with me. I know you're one hot little number when you want to be."

She laughed with delight, because he did know that about her. And he was the only one who did. "But it's broad daylight, and—"

"Oh, hey, I'm glad you mentioned that." He scrambled from the bed and hurried over to open his top dresser drawer. "I can take care of the daylight angle for you.'' He dangled a red silk scarf from one hand. ''My souvenir.''

She clapped a hand to her mouth. She'd never missed it.

He approached the bed holding the blindfold. ''I'll tie this over your eyes and you can pretend it's dark out. I don't have a feather duster, but I'm sure I can round up something to tickle you with. I think I still have that old toy headdress in my closet.''

She smiled at him. They were going to have such fun being married. ''Let's play with the blindfold later, Jonas. This time I want to look into your eyes when we make love.''

He tossed the blindfold aside immediately. ''Works for me,'' he said softly.

Jonas loved her. That was enough to make her bolder than brass. She unfastened the remaining buttons on her blouse.

His gaze drifted to her lace-covered breasts. ''As for me, I want to look...everywhere. I've been through some serious sight deprivation recently.''

She unfastened the front catch of her bra and arched her back. Then she lowered her voice to the sultry murmur she'd used at Sarah's house. ''Then be my guest.''

"Oh, yeah. That's the woman I was looking for." He grinned as he came toward her. Then his grin faded as he gazed into her eyes. His voice grew husky with emotion. "You are the woman I was looking for," he said. "All my life."

\*   \*   \*   \*   \*

*B.J. might have found her man, but her sister, Keely, is still out there looking.*
*Don't miss the fireworks when Jonas's brother, Noah, goes to Las Vegas for a wedding and ends up with Keely Branscom sharing his hotel room— and his bed!*

*Look for NOTORIOUS by Vicki Lewis Thompson, the first book in Harlequin's newest—and hottest—series yet.*

*Available in August 2001, wherever Harlequin books are sold.*

# AFTER HOURS
## Stephanie Bond

# CHAPTER ONE

"DON'T WORRY, MRS. CONRAD, the loincloth is definitely machine washable." Rebecca Valentine juggled the phone so she could talk while pinning a floor-length velvet cape hanging on a dress form. Her mind wandered to accessories she'd have to pull together—jeweled sash, vampire teeth, thigh-high boots.

"And the ankle cuffs, too, dear?"

She spoke around straight pins clamped between her lips. "Um, yes, the ankle cuffs are washable, too."

"Oh, that's grand! I was afraid we'd have to order another outfit for Marty, and this one practically brand-new. I mean, the fantasy weekend brochure mentioned mud games, but I didn't realize it would be a *pit* of mud."

Rebecca normally humored the woman as much as her modesty could withstand, but today she wasn't in the mood to hear about the Conrads' sensual adventures, not after another sleepless night pondering her own hapless love life. A bell chimed, and her shoulders fell in relief. "There's my front door, Mrs. Conrad. I have to go."

"Okay, dear, thanks for the information. And call me as soon as the harem costume arrives. I have a surprise planned for Marty's birthday."

"Er, I will. Goodbye, Mrs. Conrad."

"Toodle-loo."

Rebecca returned the receiver, marveling that a grandmother who wore tweed skirts and brought homemade cream candy every time she visited Anytime Costumes, could have such an erotic relationship with her husband of thirty years. People weren't always what they seemed.

As she headed toward the front of her shop, she smirked. Take Dickie, for instance. From all outward appearances, he'd been the perfect fiancé, not the kind of man who would elope with his pregnant mistress while his clueless bride-to-be fretted over a china pattern. And his pregnant mistress couldn't be just any boyish shopgirl, *noooooo*—she was a former Miss Illinois, 38-24-36.

"Hidy-hoo!" a deep melodious voice called from the front of the shop.

Rebecca smiled in spite of the tightness that had

seized her chest, and rounded the corner as fast as she could in the nun's habit she wore. Quincy Lyle, deliveryman extraordinaire, stood in her showroom with a large box at his feet, shaking rain from his buff brown arms. He scanned her head to toe. "Sworn off men altogether, Sister Rebecca?"

She laughed and touched the stiff headdress. "I'm testing a design. The village playhouse needs twelve nun costumes for a musical. But now that you mention it, maybe becoming a nun isn't such a bad idea." The celibacy vow would not present a problem.

"*Pshaw,* you're too beautiful to be a nun."

Sigh—if only the man wasn't gay. "You're such a sweet liar, Quince."

"Hey, in case you haven't looked in the mirror lately, you're Audrey Hepburn reincarnated."

She smiled ruefully. "Ah, but I can't twirl a baton." Since Quincy knew practically everyone in the North Chicago business district, and since Dickie's law firm was only a few blocks away, the deliveryman knew all the sordid details of her jilting.

He rolled his eyes. "*Please.* The man's name is *Dickie,* for heaven's sake. He has *issues.*"

"I know," she said, wondering why it was easier

to commiserate about the foul ordeal with a casual acquaintance than with her close friends, or even with her sister. "I'm over him." And her voice cracked only because she was probably coming down with a cold. She expelled a tiny cough. Yes, a cold.

"Sure you're over him," Quincy said cheerfully, then leaned on her counter and flashed a devilish smile. "Which is why you should treat yourself to an incredibly irresponsible fling with an incredibly irresistible specimen."

She laughed and shook her head. "Sounds fun, but it's not exactly my style."

"Styles change, honey." He lifted the edge of her voluminous black sleeve. "And you're crying out for an emotional makeover."

Rebecca bit into her lip. In truth, over the past two weeks, the urge to retaliate against Dickie's betrayal had sometimes overwhelmed her. Lying in bed late at night, listening to sad songs on the stereo, hadn't she wished she had the nerve to engage in a relationship for pure physical pleasure? To prove to Dickie, to prove to *herself* that what was good for the gander was good for the goose? Just the thought of an illicit affair made her burn with sweet revenge. Yet inevitably she would concede that even if she decided to do something so uncharacteristically wicked, how would she go about finding a...specimen? The only other man in her life, pathetically, was a mouthwatering customer she'd secretly fantasized about for years, and he was married.

Quincy clucked. "Just promise me that if someone suitable happens by, you'll be open to a little flirtation."

"I will, but he won't. Happen by, that is."

"You never know. It's the lousy weather that's making you blue." Quincy glanced at the heavy gray clouds that had taken up residence over the city, then gestured to the area above the counter where some of the most colorful costumes were displayed. "If this keeps up, I'm going to need one of those mermaid costumes of yours just to make deliveries."

She smiled at his lame attempt to lift her spirits, and nodded toward the box. "What do you have for me?"

"Don't know, but it's as light as a feather." He squinted at the label. "Lana Martina Healey, Lexington, Kentucky."

"Lana Martina Healey? Oh—Lana Martina!"

"Customer?"

Her troubled thoughts were instantly replaced with fond memories. "No, she was this genius my sister and I knew in college. Wow, she must be married now." She walked around the plain cardboard box measuring about three feet square, marked with the words Do Not Cut Open. "What on earth would she be sending me?"

"A wedding gift?"

Rebecca frowned. "I don't see how Lana could have known about the wedding. We really haven't kept in touch. Can you give me a hand with it, Quince?"

"Sure." He made short work of the strapping tape and stepped aside.

Rebecca pushed back the cardboard flaps, exposing a sea of foam peanuts.

"Whatever it is, it must be breakable," he said.

Her curiosity piqued, she stuck her hand into the packing material, sending peanuts everywhere, and found an envelope. She slid her finger under the flap and withdrew a brightly colored note card with a picture of a cup of coffee on the front.

"The suspense is killing me," Quincy said, motioning for her to hurry.

"Dear Rebecca," she read. "I got your business address from the Alumni directory. Believe it or not, I'm also an entrepreneur.'' Rebecca pursed her mouth—Lana, Little Miss Corporate, had struck out on her own? ''I gave up the accounting gig and opened a bohemian coffee shop in Lexington—which doesn't sound nearly as interesting as owning a costume shop. I just married a yummy attorney I met through the personal ads, although neither one of us placed one.''

She glanced up at Quincy. ''Interesting things always seemed to happen to that girl.'' Then she continued reading. ''Oh, well, how Greg and I met is another story. The bottom line is, I credit the good fortune of meeting my husband to my good luck charm, Harry. So, following the agreement at Angie's bachelorette party in college, I'm passing Harry on to you in hopes that he will be your good luck love charm. Take care of him and he'll take care of you. Fondly, Lana. P.S. If the directory is out of date and you're already married, please pass along to your sister, or to a single friend.'' She stopped reading—Angie she remembered, as well as the bachelorette party. But she had no recollection of any agreement having to do with a man named Harry.

''She sent you a man in a box?'' Quincy asked,

his eyebrows drawn together. "Was she voted Most Likely to Be a Serial Killer?"

Rebecca eyed the box warily, then crossed herself.

MICHAEL PIERCE PULLED HIS ball cap lower to fend off the rain. Damnable stuff. As if this week hadn't been terrible enough, what with the divorce being final, then being forced to close the restaurant to regroup. The driving rain, while appropriate, amounted to salt on his open wounds. He used the armful of employee uniforms as a shield and tried to ignore the tight, achy feeling in his head and chest. Must be getting a cold—par for the course.

At times like this, Florida sounded appealing. As did playing guitar for impromptu crowds with a lot of pocket change.

The restaurant had been Sonia's idea, and for some reason, that woman had always been able to talk him into anything. He'd been so crazy about her when they were married six years ago, he would have done anything to make her happy, including sinking his life savings into a restaurant. Sonia had loved the social aspect of running an eatery, but refused to bend to the financial demands—she would think nothing of comping an eight-hundred-dollar table if the people were friends of hers. Her bubbly personality was her greatest asset, and his greatest weakness. And because he gave in to her every whim, their personal and business bank accounts were nearly drained.

Still, he'd grown to enjoy the restaurant business, struggles and all. But he'd been completely blind-sided by Sonia's request for a divorce six weeks ago. She had taken a lover, it seemed, a wealthy real estate king who frequented the restaurant—of course, now Michael knew the man hadn't been coming back for the sea bass. The news of the affair had cut to the quick because as stunningly beautiful as Sonia was, she'd never been that interested in sex. Oh, she would never turn him down when he initiated intimacy, but he always had a feeling when they made love that she was preoccupied, the way a woman might let her mind wander during a physical exam to bide time until it was over.

Over the past few weeks, his emotions had shifted from hurt to anger, and he had now reached the vengeance stage—not the best time to make decisions affecting his future. But smart or no, he'd borrowed against his retirement savings and planned to make the restaurant a success...somehow. To prove something to himself? To stay busy? Maybe a little of both.

What he needed, his brother Ike had told him, was a fling to help him get over her. Ike should know—he'd been divorced four times. All his brothers had lousy track records with marriage, and Michael had been determined that he would be different. It was mind-boggling to think that his marriage could be dissolved in less time than it took for them to plan the wedding. It took six weeks to get a doctor's appointment, for heaven's sake. A magazine subscription. A pasta maker from an infomercial.

Maybe his brother was right, maybe a fling would take the edge off the hurt, but the thought of going to a bar to pick up a one-night stand made his stomach cramp. The awkwardness, the diseases, the morning-after scene—stuff nightmares were made of. Despite their less than electrifying sex life, he'd never wanted to sleep around, never even thought about it. So to suddenly start looking at women again as potential lovers would take some practice. There were lots of pretty waitresses at the restaurant, but he drew the line at fooling around with an employee. Customers? Too risky considering right now he needed the business more than he needed the sex.

No, he had too much on his plate to consider complicating his life even further with an affair. In fact, he vowed silently, for the next six months, he was swearing off women. No sex, no flirting, no looking.

Well, maybe *looking* was allowed, as long as it didn't lead to sex.

His mother, a devout Catholic, was a big believer in signs. "Michael," she'd say, "after you make a decision, be alert for a sign from the heavens that you've made the right one."

Michael sighed, then pushed open the door to Anytime Costumes and came face-to-face with a nun.

Apparently heaven wasn't being subtle today.

## CHAPTER TWO

REBECCA STRAIGHTENED AND smiled at Michael Pierce, the longtime object of her fantasies. The contents of the mysterious box would have to wait while she got her thrill for the day. "Hello, Mr. Pierce."

The Incognito restaurant was one of her best accounts. Mrs. Pierce made most of the costume decisions, but occasionally Michael Pierce dropped by to pick up or drop off something. His uniform of jeans, T-shirt, brown leather bomber jacket and ball cap was in sharp contrast to his wife's always-coiffed appearance. Although the casual attire suited him immensely, she'd bet he would look smashing in a dark suit. Or that Zorro costume she'd mentally reserved for him when it arrived a year ago.

His mouth turned up in amusement. "Rebecca, is that you?"

She nodded, feeling a flush coming on. He probably thought she was a kook, always dressed up in some outlandish garb. "It's me. Um, Quincy, would you mind putting the box in the storage closet?"

Quincy frowned because he was dying to know what was inside. "Sure. How are you doing, Mr. Pierce?"

Michael gave Quincy a friendly nod and dropped a pile of garments on the counter—loose pants and shirts, long twill skirts, big-sleeved peasant blouses.

"More mending?" she asked.

"Afraid so. Rips, buttons missing, et cetera."

Quincy waved on his way out the door. "See you, Rebecca, Mr. Pierce."

Michael lifted his hand. "Thanks, Quince, for letting me know that Rebecca was closing early today."

Rebecca frowned—she wasn't closing early.

"No problem. I wouldn't have wanted you to wait and maybe miss her."

Michael turned to the counter and Quincy gave her a pointed look behind the man's back. She shook her head in the tiniest—and firmest—indication of "are you out of your freaking mind, this man is married." "Goodbye, Quincy," she said through clenched teeth.

"See you tomorrow," he said with a sublime expression, then left.

She manufactured a smile for Michael, praying he'd missed that exchange. "I can have the mending back to you the day after tomorrow." She wondered about the smudges under his brown eyes and the pinch between his thick, dark brows. Not that either took away from his all-American good looks. Michael Pierce was big, solid and sexy with a boyish air, and eminently male. She had always allowed herself to spin absurd schoolgirl fantasies about him because one, she was contentedly engaged, two, he was oblivious to her existence outside of providing costumes for his business and three, he was married to a woman so gorgeous she made Rebecca feel like a boy. Okay, so now they were down to two out of three, but Michael Pierce was still handily off limits and therefore…safe.

"Actually there's no hurry," he said. "I closed down the restaurant for a couple of weeks to remodel."

"Oh, that's exciting—what are you going to change?"

He sighed, then pushed back his Cubs cap. "I'm open to suggestions."

The anxious tone in his voice caught her off

guard. She gave a little laugh. "Oh, you don't want my ideas."

He raised an eyebrow. "You have ideas?"

She blushed and realized how presumptuous she sounded—just because she'd often thought of how she might change Incognito if given the chance didn't mean that her ideas had merit, or that the Pierces would be interested. "N-no, I—"

"Because if you do, I'd like to hear them."

Michael had to be the most handsome man she'd ever seen up close. His features were large and well formed—broad forehead, strong nose, wide cheekbones, square jaw. His hair was the color of tarnished brass and he wore it cut close to his head. But it was his brown eyes that she found so compelling that she had difficulty maintaining eye contact for more than a few seconds. She stepped back to stuff the costumes he'd brought into a large cotton bag under the counter.

"The restaurant needs a new look," he said. "Something to get the public's attention. We were hoping to have a grand reopening in two weeks, but frankly, we're running a little short of 'grand.'"

"Well," she said in a little voice. "I, um—" she cleared her throat "—do have a few c-concepts that could be, um...different."

"I'm listening."

She took a deep breath and gestured to the bag of costumes. "These costumes and the Lone Ranger masks aren't...special. Maybe you could dress the servers in more elegant costumes, like vampires, or flamenco dancers. And speaking of dancers—" She stopped and bit into her lip. Had she said too much?

"Go on," he urged.

"Well, maybe you could take out some of the tables and build a stage, then have dinner dance shows. I was thinking flamenco, but Middle Eastern and African dances can be just as provocative."

"Provocative? I don't want to turn the place into a men's club."

"I was thinking of couples dancing."

"Oh." He shifted. "Well, maybe we can spice up the costumes a little, but honestly, Rebecca, I don't see anything elegant or provocative about a vampire costume. I wouldn't want it to turn into a Halloween party."

"But that could be fun," she said, her excitement building. "Invite patrons to wear their own costumes—the name of the restaurant is *Incognito*. Capitalize on it. You could put on an elegant masquerade party every night of the week. So instead of just a great meal, dining at Incognito would be an experience.''

He simply looked at her for a few seconds, his face unreadable. Her heart pounded nervously—why had she said anything at all? Her ideas sounded silly and superficial even to her own ears, and she couldn't bear it if Michael laughed at her.

''It sounds like a lot of work,'' he said. ''Costumes, a stage, dancers.''

''It would be,'' she admitted. ''But you have me as your resource for costumes, a stage would be a matter of getting a permit and installers and there are several dance troupes in the area.''

''It sounds like you've been giving this some thought.''

She swallowed and shrugged mildly. ''Entertainment is my life.'' And she'd taken a special interest in the business of her favorite customer.

He scanned her nun's habit, then pushed his cheek out with his tongue. ''Yeah. Thanks for the ideas, Rebecca. I'll give them some thought.'' Michael walked to the door. His six-foot-plus frame took up most of it. ''Did anyone ever tell you that you look like Audrey Hepburn?''

He walked out the door into the rain, leaving her

blushing to the roots of her hair at the end of the longest conversation she'd ever had with the man.

What had come over her to be so bold as to tell him how to run his business? He probably asked only to humor her, not thinking that she'd practically whip out a business plan. She covered her face with her hands. Michael would probably have a good chuckle with his wife over her wild ideas. And they'd never stop laughing if they knew she had a wild crush on Michael.

Rebecca sighed and came back to earth.

The next hour of business was typical off-season Monday traffic—returns of weekend rentals, and a few shoppers. A teen pop star named Baby something or another had made pink gloves all the rage—she'd sold four cases to date. A fortyish couple came in under the guise of renting an animal costume for their child's birthday, but wound up buying a French maid costume, complete with feather tickler.

She went through the motions of waiting on customers with a smile pasted on her face, but she couldn't stop thinking about Michael Pierce and that little pinch between his eyebrows. Or the way he moved his big body. Or that sexy ball cap. He was married, she knew, but if Dickie could take a mistress, why couldn't she indulge in an innocent fantasy about Michael Pierce? She likened it to fantasizing about a celebrity—the chance of sleeping with that person was nil, so it was harmless, right?

The phone rang, breaking into her musings. Remembering to be grateful for any customers—even late ones—she picked up the phone. "Anytime Costumes, Rebecca speaking."

"Hi, sis."

She smiled into the phone at her sister Meg's comforting voice. "Hi, yourself."

"How are you doing?"

"Oh, all the wedding and honeymoon arrangements are canceled, but I still have a few more gifts to return."

"I asked how *you* are doing?"

She exhaled. "I'm fine. I think my pride is hurt more than anything. Dickie and I just weren't right for each other, and I guess he recognized it first. I think Mom is taking it harder than I am."

"Well, you know that Mom wants us both to have the kind of marriage she didn't have."

"I know—I feel like I let her down."

"*You* let her down? You didn't ask Dickie Montgomery to take a mistress and impregnate her. Even if things weren't working out, there are honorable ways to end a relationship.''

"I just feel so foolish, Meg. Why didn't I see it?"

"You and I don't look for trouble. We want things to be...peaceful, sometimes at our own expense."

Hearing the odd note that crept into her sister's voice, Rebecca said, "I hope that my situation hasn't caused tension between you and Trey."

"Oh, no. Trey is just as solid and dependable as always."

"Are you two any closer to setting a date?"

"I'm not going to rush him into a commitment."

Rebecca wanted to point out that after five years of dating, Meg wouldn't exactly be rushing the man, but considering the state of her own love life, she decided to keep her opinion to herself. "Well, I guess I won't be taking you away from him after all to run the shop while I'm on my honeymoon."

"Actually I was sort of looking forward to the break."

"After the semester ends, why don't you come anyway?"

"I might, just for a change of scenery."

"Meg, are you sure everything's okay?"

"Absolutely—don't worry about me. And there's Trey at the door. Sorry to run."

Since Dickie had dropped the bomb, Meg seemed almost apologetic that she had a man in her life. "That's okay, really. Thanks for calling, sis."

"Call me if you want to talk."

"I will." She hung up the phone, grateful that her sister cared enough to call, but wishing everyone would stop worrying about her. People got their hearts broken every day—she wasn't so special.

Rebecca locked the front door, added the day's receipts, then lowered the lights, frowning because there was something she'd been meaning to tell Meg, but couldn't remember what it was. She decided it must not have been important, then carried the trash past the dressing rooms and through the workroom to the back door. The parking lot was deserted except for her van and the Dumpster where she tossed the garbage bag. The sky was still drizzling rain, and the temperature was bone-chilling. A good night to stay in and catch up on a few special projects. She returned to the workroom to survey her current work-in-progress.

The purple velvet hooded cape hung benignly on the dress form, begging her to bring it to life. This was her favorite part of owning the shop—assembling just the right components of a costume. She wheeled the dress form around the workshop, poking into huge wire bins of hats, masks, shoes, shirts, blouses, pants, wigs, lingerie, shoes and countless accessories. If something caught her eye, she held it up to the cape. If it worked, she moved on. She had abandoned the idea of a jeweled sash and thigh-high boots for a more seductive vampire look—a black leather renaissance corset, G-string, garters, hose and black heels. With the outfit decided, she discarded one mask after another, finally choosing a black sequined model that covered only the eyes.

She walked into a changing room, a familiar warmth growing in her thighs, along with a familiar guiltiness. At times she felt just as naughty as some of her customers, dressing up for the mirrors. She blamed it on her background in drama and dance, this penchant for sensual costumes that took her out of a small shop in North Chicago and set her down in ancient Greece or medieval France or Victorian England.

Donning the clothes reminiscent of times gone by was the closest she would ever come to having magic in her life. Few women would understand her delicious little pastime, but surely no man. Dickie? She laughed softly. Dickie had no idea that his mousy little Rebecca was a hundred different women, all of them yearning to pleasure him. He had directed their lovemaking, which had been sparse and no-nonsense.

No, they hadn't been perfectly compatible physically, but she cared about him. He was intelligent and attentive and successful. In the three years they had dated and the year they had been engaged, she had been content. Sex was not the mainstay of a relationship.

Or so she'd thought. She wasn't sure what hurt the most—the fact that he'd gone elsewhere for fulfillment, or the fact that she hadn't been confident enough to expect it herself in their relationship. Maybe if she'd been more assertive…

It didn't matter now. Dickie was off to greener pastures, and she was alone with her fantasies. Mere weeks before her wedding and she was starting over. When tears threatened, she pinched herself hard on the back of her hand. The only way she'd gotten through this miserable humiliation was by designating a "crying zone" between 10:00 p.m. and 2:00 a.m. During those hours she wailed and flailed and listened to sad songs and went through a tree's worth of tissues. Then she'd pull her dehydrated self together enough to face customers the next morning.

The three dressing rooms separating the showroom from the workroom were all nicely furnished, but the red room was Rebecca's favorite—soft lighting, a three-way mirror, red velvet upholstered cushions on the benches and plush red carpeting. She didn't bother pulling the tapestry curtain because the dressing rooms opened into the shop and weren't visible from the windows even if a Peeping Tom were persistent. Besides, with the curtains open she could hear the strains of the medieval music CD playing over the stereo speakers. The melancholy strum of a mandolin, the haunting lilt of a flute, the moody throb of a primitive drum—all of it helped set the stage for Rebecca, mistress of the night.

She slowly removed the nun's habit, then her underwear. The plastic teeth went in first because to begin the ritual of dressing like a vampire, she had to first assume the role. The fangs were barely visible with her mouth closed, but when she opened her mouth, she looked catlike and dangerous, and a thrill ran through her naked body. The air was tinged with a chill, bringing the peaks of her breasts to rapt attention. She stood quietly, imagining herself to be a she-vampire, admiring the slight flush of her breasts, the flat planes of her stomach, the triangle of dark hair at the juncture of her thighs.

Arching her back, she skimmed her hands over her body, grazing the tips of her breasts, the dimple of her navel, the swell of her hips. The image of Michael Pierce's face came to her in emphatic detail. As she imagined his hands covering the same ground, her body became engorged with desire. She somehow knew that Michael was a luxurious lover.

She applied dramatic eye makeup and red lipstick, then slipped on a black G-string, and cinched the corset tight enough to push her breasts high. The barest hint of the pink skin around her nipples showed at the top of the binding garment. She rolled on black thigh-high stockings and attached garters to the corset. Three-inch black heels accentuated the curve of her calves and ankles.

She swept her dark hair up into a loose knot, added dangling earrings to her lobes, then settled the sumptuous cape around her bare shoulders. The soft brush of the velvet sent goose bumps over her arms, and the budded tips of her breasts emerged over the top of the corset. She slipped on the sequined mask and, finally, raised the hood of the cape. Mistress Rebecca looked sinister and sexy and ready to take on the night. The costume was so convincing, she could almost imagine taking flight.

She stepped out of the dressing room and fairly floated down the hall and into the brightly lit workroom. She turned quickly to the beat of the music, the fabric swishing around her ankles and stirring a breeze to fan her body. She reveled in the knowledge that this outfit would stop any mortal man in his tracks, even Michael Pierce who had doubted that such a costume could be provocative. A languid smile curved her mouth. If he could only see her now....

At a sudden noise behind her, Rebecca inhaled sharply and whirled, sending the cape swirling. At first she thought her mind was playing tricks on her, conjuring up an image of Michael Pierce standing just inside the back door. But if so, his apparition looked just as stunned as she felt. Her panic turned to mortification when she realized that she'd left the door unlocked when she'd taken out the trash.

And that the man she'd been spinning fantasies about for years had just caught her playing dress-up.

## CHAPTER THREE

IT TOOK A FEW SECONDS FOR Michael to assimilate the facts of the situation. Fact: He'd been drawn back to the costume shop to talk to Rebecca about her ideas for the restaurant. Fact: He'd seen her van parked in the back and had heard music coming from inside the shop. Fact: He'd knocked on the door, waited, then entered, expecting to find Rebecca bent over a sewing machine. Fact: He hadn't imagined in a thousand years that he'd find her dressed in an outrageously sexy costume.

The purple velvet cape hung open, revealing a long, lean body encased in a corset, thigh-high stockings and garters. In fact, he had to look twice to make sure the masked siren before him was Rebecca Valentine. The same Rebecca Valentine who reminded him of a pixie and who, the last time he'd seen her, had been dressed in a nun's habit? Yes— same big green eyes, albeit now bugged out of her head. Same small shapely hands, now frozen in front of her. And same full mouth—now distorted by...fangs?

He stared and she stared, both speechless. Michael didn't have to look down to know his body had reacted to her skimpy outfit. His instincts told him to seek and touch and feel. But his brain told him that the horrified look on her face was not the expression of a woman who wanted to be sought and touched and felt, at least not by him. Hadn't Sonia mentioned once that Rebecca was engaged?

Michael opened his mouth to defend his presence, to defend his body's reaction, to defend the wicked thoughts stampeding through his brain. "I...wanted to talk...didn't answer my knock...door was unlocked...I was concerned."

So much for coherency.

But at least his words shocked her into movement. She yanked the cape closed, although her image was now forever branded on his mind.

"Vish isn't a guud time," she said, her speech somewhat hampered by the fangs.

"I...can see...that," he remarked, then gestured vaguely. "Not that I saw...anything." Only that she was bursting out of her corset. "I'm going now."

She nodded, his cue to head for the door, Michael

knew. But he couldn't ignore the sexually charged atmosphere—the low lights, the pulsing music, her incredible outfit, his awakened needs. His feet seemed rooted to the floor in some juvenile hope that...what—she'd ask him to stay?

He finally mustered the strength to back out the door and pull it closed behind him. He stood dazed until the cold rain crept under his collar and trickled down his back. Michael turned and walked to his SUV. Dusk had fallen prematurely because of the low cloud cover. Horns sounded from the distant highway rush hour traffic. Just an ordinary rainy Wednesday evening.

He had pulled out of the parking lot with both hands welded to the wheel when a big, goofy I-can't-believe-that-just-happened smile spread over his face. Seeing Rebecca dressed in an erotic costume was like a teenage fantasy come true—without the explosive ending, of course. But still amazing. What kinds of things was she doing in her costume shop after hours? And did she do it often?

The thought of her playing dress-up alone among all those...*props* sent his blood pounding. His arousal still strained against his fly. Who could have known that under the big fuzzy animal costumes and the funky fruit costumes and the nun's habit lurked a stunning figure and a penchant for revealing lingerie?

Then his fingers tightened around the steering wheel—what if Rebecca had been waiting for her boyfriend? Maybe they indulged in role-playing games in the shop after hours. He'd heard of those things before, and considering Rebecca's line of work, it seemed likely. That would explain why the door had been unlocked.

But for some reason, the thought of Rebecca dressing up—and being undressed—by some faceless man irked him beyond reason. She was young...wasn't she? And innocent...wasn't she? Hopefully the boyfriend wasn't some pipsqueak greenhorn who fumbled his way through intimate encounters.

Then Michael shook himself mentally. What Rebecca Valentine did and who she did it with was no business of his—he barely knew the girl, er, woman. And just today hadn't he sworn off women? They did things to mess with a man's mind, like completely blow a preconceived image by dressing up like a prowling she-vampire.

He squirmed in his seat and tried to push away the naughty images of Rebecca, but snatches kept creeping in—her trim ankles, her toned thighs, those garters, that corset and the sexy, plush cape that would have made a virtual bed for them if he'd—

*Enough.* He had to put his business first, and if he were going to implement some of Rebecca's ideas, he would need her help. He'd just have to…handle everything over the phone.

REBECCA WOULDN'T EVEN LET herself think about what had just happened until she locked the door. Then every muscle in her body collapsed. She leaned against the door as waves of humiliation rolled over her. For whatever reason, Michael Pierce had come back to talk to her and instead had gotten the shock of his life. How could she ever face him again?

With wobbly knees, she extinguished the dressing room and workroom lights, and climbed the stairs that led to the door of her tiny apartment. She wanted to go to bed and hide her head under the covers for a few months.

The apartment over the retail space was one of the attractions when she purchased the building. Admittedly it was cramped, livable only because the Murphy bed disappeared into a wood cabinet in the sitting room to allow foot traffic to the bathroom and laundry closet. To call the room on the other side of the sitting room a kitchen required a stretch of the imagination, but a toaster oven, microwave, compact fridge and freestanding pantry was enough to store and prepare a passable meal.

Dickie disliked the ''attic,'' as he referred to her apartment, but next to his posh condominium, Rebecca found her little nook quaint and intimate. Miss Illinois probably lived in a penthouse somewhere, with a big stationary bed and a commercial-grade kitchen that she never used.

A fresh well of tears threatened to surface, but it was only six-thirty—she had hours to go before she could have a good cry. Rebecca stripped the vampire costume, burning with shame. She donned sweatpants and a T-shirt and sneakers, then fell onto the couch and pressed a pillow over her face. If there was a God, she'd be able to travel back in time to thirty minutes ago and stop herself from looking like a colossal boob.

Maybe Michael had thought about her suggestions and wanted to discuss them further. If so, she'd blown any credibility she might have had. He was probably talking to his wife on his cell phone at this very moment, guffawing over the little scene he'd stumbled onto. Good grief, she hoped Mrs.

Pierce didn't think that she was trying to seduce her husband. She banged the pillow against her forehead. Every time she replayed the scene in her head, she could more clearly see the expression on Michael's face—bewilderment, shock, dismay. She groaned and squeezed back tears. And of all people who might have stumbled in the back door—burglars, bums, serial killers—why did it have to be Michael?

Desperate to expel her nervous energy, Rebecca grabbed an apple, then headed back down to the shop to dive into the Pierces' stack of mending. Somehow the tedium of sewing on buttons and repairing rips made her feel as if she were paying penance to the Pierces for what she'd done. She'd probably lost their business for good anyway, so she might as well tie up all the loose ends.

By 9:00 p.m., she'd finished the mending and dropped the clothes into the chute for the cleaners to pick up. She rolled her tired shoulders and stretched tall, looking for something else to occupy her hands and mind. When her gaze landed on the closet, she suddenly remembered the mysterious box and that she'd meant to tell Meg that she'd heard from Lana.

She pulled the box from the dark closet out into

the light, then dropped to her knees to dig through the bothersome packing material. Her fingers came into contact with something pillowy and plastic. Rebecca lifted the item from the box, displacing foam peanuts everywhere, and stared into the face of a male blow-up doll.

Harry. A wry smile pulled at her mouth as memories came flooding back. She did remember Harry at the bachelorette party. Angie had passed him off to some girl whose name escaped her, joking that when the girl got married, she'd have to pass the anatomically correct doll on to another single friend. Apparently Lana had gotten the doll and now that she was married, she was passing it on to Rebecca for "good luck."

Rebecca scoffed. Good luck? Where was Harry a month ago before her life went into the toilet? She extracted the pajama-clad doll from the box and shook him free of the staticky peanuts. He'd been underinflated in lieu of his trip through the postal system, which made his hard plastic erection all the more prominent beneath the striped pajama pants. He'd been repaired in at least one place.

Out of curiosity, she pulled out his waistband for a look—make that two repairs, although the equipment seemed to be in good working order. She pondered the kind of aggressive interaction that would have led to the doll's blowout, then discarded all the notions that flitted through her mind. Not *everyone* had to rely on private little games to get their jollies, she reminded herself.

"Sorry, Harry," she said, pushing him back into the box. "As much as I could use a little luck right now, I do not need a good luck *love* charm, so you're going back into the closet until I can figure out what to do with you." After she returned the box, she closed the door and shook her head. Good luck love charm—right.

She turned off the lights as she headed back to her apartment with a heavy heart and heavy feet. The cable was out again, probably due to the weather, so she decided she might as well go to bed. She flipped on the radio and lowered the Murphy bed, then clapped off her lights and crawled under the covers.

Being at the top of the old building meant that she sometimes went to sleep to, and woke up to, the soothing tune of rain on the corrugated roof. But tonight the rain seemed to mock all the tears she'd shed over the past few weeks. And on top of everything, tonight's humiliation in front of the man she least wanted to make a fool out of herself in front of. Her chest ached with frustration and defeat. She curled up into a ball and tried not to think about the next time she'd see the Pierces.

Especially Michael.

# *CHAPTER FOUR*

MICHAEL STARED AT THE spreadsheet on his desk that represented the changes he wanted to make to the restaurant. But the numbers kept blurring as his mind wandered to figures more entertaining—Rebecca Valentine's, to be exact. He simply couldn't stop thinking about her. The last day and a half his body had been in a constant state of readiness, as if it might be called into action at any moment. And he was ready to explode from wanting her.

It was as if the sight of her in that erotic costume had flipped some kind of switch in him, igniting a sexual surge he hadn't experienced in years, if ever. Before Sonia, he'd slept with an average number of women, and found the experience to be very... *average.* No woman had ever captured his imagination as completely as the sweet-faced shopgirl had. The fact that he'd stumbled onto her in such a vulnerable situation made him feel oddly protective of her. He wanted to see Rebecca, to reassure her that her secret was safe, but frankly he was afraid he might betray his rampant fascination.

He picked up the phone for the twelfth time with the intention of calling her, but since he still couldn't think of anything brilliant or even reasonable to say, he set the receiver down again.

Damn, he'd have to face Rebecca sooner or later—sooner if he were going to get these changes implemented within two weeks, later if he didn't get his libido under control.

REBECCA STOPPED IN FRONT of the Incognito restaurant and inhaled, then exhaled. She could do this. She'd been giving herself pep talks for the past day and a half and had determined she'd be less miserable if she delivered the mended and cleaned costumes herself rather than cringing every time the bell on her door rang.

She shifted the clothing to one arm and pushed the door open with the other. At this point, outright laughter in her face would be better than the slow torment of wondering what the Pierces were thinking. She swallowed. Especially Michael.

Her skin tingled as she entered the brightly lit foyer. The noises of electrical tools and workmen sounded from another part of the restaurant. A dark-haired man dressed in chinos and a button-down shirt emerged and smiled.

"May I help you?" He spoke precise English with a slight Hispanic accent.

"I'm Rebecca Valentine from the costume shop. I have a d-delivery for Mrs. Pierce."

The man frowned slightly. "Mrs. Pierce...isn't here."

Dread filtered through her—if possible, she didn't want to see Michael. "When would be a better time to speak with her?"

He hesitated, then held up a finger. "Just one moment."

The man disappeared down the hallway. Rebecca took the opportunity to look around and try to calm her thudding heart. The building was old and beautifully maintained, heavy with ornate woodwork and moldings, blessed with high ceilings, black and white marble tiled floors, and brilliant chandeliers. Immediately her mind took flight—she could see elaborately costumed couples milling arm in arm under sparkling lights.

Then she shook herself—this was the line of thinking that had gotten her in trouble the other night. At the sound of footsteps behind her, her heart jumped to her throat. She turned and, to her horror, Michael Pierce was striding toward her looking superb in jeans, red T-shirt and athletic shoes. She willed the floor to open and swallow her, but she wasn't to be so easily saved.

"Hello," he said, his expression passive, just as if she'd been fully clothed the last time he'd seen her.

Rebecca wet her lips. "I, um…brought the mended costumes to…save you and Mrs. Pierce a trip."

"That's kind of you," he said, stepping forward to relieve her of the hanging garments.

She caught a whiff of his masculine scent— woodsy and clean, almost minty. Their hands brushed as he collected the clothes, and the contact was enough to set her on edge. She was fairly shaking, and her cheeks felt warm.

"Rico said you wanted to talk to Sonia."

"I wanted to make sure the costumes were satisfactory," she murmured. "And I didn't want to…bother you."

He held her gaze for several long seconds, then said, "I'm glad you're here. Do you have a few minutes to talk?"

No, she needed to get back to the shop, and the last thing she wanted to do was relive the humiliation of the other night. But she'd come for closure. "Sure."

He gestured for her to precede him down the hall. She was self-conscious about walking in front of him, but she'd dressed carefully in nondescript navy slacks, a yellow turtleneck and a bulky sweater. No unnecessary skin exposed anywhere.

Michael stopped at a supply closet and hung the costumes alongside others. "My office is down on the left."

Those last few steps seemed like the longest walk she'd ever taken. But finally they were at the door of an unremarkable ten-foot-square office. Michael Pierce was not caught up in the trappings of owning a business—his furniture consisted of a simple desk, a worn leather desk chair, a credenza, a wall of file cabinets and two visitor chairs. He gestured to one as he closed the door. "Have a seat."

She sat, but her mind raced.

"Would you like some coffee, iced tea?"

"No, thank you."

He eased down in his seat with a sigh. "Rebecca..."

She looked down at her hands, holding her purse in a white-knuckled grip.

"Sonia and I are divorced."

Rebecca jerked her head up, genuinely stunned. "What? When?" Then she held up her hand. "I'm sorry—that's none of my business."

He shook his head. "It's no close-held secret. In fact, I'm surprised you hadn't heard through the grapevine."

Under other circumstances, she might have, but since she and Dickie had been fodder for the grapevine lately, she'd been excluded from the community gossip circle. Then Quincy popped into her mind—of course *he* knew, which was why he'd encouraged Michael to stop by her shop that day. The sneak.

"The divorce was final this week."

Remorse wallowed in her stomach—she could tell from his eyes that Michael was hurting. "I'm so sorry."

He nodded as if he were sorry, too. "Well, now that that's out in the open, we can get down to business."

Rebecca lifted her eyebrows. "Hmm?"

"I've given your ideas for updating the restaurant a lot of thought. My manager Rico and I talked it over, and I've decided to give them a try."

A smile spread over her face.

"If you'd be willing to help, that is."

Her smile vanished. Help? As in be in close quarters with a sexy divorced man who had seen more of her than was professionally acceptable?

"I've already ordered construction of a stage," he said. "And I'll pay you for your consulting, of course."

"I..." Her mind raced in circles. "I don't know..."

He leaned forward. "Listen, Rebecca, about the other night—"

"I was simply trying out a new costume," she cut in with a little laugh. "I'm s-sorry if I embarrassed you. I assure you, I was even more embarrassed." Her cheeks flamed.

"You don't owe me an explanation. I had no business barging in like that." He cleared his throat. "I've already forgotten it happened."

She nodded with mixed emotions—relief and a little remorse. Her accidental peep show hadn't even been memorable. Of course when compared to the stunning Sonia, she was bound to come up short.

"What do you say about us working together?"

She could certainly use the extra money, and the exposure the new format of the restaurant would give to her shop. And she had to admit that the idea of working with Michael was irresistible. "I could only work after my regular store hours."

He nodded and smiled. "Fine. Can you start this evening?"

"I...suppose."

"Good. I don't have much time to get this off the ground. What time shall I stop by?"

Of course he'd be coming to her shop since all the costumes and sketches were there. But it was strictly business. She stood and straightened her shoulders. "How about six-thirty?"

He stood. "I'll see you then."

He extended his hand. Rebecca hesitated, then decided she was overreacting. She put her hand in his, hoping he couldn't feel her trembling. When his fingers closed around hers, she bit her tongue against the current that passed through his warm hand to hers. She had no explanation for why this man moved her, but the mere thought of Michael Pierce was an aerobic workout. The Surgeon General would definitely approve.

"Until later," he said.

Had she imagined a husky note in his voice?

A casual smile warmed his brown eyes.

Yes, she had imagined it. Rebecca withdrew her tingling hand. "Goodbye."

She turned and calmly fled.

## CHAPTER FIVE

REBECCA SHOOK HER FINGER at Quincy. "You're up to something."

Quincy pulled an innocent face and pressed his hand against his chest. "Me?"

"Yes, you."

"Can I help it that the man's divorce is final the same week you're looking for a divine diversion from Mr. Dickie?"

"I'm *not* looking."

"Don't you see, it's perfect—your heart is broken, his heart is broken."

She bit into her bottom lip. "Did she have an affair? No wait, don't answer that."

"Yep, the guy was a customer at the restaurant, and he's freaking loaded."

She stuck her fingers in her ears. "I don't want to hear this."

"Mrs. Pierce dumped Mr. Pierce and left him holding the bag."

She unplugged her ears. "What bag?"

"The restaurant—it's going under."

Rebecca's eyes bugged. "How do you know that?"

"Most of the restaurant's vendors will only ship 'cash on delivery.' It's a sure sign."

She frowned. "You're not supposed to tell things like that."

He sighed dramatically. "I only divulge information on an as-needed basis, and you need the whole picture if you're going to have an affair with him."

"You're not well."

"Don't tell me you don't find the man attractive."

"Is he? I hadn't noticed."

"Right. Are you blind? The man's gorgeous."

She carried the special-order costumes he'd delivered to the closet. "Michael and I are working together on a project, Quince. I don't mix my personal and professional lives."

His ears fairly grew before her eyes. "What kind of project?"

"If you must know, he's asked for my help in the evenings to give the restaurant a new look—and that little tidbit is not for public consumption."

Quincy grinned. "That's great news—he's going to fight to keep the place going." He wagged his eyebrows. "And the two of you working elbow to elbow, knee to knee—you never know what could happen."

"Nothing is going to happen, Quince. End of discussion."

He nodded to the box that held Harry. "What did your friend send you?"

She kicked at loose foam peanuts on the floor. "A male blow-up doll."

He blinked. "Okay."

"It's dumb—he's supposed to be a good luck charm, but I don't buy into that bunk."

"I don't know, it sounds like a fun little tradition to me."

"I don't have time for nonsense."

"I guess not, now that you'll be working after hours with Michael Pierce."

She gave him an exasperated look. "Don't you have a route waiting?"

"Alas, yes." He headed toward the door, then gestured to her front window. "By the way—the vampire costume is *hot*."

"Thanks."

Rebecca sighed. She had already taken a couple

of orders for the racy outfit—a bonus because she'd actually dressed a mannequin in the costume to convince Michael that she hadn't been simply, um, entertaining herself.

She called Mrs. Conrad and left a message that her order had arrived. Then she rented several costumes for a party at a nearby community college. A magician came in looking for skimpy show outfits for his two assistants. A local club singer came in to buy a glitzy hat. Meanwhile, the clock hands seemed to creep toward six-thirty.

And if she hadn't been edgy enough since her earlier talk with Michael, the information that Quincy had leaked only heightened her anxiety. Michael needed for her ideas to work. When he'd asked offhandedly for her input, she'd been talking from the top of her head with no inkling that his business was at risk. If she'd been harboring any deep-seated schoolgirl fantasies about Michael Pierce's motivations for meeting with her, they were now dashed. The man was looking for a miracle, not amusement.

The bell on the door tinkled, and Mrs. Conrad walked in wearing brown tweed and a fussy cardigan, and bearing a little tin—more cream candy?

"More cream candy," she sang. "Oh, and it

looks like another storm is blowing in just in time for rush hour."

Rebecca thanked her for the candy and fetched the package from the closet. Another peanut followed her out, riding on the static electricity around her shoe. Darn pesky box.

"Here you go, Mrs. Conrad. One harem costume."

The woman beamed. "I'm so happy the outfit made it in time for Marty's birthday."

"Would you like to try it on?"

"Absolutely."

Rebecca escorted her to the yellow dressing room and closed the curtains. "Yell if you need me."

"Oh, stay here, I want to tell you about the most wonderful time Marty and I had last night at a club called Rapture."

"Er, Mrs. Conrad, I don't think—"

"It was body paint night and—"

"Mrs. Conrad, do you mind if I ask you a question?"

"No dear, go right ahead."

"How did you and Mr. Conrad meet?"

"In high school."

"Oh, you were high school sweethearts?"

"No, we met by the bathrooms at my prom. I

dumped my date and he dumped his, and we spent the rest of the night in the back seat of his Buick.''

Rebecca lifted her eyebrows.

''Not what you expected to hear?''

''Well…''

The curtain zipped open and a veiled Mrs. Conrad shook her hips to make the coins around her waist jingle. ''What do you think?''

''It's great.'' The woman's body was still trim and firm. ''I'm sure Mr. Conrad will love it.''

The woman angled her head. ''That's the secret, you know.''

Rebecca squinted. ''The secret to what?''

''A happy relationship. Do you have a boy-friend?''

''No. I was engaged…until a few weeks ago.''

Mrs. Conrad looked sorrowful. ''Was the sex dreadful?''

Her neck burned. ''Well, um, I always thought our physical relationship would…develop.''

''Wrong.'' The woman lifted her hand in the air and looked to an imaginary horizon. ''From the get-go, there has to be a spark between the two of you, an awareness of each other that is so unique, you simply can't bear to be away from each other.''

Far different from the advice her mother had

drilled into her and Meg's heads so they wouldn't fall for a man who would abandon them with two small children. "What about friendship, emotional intimacy?"

"Overrated. Those things will grow out of your physical bond if it's right. You'll have many friendships, Rebecca, and other people in your life to whom you'll be emotionally close. But physical intimacy is unique to the relationship with the man you love. You'll share the deepest thoughts with your heads together on a pillow after great sex."

Dickie never talked immediately before, during, or after sex. In retrospect, the man turned into a mime when he was aroused. "But I'm not...I mean, how do you..."

"How do you find out if a man is *the* one without compromising your principles?"

Rebecca nodded.

Mrs. Conrad gave her a rueful smile. "You have to take a chance, dear. And when you find the man who makes you forget your name when he walks into a room, you hope against hope that he feels the same. Then it's magic." She shook her hips again, sending the spangles on her outfit dancing under the lights. "I'll take it," she said, then pulled the curtain shut.

The woman's words stayed with Rebecca until after she turned the Closed sign on the door at six. If Mrs. Conrad was right, her and Dickie's relationship had been doomed from the beginning. They had met at a benefit dinner, and although he was nice-looking, she remembered thinking after the first date that he was the kind of man she *should* fall in love with. His gentle kiss on the third date had set the pace for their love life, and she had acquiesced. Why she'd gone against her natural inclinations, she wasn't certain, other than she didn't want him to think she was odd. It hadn't occurred to her that Dickie might be the odd one, or that their chemistry was simply all wrong.

Shaking the melancholy thoughts from her head, she tallied the day's receipts and straightened the table in her workroom in anticipation of Michael's arrival. She pulled a catalog of fabric swatches from her shelf, and sketches from her ''fantasy'' file, elaborate costumes she ordered or made by request only. From her Rolodex file, she withdrew cards for local dance troupes. To calm her nerves, she put on a fresh pot of coffee. She turned off the overhead music, but it seemed too quiet, so she turned it back on and settled on a Spanish station—upbeat, but not distracting. At sixty-thirty exactly, a knock sounded on the front door.

Rebecca inhaled deeply and rounded the corner. Michael stood outside the door hunched against the rain that had blown in. She jogged to the door and unlocked it, waving him inside. "Did you walk?"

He nodded and set down his dripping briefcase. "I was halfway here when the sky opened up. I figured I might as well keep going." He yanked off his cap and banged it against his knee, then wiped his shoes on the doormat and shrugged out of his jacket. His damp T-shirt was plastered to his chest. "Filthy night."

The picture he created—big and masculine and easygoing—set her stomach churning, and God help her, she was already imagining things that shouldn't happen. Even the simple act of locking the door behind him seemed intimate, as if they were shutting out the world. She reminded herself that Michael was there on business, and was counting on her help to turn the restaurant around.

He bent to scoop something off the floor—a foam peanut. Those things were everywhere—she'd found one in her bathtub, for heaven's sake.

Rebecca held out her hand and he dropped it on

her palm. "Thanks," she said. "These things seem to be reproducing."

At his wry smile, she swallowed—an unfortunate choice of words.

She shot a look toward the closet where the "good luck charm" was stored. To be packed away, Harry was doing a good job of finding his way underfoot. She closed her fingers around the peanut and tried to ignore the pull of Michael's body on hers. "Let's get started."

# CHAPTER SIX

MICHAEL'S MIND JUMPED all around, bombarded with images of the woman walking in front of him dressed in the outfit now on display in the window—the mannequin certainly didn't do it justice. In contrast, Rebecca's trim figure was clad in the same prim outfit she'd been wearing earlier—by design? Her black hair was pulled back from her face with a dark headband, and her face was devoid of makeup. By all appearances, a demure shopgirl. And if not for the citrusy scent she wore, the same one he remembered being stirred up by the swirling hem of a velvet cloak, he might have convinced himself the incident had been a figment of his overactive imagination.

All afternoon he'd told himself that he'd asked for Rebecca's help for the sake of the restaurant. And while he did respect her opinion, he was a liar, liar and his pants were on fire—he simply wanted to be near her. But dammit, it felt good to think about something other than his failed marriage.

"My office is in the back," she murmured.

He followed, focusing on the surroundings to keep his mind and eyes off her willowy figure. An up-tempo Spanish instrumental played on the radio, the recording occasionally interrupted by a zap of static that revealed the proximity of lightning. Indeed, the air had an electric quality that heightened his senses, and magnified his awareness of the woman in front of him. The fact that she was oblivious to his raging hormones was both a relief and a frustration.

They left the showroom, passed three dressing rooms on the left, then walked through swinging doors bearing a sign that read No Customers Beyond This Point. The expansive area on the other side of the doors he recognized as the large room he'd entered the night before last by way of the back door. The floor was shiny sealed concrete, the ceiling exposed pipes and conduit. Colorful costumes hung on rods spanning two walls, and a half dozen wire bins were stacked with clothing, wigs, hats and other items not readily identifiable. Dress forms and mannequins were too numerous to count.

The room had a mischievous feel—as if at night

the inanimate objects might spring to life. He could see how Rebecca might fall under the spell of the compelling atmosphere, how even he might himself.

She walked over to a large drafting table with an adjustable lamp clipped to the edge. A bench seat was tucked underneath. Three file cabinets and a computer workstation sat adjacent.

"My office," she indicated with a sweeping gesture.

"Nice."

"Efficient," she corrected with a laugh. "I made coffee."

"Sounds great."

"Have a seat."

He pulled out the bench seat and sat down feeling like a teenager who'd just discovered he was going to share a science lab table with a cute girl. She returned from a makeshift coffee station and set down two brimming cups, then eased onto the bench. He noticed that she didn't seem to be as affected by their nearness as he. He was a mess, Michael decided. A horny mess. He lifted his briefcase onto his lap and flipped opened the closures. "I brought a diagram of the store."

"Great. And do you have a staffing chart?"

''Right here.''

The tip of her tongue emerged as she studied the diagram. Michael was riveted. Suddenly everything the woman did seemed sensual.

''You've already drawn in the stage, I see.''

He dragged his mind back to the matter at hand. ''Yes. But we lost six tables, which took a chunk out of the seating capacity.''

''Hmm. What if you try this?'' She sketched an alternative table arrangement in pencil over the diagram. He was drawn into her enthusiasm, taken by her animation. She moved over the diagram systematically, making suggestions for color schemes and lighting. By scheduling carefully and streamlining the menu, two dinner seatings with floor shows could be accommodated on weeknights, three on Friday and Saturday nights.

''But leave the artichoke salad,'' she said with a smile. ''It's my favorite.''

He leaned one elbow on the table. ''You've eaten at my restaurant?''

''Several times.''

''When we reopen, I'd like to treat you and your fiancé to dinner.''

Her smile faltered. ''I'm not engaged, Michael.''

''I'm sorry. Sonia told me—''

"I'm *no longer* engaged."

The news made his gut clench. "Oh."

"He found someone else."

"Oh." He studied the lines of her face, and her understated beauty hit him hard. And while his mind argued that her announcement changed nothing, his body knew different. It changed everything. "I guess we're both on the mend."

"I guess."

"It's hard, suddenly being single."

She nodded. "Everyone just expects you to move on to another relationship as if the last one didn't exist."

"When you're not even close to being ready for an emotional commitment."

"Right."

He pulled his hand down over his face and laughed. "My brother thinks I should have a fling to make myself feel better." As soon as the words left his mouth, he wanted them back. He hoped she didn't think he was flirting or something.

One side of her mouth pulled back. "I've been told the same thing."

As the silence stretched between them, his mind raced—it was his turn to say something. "Were you in love with this guy?"

She looked away. "I thought so, but now I wonder how much of it was simply convincing myself that he was a good catch. I mean, I miss him, and it'll take me a while to get over the hurt, but when something you were banking on gets snatched away, it makes you question if it was ever real."

He stared at her profile.

She looked back and smiled. "I didn't mean to get all sappy."

"No, it's...fine." Actually she could have been reading the words engraved on his heart. He looked into her brilliant green eyes and saw the same shadows of rejection he'd been wrestling with. "It's nice to talk to someone who understands."

"I wouldn't presume to compare my engagement to your marriage."

He made a rueful sound. "Things hadn't been right between us for a long while, but my stubborn pride wouldn't let me see it." Then he clapped his hands together. "But now I plan to sink all my energy into getting the restaurant back up and running."

She smiled. "I'll help all I can."

How many times had she smiled at him over the past few years, yet he hadn't noticed how her entire face lit up, how the entire *room* lit up. "Thank you, Rebecca."

She inclined her head in that quiet, confident way that was so…comforting. So different from Sonia's manic behavior.

"Here are some sketches of what the staff might wear," she said, passing him several sheets of stiff paper.

Michael reviewed colorful drawings of a gladiator, an African princess, an Asian emperor, and numerous others, all elaborate and impressive. He was starting to visualize the sensory impact her ideas would have on patrons. "Did you draw these?"

A blush tinged her cheeks. "I studied fashion illustration in college."

"They're quite good."

"Thank you. Excluding the cooking staff, I figure you'll need twelve female costumes and twelve male costumes to span shift changes, laundry turnover, et cetera."

"Can you have them ready in two weeks?"

She nodded. "I have pieces of some of them on hand." She stood and walked over to one of the racks and removed a high-waisted gown made of a pale blue iridescent fabric. "This…plus this." She removed a cone-shaped white hat from a bin.

"Equals a medieval maiden." She grinned. "With a little work, and a few accessories. And every costume must have a mask, of course."

He stood and walked over to join her because he simply missed being close to her—red flags waved in his brain. He lifted the sleeve of the gown she held. "Nice. But I notice you didn't include the vampire costume in the sketches."

"Because you said you couldn't imagine a vampire costume being elegant or provocative."

He dropped the sleeve of the garment. "After seeing you the other night, I stand corrected."

Her eyelashes fluttered. "I was just fooling around."

Michael gestured toward the racks. "Do you fool around often?"

Her tongue flicked over her lips, but she didn't look away. She was probably trying to decide if he was making a pass at her. So was he.

"I like the costumes," she said softly. "They let me be anyone I want to be."

Michael planted one hand on the wall and leaned forward to whisper against her temple. "Who do you want to be tonight?" He heard her swallow, sensed her hesitation. "Tell me, Rebecca."

"Who would you like for me to be, Michael?"

His sex stirred. ''Surprise me,'' he murmured, then gently lifted her chin. Their lips were so close, her breath mingled with his. He paused to give her a chance to pull away, but she didn't. When her mouth twitched, he took it as a sign of acquiescence and lowered his mouth to hers. The unfamiliar textures intrigued him. Her mouth was plump and accommodating, and she tasted of sweet creamed coffee. Their warm tongues parried, and her enthusiasm evoked a rigid response from his body. Powerful.

She tipped her head back and looked at him steadily. ''Are we ready for this?''

He inhaled sharply and brushed her hair back with his thumbs. ''I can only speak for myself. I can't stop thinking about seeing you the other night in that outfit. It took everything I had to walk out of here.''

Her eyes glittered, then a slow, feline smile curved her lips. ''I've been saving a costume that would be perfect for *you*.''

''Me?''

She nodded and wet her lips. ''If we're going to do this, let's make it memorable.''

Michael swallowed hard. He wasn't exactly comfortable with the thought of dressing up, but if it would excite Rebecca the way he'd been excited the other night, the way he was excited right now...

"Show me."

## CHAPTER SEVEN

IN THE RED DRESSING ROOM, Rebecca trembled as she dressed in a sumptuous off-the-shoulders black-and-yellow Spanish gown. She moved slowly, afraid that at any second Michael, who was next door, might abruptly change his mind about what they were planning to do. But the slide of his zipper both reassured and terrified her. What if he laughed? What if he thought she was strange? What if he were disappointed by her body or by her...performance?

With her blood pounding in her temples, she lifted the lavish skirt and fastened the garters to her black stockings, then slipped her feet into heels. She pulled her hair up into a topknot, then fastened it with a Spanish comb and a black lace fall.

Standing on wobbly knees, she smoothed a hand over the bodice of the provocative satin dress. Hadn't she dreamed of this, of dressing up—and down—with Michael? What had Mrs. Conrad said?

*You have to take a chance.* Well, no matter how scared she was, this was her chance, and she was taking it. They were both available, consenting adults—no one would get hurt.

Physically.

Her heart jumped wildly in her chest as she opened the curtain. Michael was waiting for her, leaning on the counter in near darkness, magnificent in the Zorro costume, just as she knew he would be. Snug black pants, black boots, white shirt with full sleeves, red sash at his waist. With the haunting Spanish guitar music as a background, he might have walked off the page of an adventure novel, except he was heartbreakingly real. And to her relief, he didn't seem embarrassed or self-conscious. He straightened, then swept an appreciative glance over her costume, lingering on the slit in her skirt that was high enough to reveal a garter.

"I've never done anything like this before," he said.

"Me, neither," she murmured. "At least not with someone else."

Passion flared in his eyes. "You're beautiful," he said, reaching for her.

She warmed, but dodged his arm playfully. "Where's your mask?"

He held up the black Zorro-style tie-on mask. "Will you help me?"

Her chest swelled at the realization that he was enjoying the game. She dangled a similar mask from her fingertips. "If you'll help me."

He stepped behind her, then lowered kisses on her bare shoulders and neck that sent shivers cascading over her. She groaned and arched into him as he wrapped the strip of black fabric around her eyes and temples, adjusting the holes before gently tying the ends. He splayed his hand over her stomach and pulled her against him. With his thumb he stroked the underside of her breast. His male hardness was evident against the small of her back even through the layers of their clothing. Her thighs quickened in anticipation of what was to come. She wanted the night to last and last.

"Now yours," she murmured, then spun around behind him. She situated his mask and tied it. His hair was soft beneath her fingers, his body still except for his chest moving up and down rapidly. She pressed her cheek into his back and wrapped her arms around his waist. With a delicate touch, she explored the firm contours of his chest through the thin fabric of his loose shirt. He moaned and covered her hands with his, sliding them down to his stomach, then to his waist, then lower.

Rebecca sighed as her fingers closed over the bulge of his sex. She allowed him to guide her hand, massaging his arousal through his clothing. After a few seconds, he stopped her hand with a groan. Then he turned and drew her into his arms.

"A dance, *señorita?*"

Her mouth parted because the mask he wore took her breath away. "You dance?"

"Nothing too complicated," he said with a little laugh. "And I haven't in years."

Still, she couldn't have been more surprised— until she realized that he was a very good dancer. He waltzed her around the room, holding her tightly against him with a strong arm around her waist. She stayed on her toes to be responsive to his moves, but their bodies melded perfectly, curve to hollow. Rebecca had never been so in tune with a man physically, and the experience was heady.

When the music slowed, he pulled her against him for a leisurely rasp of their bodies. She lifted her leg and hooked it around the back of his knee, exposing the garter he so admired. The mask made her feel mysterious and anonymous, as if they'd met at a Spanish ball a hundred years ago. Rain pounded the roof, cocooning them inside.

He kissed her hard, thrusting his tongue against hers. The blood rushed to her breasts and loins, weighting them, whetting them. He unzipped the back of her dress, allowing the bodice to fall and expose her breasts. Rebecca closed her eyes and held her breath until a low growl of appreciation came from his throat.

"Beautiful," he whispered against a budded pink nipple before he pulled it into his warm, wet mouth. Desire shot through her and she encouraged him by holding his head.

"Harder," she whispered. He pressed her breasts together so he could move from one to another with a flick of his tongue. Then he drew upon each nipple, kneading with his hands, pulling as much sensitive skin into his mouth as possible. Rebecca threw her head back and murmured a long "ah" of delight.

"I want you," he breathed against her breasts. "Now."

"Yes," she said. "Yes."

He lifted her as if she were feather down and carried her into the red dressing room. He pulled the curtain, and they were tucked away in a private nest, surrounded by mirrors. Seeing herself naked from the waist up while his gaze devoured her was rapturous. His hands moved against her skin, dark on light. His wide, long fingers circled the engorged skin at the tips of her breasts. She was mesmerized, chest heaving. And she was ready for him.

Rebecca turned and loosened his waistband, allowing his erection to spring free into her hand. Slick moisture transferred to her fingers—he was ready for her, too. He pressed her back on the padded seat, pushing her skirt up to her waist. He knelt between her legs, kissing her thighs above the stockings. The mask he wore heightened her anticipation because it gave him a dangerous air—she didn't know what he might do next. She closed her eyes and undulated her hips in time to the music around them.

He flicked his tongue against her panties, then fastened his mouth over the mound that housed the sensitive bead of her desire. Through the skimpy layer of black sheer fabric, his hot breath scorched the vulnerable nub, sending her hips bucking. But the barrier of her panties diluted the pleasure of his tongue just enough to make her wild with frustration. "More," she pleaded. "More."

He unhooked the garters and inched the tiny

black panties down over her twitching legs. Then he lifted his shirt over his head and flung it off. He produced a foil packet, ripped it open and rolled on the condom in record time.

Rebecca opened her knees shamelessly. His eyes were hooded with desire as he lowered his body over the length of hers. He guided the knob of his thick arousal up and down her wet channel, clenching his teeth in restraint as she moved in little circles against him. She clawed at his bare back as her release engulfed her and she cried his name. At her pinnacle, he entered her in one long stroke. The breath squeezed out of her lungs as her muscles contracted around him involuntarily. Their moans mingled and she wrapped her legs around his waist. They swayed in perfect rhythm, as if they'd made wild love together many, many times.

Rebecca knew she would never forget their reflection—she bare-breasted with the dress rucked up to her waist, and he driving into her, shirtless and masked. He sheathed and unsheathed himself with increasing urgency until he stiffened and emitted a long, satisfied groan. He relaxed into her, breathing her name over and over.

The only thing better than the sex itself was having the weight of his spent body on hers. So comforting, so erotic. Neither of them moved for several long minutes, recovering. Rebecca closed her eyes and let the wonder of what had just happened course through her. She hadn't known it could be so utterly fulfilling, so completely draining.

He roused and withdrew slowly, then rolled to her side. A chill ran over her body when the air hit her skin, moist wherever they'd touched. She held her breath—the moment of truth: Regret? Remorse?

He lifted onto his elbow, propped his head with his hand and looked down at her.

"It's a good thing we got most of the business out of the way," he murmured, pulling the mask off and down to his neck. "Because I'm exhausted."

Relief flooded her. Michael didn't think she was strange.

"You're amazing," he said. "I never imagined...did I mention that you're amazing?"

A flush of female satisfaction spread over her body. "I think it's called chemistry." She lifted her head and untied her mask.

He gasped. "Oh my God, it's the girl who runs the costume shop."

She laughed and propped herself up to face him.

Thunder boomed overhead. "It's really storming out there."

"The roof could have blown off and I wouldn't have noticed."

The lights blinked, then went out. Every electric buzz in the building fell quiet, increasing the volume of the rain pelting the building. "That old transformer is temperamental," she murmured. "The generator will kick on in a few minutes." They lay in pitch-black for a few seconds listening to the wind howling.

"Hell of a storm," he said quietly. "I used to dig storms when I was a kid."

"Where did you grow up?"

"South Side, rough part of town. You?"

"Little town called Madison about a hundred miles from here."

"I've heard of it." He shifted. "How did you get into the costume business?"

She pressed her lips together, and the years melted away. "My mother worked most of the time, and my younger sister and I had to entertain ourselves. Meg read books, and I played dress-up." She smiled in the dark. "I guess it stuck."

"No father?"

"No. He split when we were little. But Mom still lives in Madison."

"Where's your sister?"

"She's a schoolteacher in Peoria."

"I always wanted a sister. I have brothers. Three of them."

Her eyes had adjusted to the darkness enough for her to pick up the glint of his eyes. "Are you close to your brothers?"

"I suppose, as close as you can be after everyone grows up and has their own family, their own problems. They're all divorced." He made a rueful sound. "I guess we're all divorced now."

A reminder why they'd done what they'd done— sexual healing. "How did you get into the restaurant business?"

"It was my w—Sonia's idea. I owned a small wireless telecommunications business, and a big company offered to buy me out. We took the money and sunk it into the restaurant." He gave a small laugh. "I hated it at first, but then I grew to really like it. I think the place has a lot of potential now that…I have more control." His mouth moved closer to her ear. "And with your help."

"You should call the directors of the dance troupes tomorrow."

"It's on my list."

"And the invitations for the masquerade ball should go out immediately to everyone you know, and to the press."

"It's on my list."

"And a graphic artist—"

"It's on my list." He nuzzled her ear. "God, I wish we didn't have to get out in that storm."

She hesitated to offer him her bed. Sure, they'd had sex, but somehow sharing sheets seemed more intimate. And there was that whole morning-after awkwardness to deal with. Better to part now during the afterglow?

"I'll drive you home whenever you're ready," he said through a yawn. "I'll walk back to pick up my Explorer first."

She swallowed. "Michael, my apartment is upstairs. You…don't have to go."

He shifted. "Are you asking me to spend the night?"

*Be breezy.* "I wouldn't want to be responsible for you having an accident on the way home."

He inhaled noisily. "I'm sorry, but this is all new to me. Again."

"Don't feel obligated—"

"I don't. I mean, neither one of us—"

"—is looking for—"

"—a serious relationship."

"Right." She bit into her lip. Good thing that was out in the open.

A terrific crack of lightning lit the shop for a split second, and rolling thunder followed in waves, like fireworks.

"Is that offer to stay still open?" he asked.

"Yes."

"Then I accept."

She sat up and pulled the bodice of the dress around her. He offered to zip her up, and when his warm fingers brushed her skin, Rebecca felt the first stirrings of trouble in her chest. No...she wasn't falling for Michael. She was on the rebound, and he was still in love with his ex-wife. They had just made each other feel better, that was all.

Yes, that was all.

"Ready?" she asked.

"Right behind you."

They felt their way out of the dressing room, and she rooted a flashlight from beneath the counter, along with the tin of Mrs. Conrad's cream candy. She was starving. They were almost at the bottom of the steps leading up to her apartment when Rebecca stepped on something round and slipped. Mi-

chael caught and steadied her, then shined the flashlight beam at the floor.

A foam peanut.

Rebecca cut her gaze toward the supply closet.
*Mind your own business, Harry.*

# CHAPTER EIGHT

"I CALLED YOU LAST NIGHT," his brother said. "You screening your calls?"

Michael squirmed in his desk chair. "No, Ike."

"What then? I've called every night this week."

"I've been busy with the restaurant. We're re-opening in a couple of days."

"I've been calling the restaurant, too, and Rico said that come six o'clock sharp, you're outta there. What's going on?"

"I've been busy, that's all."

"You got a woman, don't you?"

In a previous life, Ike had been a bloodhound. "Don't, Ike."

"I knew it, I *knew* it. Who is she?"

"None of your business."

"Waitress? Customer? Somebody you picked up at a bar?"

Michael remained silent, hoping his brother would wear himself out.

"And I bet you feel a whole lot better about the divorce, don't you?"

"A little," he admitted. Actually a lot.

"I knew it, I *knew* it. Didn't I tell you?"

"Yes, Ike, you told me."

His brother hooted. "Will I get to meet her at the reopening? I was calling to RSVP, by the way."

"We'll see," he hedged. "And I'll put you down for two?"

"Yeah, I can probably scare up a date within two days."

"I'll see you then."

"Later, bro."

Michael hung up, shaking his head. Ike meant well, but he was just so...*base*.

Then he puffed out his cheeks—he was a good one to talk. For the better part of two weeks, he'd spent every evening with Rebecca under the guise of working. And true, they had made a lot of progress on plans for the reopening. More often than not, though, she'd try on one of the costumes she was making for his employees or she'd ask him to try one on, and things would...digress.

Or they would accidentally brush against each other and...digress.

Or she would drop a pencil and they would...digress.

He wiped his hand across his mouth. God, sex with Rebecca was like salve to his soul. It was exciting and comfortable at the same time. He would lie with his head between her breasts, utterly sated, yet hours—sometimes minutes—later, he'd crave her lovemaking again. The incredible mix of tenderness and enthusiasm she exuded reminded him of younger days, when sex was new and wondrous.

In fact, he decided, it was the mind-blowing sex that was messing with his mind. It was simply too soon to care about Rebecca—they'd never even been on a date, for heaven's sake. She was getting over her fiancé, and he was getting over Sonia, that was all. Exorcising grief. Seeking comfort. Restoring confidence.

The reason he and Rebecca could talk so easily, he reasoned, was that the situation wasn't threatening—they both knew it was temporary.

A knock on his door was a blessed rescue from the possibilities plaguing him. Of course for a second he entertained the hope that Rebecca had come to see him. Not a good sign.

"Come in."

Rico stuck his head inside the doorway. "The

director of the dance company is here…she wants to discuss Friday night's lineup.''

He nodded. "Let me grab a file."

The door closed and he thumbed through the stack of folders associated with the reopening—contractors, interior designers, ah…dancers. He glanced at the phone and wondered what Rebecca was doing for lunch. There was a place over on Shively Street that he'd always wanted to try, but never seemed to get around to it.

Then he frowned. What if she construed the offer as a date, as an invitation to take their…*liaison* to the next level? And what if the next level led to another level, then another? When he looked to the future, he could picture Rebecca at his side. But start with slim odds for a successful marriage, and add his track record, and he was most likely looking at a second divorce down the road. Every time Ike met a woman, he was convinced she was "the" one. Now, his brother kept a divorce attorney on retainer.

No, it was too soon to become involved with Rebecca, to drag her into the aftermath of his divorce. Best to keep things clear-cut. Untangled. Simple.

That decided, he picked up the file and headed

toward the front of the restaurant. Rico stood talking to an attractive middle-aged black woman dressed in a bright yellow dress.

"This is Ms. Crema Carroll," Rico said. "From the dance studio."

"How do you do, Ms. Carroll." Michael shook her hand. "I'm—"

The front door opened behind the woman and to his amazement, Rebecca appeared, then flashed him a secret smile across the room. His heart lifted crazily. She wore snug jeans and a red windbreaker and navy tennis shoes. Fabulous.

"I'm, um—"

Her hair was pulled back into a ponytail, and her cheeks were pink. Just looking at her made him think of spring. And bedsprings.

"He's Michael Pierce," Rico explained to Ms. Carroll, giving him an odd look.

Michael shook himself, then turned his attention back to the woman. "Yes, I'm Michael Pierce. Thanks for stopping by. Would you excuse me for just one minute while I speak with a vendor?"

Ms. Carroll nodded, and Michael suggested that Rico show her the finished stage in the dining room. Then he turned to Rebecca, shamelessly pleased to see her. "Hi."

"Hi," she said, then nodded toward the parking lot. "I brought the costumes."

"You're finished? Great."

"Yeah," she said, then shoved her hands in her jacket pockets. "And I was wondering...if maybe you had time to grab lunch."

At her hopeful expression, alarms sounded in his head. It was happening—complications. Today lunch, tomorrow, meet the parents. After all, she probably still had a wedding gown hanging in her closet. Panic reared.

"No, I'm sorry, I don't," he said, although he barely recognized that tinny, forced voice as his own. He cleared his throat and gestured vaguely after Ms. Carroll. "Last-minute details."

"Sure. Some other time, maybe."

"Hmm." He jerked his thumb toward the dining room. "I have to run, but I'll send Rico out to carry in the costumes."

"Okay," she said with a little smile. "See you later?"

More alarms. He pushed back his cap and scratched his temple. "I was thinking I might have to work late tonight, considering we're getting down to the wire."

Another little smile. "I understand." She lifted a hand and turned toward the door.

His chest squeezed painfully. "But you're still coming to the reopening party?"

She opened the door and looked back. "Wouldn't miss it."

REBECCA UNLOCKED THE DOOR of her shop and removed the Back In One Hour sign. Her chest tingled from Michael's rebuff—it was obvious that he didn't intend to see her again. Their affair had run its course, as she'd known it would.

They had an unspoken understanding, she and Michael. Help each other past the rough spot of a breakup. Indulge in great sex with no strings attached. Talk endlessly afterward because they weren't trying to impress each other.

She bit down on the inside of her cheek. Before their affair had even begun, she knew it wouldn't last. So why did it hurt so much?

A cleansing inhale put her mind back on business. She had to finish those nun's habits by the weekend, and the costume she was going to wear to the reopening of Incognito. No matter how things had ended with Michael, she wished him well.

Battling tears, she went to the cash register and

broke open the coin wrappers of pennies and dimes she'd gotten from the bank. In the dimes compartment lay a foam peanut.

Rebecca shot a glance toward the supply closet, then sighed. "Okay, Harry, you win." She closed the cash register drawer, walked to the closet and dragged out the box Lana had sent to her. Harry had deflated a bit more, so, feeling like an idiot, she put her mouth over the air nozzle in the side of his head. He expanded appreciably as she blew several long breaths into him. Those darn peanuts were everywhere.

The bell rang on the door. "Hidy-hoo."

She winced—caught. She replaced the rubber stopper and turned sheepishly.

Quincy grinned across the showroom, his gaze on the doll. "I take it this is Harry, your good luck *love* charm." His rich laugh rolled out.

"Don't rub it in."

He set a parcel on the counter, then walked closer. "Hey, he's cool. But why the sudden change of heart?"

She frowned. "Let's just say he's difficult to ignore." She stood Harry against the wall and signed on the clipboard Quincy extended.

"Everyone is all atwitter about the masquerade

ball,'' he said. ''Looks like your little after hours project with Michael Pierce was a success.''

Her heart squeezed, but she tried to look casual. ''I guess we'll know Friday night.''

He angled his head. ''You all right?''

''Sure.''

''Dickie been causing trouble?''

She laughed dryly. ''No. Dickie has moved on to his new life and new wife.'' Everyone was moving on, it seemed. She blinked furiously to stem the tears that assailed her.

''Oh, honey, what is it?'' he asked, rubbing her shoulder.

''It's nothing,'' she said, but her voice was clogged with emotion.

He squinted at her. ''It's Mr. Pierce, isn't it?''

She sniffed mightily, afraid to answer.

He sighed. ''So, you took my advice, and now you've gone and fallen in love with the guy.''

''Oh, no,'' she protested. ''I'm not in love with him. It's just that…I thought our time together meant something, that's all.'' She wiped at her eyes and smiled. ''Don't mind me—I'm in a bit of a slump.''

''If I thought it would turn out like this,'' he murmured, ''I would've kept my mouth shut.''

"It's okay," she said, pulling herself together. "Really. If nothing else, it helped me to put things with Dickie in perspective." In short, Michael had likely ruined her for all other men. "I'll be fine."

He nodded sympathetically, then snapped his fingers. "Hey—I need a costume for the masquerade party."

She smiled, glad for the change in subject. "*That* I can do something about."

"You're still going, aren't you?"

"I told Michael I would, although I'm not so sure he really wants me there. It could be awkward, I suppose."

"I'll bet you're wearing something fabulous, aren't you?"

She walked behind the counter and uncovered a mannequin dressed in the silver beaded flapper gown and turban she'd spent hours making.

"Wow," he breathed.

She was pleased with the outfit herself—she'd wanted to create something special to commemorate the occasion. And she'd wanted to look wonderful for Michael.

The bell on the door rang and Rebecca turned to wait on her customer. But her feet faltered at the sight of Sonia Pierce, looking like a designer-clad lioness in all her blond glory.

# CHAPTER NINE

"THE *TRIBUNE* IS HERE," Rico reported excitedly. He looked resplendent in a matador costume and red mask. "Everyone loves the new format."

Michael had chosen the Zorro costume for himself—it held good memories. He looked out over the dining room, packed with patrons dressed in elaborate costumes, their gazes riveted on the flamenco dancers on stage, swirling in colorful outfits and stomping to the rapid beat. "It looks like a success, all right."

"We've booked weekends for the next four months," Rico said. "And the line on the sidewalk is a hundred deep just to come in and mingle."

He nodded. "Great."

Rico squinted at him. "Boss, you don't look so good."

Michael rubbed his neck, which was sore from craning to look for Rebecca, which was ridiculous because he probably wouldn't recognize her since everyone wore masks. "Rico, have you seen Ms. Valentine?"

"No, sir."

"Is it possible she's in the crowd outside?"

"I gave her a VIP pass, sir."

Maybe she'd decided not to show after all. "Excuse me, I need a drink." He strode over to the bar and signaled for a whiskey and Coke.

He didn't miss Rebecca—he couldn't. He missed the sex, that was all, which he could get anywhere.

*You know better,* his mind whispered, but he drowned the thought with a mouthful of the mixed drink.

The performance ended, and the applause was thunderous. Gratification welled in his chest—if tonight was any indication, Incognito was on its way to recovery. Thanks to Rebecca.

"There you are, little brother." Ike came up and slapped him on the back. "Nice pants."

Michael glanced at his brother's jeans and leather jacket. "Where's your costume?"

"This is it—I'm James Dean."

"Right."

"So where is she?"

Michael took a drink from his glass. "Who?"

"The girl. The hottie. The woman you're screw—"

*"Shut up, Ike."*

His brother's eyebrows dove. "What's wrong with you?"

"Nothing."

"Oh, no." Ike laughed. "You didn't go and fall for your rebound fling?"

"Ike, please."

"My God, man, don't you know anything about being divorced? The first woman you take to bed is a throwaway."

He frowned. "Gee, I can't imagine why you've never had a relationship that worked."

Ike shrugged and said something, but Michael's attention had gone to the back of the room where the crowd parted to make way for a woman wearing a magnificent silver flapper gown and a pink feathered mask that obscured most of her face. A silver turban covered her hair. It was easily the most elaborate costume in the room and even garnered a smattering of applause. The woman panned the room, then stopped when she looked in his direction and made her way across the room.

He smiled, not caring if Rebecca knew that he'd been waiting for her. The night now seemed complete somehow. She stopped in front of him and pulled up her mask. Michael's mouth went dry.

"Sonia."

Ike grunted. "I'm outta here."

Sonia smiled, gorgeous and golden. She'd painted a mole high on her cheek. "Hello, Michael, how are you?"

"Fine," he said stiffly. "I didn't realize you were on the guest list."

"Michael, I couldn't *not* come. You know that the restaurant was always more my pet than yours."

"It's *all* mine now."

She sighed. "I'm sorry the way it all washed out. I miss you."

His laugh was harsh. "Is your boyfriend out of town?"

"Edward and I aren't seeing each other anymore."

A tiny sliver of vindication stabbed him and he took another drink from his glass. "What happened?"

She shrugged prettily. "I guess the novelty wore off."

Meaning the attraction was purely physical, like his attraction to Rebecca, and vice versa.

"Don't you like my costume?" she asked, turning around.

"It's beautiful," he agreed.

"I went to the costume shop and told Rebecca I needed something special. She said a customer hadn't needed this costume after all, so I bought it for a song."

"You saw Rebecca?" he asked carefully.

"Yes." She reached forward to pick something off his shirt—a favorite flirtation of hers. "You look rather fetching yourself, although that mask is a little fearsome." When he didn't respond, her mouth went contrite. "Michael, I know I handled things horribly, but I was hoping that you and I could give our marriage another try."

His heart pounded faster. Hadn't he fantasized that Sonia would come back begging for forgiveness? Did he really want to see more than six years of his life go down the drain? These...*feelings* for Rebecca would probably wear off, so why would he let them get in the way of repairing his relationship with Sonia? Maybe he could salvage one failure from the Pierce brother broken marriage heap.

Indecision gripped him like a steel band. He shifted his weight and something crunched under his boot. Michael moved his foot and looked down.

A smashed foam peanut.

## CHAPTER TEN

REBECCA SPRAYED HARRY'S striped pajamas with wrinkle remover, then smoothed her hand down his arm. "So, Harry old boy, when exactly does your good luck kick in? Do you have a switch or something, because I'm getting a little desperate here."

He grinned back and she sighed. Judging from the number of costumes she'd rented for the party tonight, it was going to be a roaring success. And Sonia would look spectacular in the outfit she'd made, better than she would have looked in it. The woman had hinted that she and Michael were going to reconcile, but Rebecca hadn't commented—and she'd silenced Quincy with a glare.

She was happy for Michael, because he'd told her one night with their heads on a pillow how he'd had high hopes for his marriage, that he'd taken his vows seriously. She hoped to marry a man like him someday.

"There," she said, giving Harry a finishing pat. "If I'm going to keep you around, you must at least look presentable." She shook her head over the striped pajamas. "And I'll see what I can do about some new duds."

She sighed and walked around the showroom, turning off lights and admiring the quirky space that she'd made her own. The costume business wasn't for everyone, but she truly loved it. She fingered the purple velvet cape of the vampire outfit in the window, remembering the night that Michael had walked in on her—the beginning of the end of something special.

Rebecca angled her head.

Why not? The last time she'd put it on, she'd been interrupted. But she hadn't forgotten how sexy it had made her feel, and right now, she could use an ego boost.

Rebecca undressed the mannequin, then moved into the red dressing room to don the decadent outfit. The mirrors and soft cushions sent a heaviness to her midsection—how many times had she and Michael made love here? She'd lost count.

Regret was a bitter taste in her mouth. Maybe if she hadn't been so forward, a relationship could have developed more slowly as they worked together. Maybe for him the novelty had worn off and now he was embarrassed. Maybe he was one of those guys who thought there were two kinds of women—women you sleep with, and women you have a relationship with.

No, deep down she knew Michael was different, that his sensitivity ran as deep as his passion. He must love Sonia profoundly if he was considering getting back with her, and that kind of love she could only admire.

She undressed, then redressed in the costume slowly, and pretended she was readying herself for Michael. She certainly had enough memories to last a while—the way his fingers slid over her skin, the way he breathed her name during his release, the way he slept sprawled in the nude.

And she'd come to appreciate her own body more—the sensitivity of her breasts and neck, and her ability to pull the most exquisite orgasm from his body.

In her life, Michael Pierce would be the one who got away. Then she scoffed at herself—she'd never really had him to begin with. But it had been delicious while it lasted.

Just as she settled the cape around her shoulders, a knock on the door sounded. She frowned—probably Quincy coming to try to drag her to the party. Or Mrs. Conrad, who couldn't comprehend the word Closed when she needed something.

She fastened the cape's front closures and headed toward the front door, then stopped when she saw Michael on the other side. Her stomach pitched and quick tears sprang to her eyes. Had he come to tell her about Sonia?

She pressed her lips together as she unlocked the door. A cold breeze blew in when she opened the door, lifting the hem of the cape.

"Hi," she said.

"Hi." He scanned her from head to toe. "You're wearing my favorite outfit."

Rebecca bit the end of her tongue and said nothing. "I...I missed you at the party."

"How's the party going?"

"We're a big hit, thanks to you."

She returned his smile. "I'm glad." And she was.

"Can I come in?"

Rebecca nodded and stepped back. He was wearing the Zorro costume, sans the mask. She closed her eyes briefly and steeled herself. "Is something wrong?"

"Yes," he said, coming to stand in front of her. "I was at the party surrounded by friends and customers—"

"And your wife," she cut in softly.

"My *ex*-wife." He exhaled noisily. "I was standing there, and I should have been thrilled that my business is back on track, and that everyone was having a great time, but all I could think about was you."

Her heart bobbed.

He cupped her jaw and caressed her cheek with his thumb. "Rebecca, I don't know where this is going, or if you even want it to go anywhere, but I'm crazy about you, and I want you in my life."

She swallowed hard, afraid to hope. "Not just in your bed?"

"No." Then he pulled her close and stroked her hair.

She inhaled the minty scent on his neck and clung to him, joyous disbelief coursing through her.

"But," he added, "you do realize, don't you, that we spend a third of our lives in bed?"

She laughed and tipped her head back. "You were so distant to me the other day."

He made a rueful noise. "I could tell I was getting in too deep, and it scared me."

"So what made you change your mind?"

Michael pursed his mouth. "It's hard to explain, but my mother told me once to look for signs when I make a decision, and I'll know if I'm making the right one."

"And?"

"And tonight I got my sign."

She frowned. "What was it?"

He released her long enough to retrieve something out of his pocket, then held out a smashed foam peanut.

Rebecca gasped and took the peanut, dumbfounded at the implication. Lana would never believe this story—or maybe she would. Closing her fingers over the flattened little piece of nothing, she whispered, "Thanks, Harry."

Michael lifted an eyebrow. "Who's Harry?"

"It's a long story," she said, throwing her arms around his neck. "But it has a happy ending."

\* \* \* \* \*

*Good Luck Harry gets a chance to next work his matchmaking magic on Rebecca's sister. Don't miss the fun when mousy schoolteacher Meg Valentine comes to Chicago to run Anytime Costumes in Rebecca's absence. But Meg's life is quickly turned upside down when she's obliged to become a body-double for a celebrity sex kitten who's in town. Wearing provocative clothing and evading paparazzi are eye-opening experiences, but Meg soon discovers the most risqué part of the job is dealing with bodyguard Jarrett Miller.*

*Look for TWO SEXY! by Stephanie Bond, part of the exciting new Harlequin Blaze series scheduled to launch in August 2001! For a complete list of Stephanie Bond's previous and upcoming titles, visit www.stephaniebond.com.*

# SHOW AND TELL
## Kimberly Raye

## CHAPTER ONE

"DESCRIBE YOUR *ULTIMATE* fantasy."

Laney Merriweather nibbled the tip of her pencil as a dozen possibilities raced through her mind. Everything from a candlelit dinner for two to a satin-covered bed full of red rose petals. Like most women, she'd entertained each scenario at one time or another in her private thoughts. They were okay, but *ultimate?* That implied special. Different. Her *most* secret longing.

Her gaze went to the woman who'd read the latest instruction in the ten-question test to win a basket of free body essentials—everything from chocolate body paint to strawberry massage oil. A smile tilted Laney's lips. Decked out in a neon purple lace teddy with a matching garter and fishnet stockings, Karen Donahue was a walking advertisement for her newest moneymaking venture—Wildchild Lingerie. Wildchild was a cross between Tupperware and Victoria's Secret where women booked parties in their homes, primarily on Tuesday nights when the local *VFW* had its weekly meeting and poker extravaganza. While the men got together and played cards, the women gathered to shop and scarf down pigs in a blanket. Or, in this case, peanuts and pretzels since Eden Hallsey—tonight's hostess—lived above The Pink Cadillac, the only bar in Cadillac, Texas, and the location for this particular party.

Karen had arrived an hour ago, suitcase in hand, and put on quite a show, featuring a collection of racy lingerie, scrumptious body lotions and oils and even a few naughty "toys," such as feather body massagers and a sexy board game called Around the Bedroom in Eighty Ways.

Laney's gaze lingered on the Wildchild demonstrator. It wasn't so much that Karen had a fairly attractive body for a forty-year-old mother of three that stirred Laney's admiration. It was the fact that she sat on the edge of the bartop, calling out intimate questions without so much as a hint of self-consciousness. She might well have been wearing jeans and a Western shirt, calling out N24's and B9's down at the bingo hall, rather than sitting half-naked in front of a barful of women. She was "out there," open and honest with her likes and dislikes, and she wasn't the least bit embarrassed about it.

Laney glanced down at her own white button-up blouse, expensive but painfully low-key, her boring gray slacks and her low-heeled pumps. A sigh vibrated up her throat. To have even half of Karen's freedom. Now *that* was Laney's ultimate fantasy.

Laney penned her answer, grabbed a handful of peanuts and waited for the next question.

"Okay, girls. Now I want you to describe the ultimate man to go with that fantasy." The instructions met with a round of hooting and hollering. "And don't forget, the hottest description wins an extra door prize." She held up a pair of fuzzy red handcuffs and winked. "To keep that man right where you want him."

Before Laney knew what she was doing, she started to write. This answer was a no-brainer, since she'd fantasized about the same man for as long as she could remember. It didn't matter what sort of scenario she set up in her head—from a rough and tough cowboy to Tarzan himself—the man who played the lead always had the same dark hair, the same greener than green eyes, the same charming,

slide - off - those - undies - and - let - me - take - a - peek
smile.

A flush of heat crept up her face as she wrote
and she took a swallow of punch. Just thinking
about him always generated the same effect. Heat.
Lots of heat.

"The tough part is over," Karen finally announced after a few more questions regarding setup
for the fantasy and the appropriate clothing—if any.
Her eyes gleamed as she rubbed her hands together.
"Let's hear the juicy details."

Karen went around the bar, asking for volunteers
to share their fantasies. Laney bit her tongue and
suppressed a strange sense of longing as she wadded up her piece of paper and tossed it into the
nearest ashtray. She'd learned a long time ago not
to waste her time wanting what she couldn't have.
She had her hands full as it was, walking the
straight and narrow path as the only child of ultra-
conservative, small town judge Marshall Merriweather.

Turning her attention back to Karen, she blinked
her eyes against the sudden stabbing pain of an on-
coming migraine and tried to concentrate on the
titillating answers being called out.

"I didn't hear any naughty answers from you." The comment came a half hour later from a tall, voluptuous blonde who wore a black tank top and shorts and a bar apron with The Pink Cadillac emblazoned in neon pink lettering.

The game had just ended and all the party attendees had disbursed, some crowding around Karen and filling in their order forms, while others scarfed down the snacks laid out across the bar top.

"'Naughty' isn't in my vocabulary."

"Well, it should be. 'Naughty' makes the world go 'round, honey." Eden fingered the pile of lingerie Karen had deposited in front of Laney a few moments ago for her browsing pleasure. "Although I have to admit that some of this stuff gives new meaning to the word."

"Careful, otherwise the entire town's liable to realize that you aren't half the bad girl you make out to be. This bar is just a front."

Eden Hallsey had been the owner and operator of The Pink Cadillac for ten years, since her parents—the previous owners—had retired to New Mexico and left their only daughter to carry on the family legacy. Eden continued to serve up the best drinks in town and, thanks to her appearance and her bad girl attitude, gave the local church ladies plenty to wag their tongues about.

Laney's gaze shot to Martha Pennburg, one of the women in question, who sat in the far corner and did her best to look appalled by the risqué items spread on the table before her. Laney had no doubt Martha had come out of pure nosiness. First thing tomorrow, she'd be on the phone to her friends, discussing tonight's "disgraceful exhibition" at length.

Laney also knew she would be included in the gossip, but she could withstand a little heat if it meant seeing Eden. Laney was so busy in Austin that she rarely had time to get home for anything other than major holidays, and those were spent attending the expected round of parties and other functions with her father. A few years ago, she'd done the party circuit with both her parents, but her mother—God rest her soul—had passed on a few years ago. Now it was just Laney and her dad.

Since arriving home two days ago, she'd had her hands full setting up interviews to find her ailing father a capable assistant to relieve his caseload. Eden had been busy, as well, with preparations for the Cadillac Car Cruise scheduled for this coming

Sunday. The Car Cruise was an annual event where classic car owners from all the nearby counties gathered on Sunday afternoon to have an old-fashioned, fifties-style drive down the main strip through town. As the only bar owner in town, Eden was responsible for providing the beer for the kick-off barbecue on Friday night, not to mention the campaign for Saturday Night's Miss Cadillac pageant. She'd been up to her armpits stocking supplies and Laney had barely talked to her on the phone, much less seen her in person. Tonight had been the first chance for a face-to-face meeting. Laney had chucked convention, closed up her father's office a few hours early and headed for the party.

They'd been friends since the first moment Laney had found Eden crying in the girls' locker room after Jake Marlboro had spread a nasty rumor about her. The entire world had believed the worst of Eden, Laney included. Until she'd seen the pain in the girl's eyes. As much as Laney had been tempted to turn her back on Eden for her own reputation's sake, she hadn't, despite her parents' disapproval. After all, Laney had been one of the fortunate ''haves'' in Cadillac, while Eden had been from a poorer than poor family, a ''have not'' all the way.

Laney's parents had finally accepted the friendship, however, dismissing it as an act of charity on Laney's part. But Laney hadn't felt sorry for Eden. She'd felt connected to her. She knew firsthand what it was like to pretend to be something she wasn't.

While Eden had always done her damnedest to live up to everyone's expectations—if you can't beat 'em, join 'em was her motto—Laney had lived up to her family's. She was every bit a cultured, refined Merriweather, as if she'd been born to it rather than adopted.

*If only.*

"Listen here, I'm bad with a capital *B,* and don't you forget it. I just wouldn't be able to breathe in some of this stuff, that's all." Eden fingered a teddy with the tiniest straps Laney had ever seen. "Personally—" she lifted her own ample bosom and shot a wink in Martha Pennburg's direction "—I need more support for these babies." The woman flushed a bright red and averted her gaze. Eden gave a satisfied smirk.

Laney tried to hide her smile. "You really shouldn't do that. You're liable to send her blood pressure soaring, and at her age I don't think that's a good thing."

"She shouldn't be so nosy and you—" Eden pinned Laney with a stare "—shouldn't worry what those old busybodies think."

But those busybodies were family friends. Her father's friends. She blinked against another twinge from her building migraine.

"What do you think?" Laney indicated a red slip of nothing. "My secretary's getting married in a few weeks and since I know her the best, I got stuck with choosing the bachelorette gift. I voted for a Crock-Pot, but the other women picked slinky lingerie."

"They put *you* in charge of buying naughty nothings?" Eden winked. "Kind of like sending flat-as-a-pancake Mary Moore to pick out a double D bra, don't you think?"

"You're a regular riot." Laney studied the teddies before picking one in particular. She pulled out her checkbook and dashed off a check. "I like this red myself."

"Careful, Melanie Margaret. Otherwise the whole town's liable to know that beneath that conservative suit lurks the heart of a real wild woman." The deep voice came from directly behind Laney and sent a wash of familiar heat skimming her nerve endings.

*Please, God, no.* The prayer echoed through her head for a long, breathless moment before she accepted what a hopeless cause it was. She'd spent her entire high school career praying the same desperate plea and not once had Dallas Jericho ever miraculously disappeared.

Her gaze snapped to the wall-length mirror behind the bar and she caught her first glimpse of the man himself. *Man* being the key word. Gone was the tall, lanky boy she remembered. Dallas stood directly behind her, wearing tight faded jeans, a white T-shirt that emphasized a broad chest and heavily muscled biceps, and a smile rumored to have charmed Pastor Standley's most pious daughter right out of her undies. The too long, dark hair that had always been his trademark was now gone. A short, cropped cut framed his face and made his features seem stronger, more mature, more masculine.

One thing hadn't changed, however. Even as a boy, his entire persona had screamed Hot Stud Alert! and now was no different.

She gathered her courage and drew in a deep, steadying breath, determined to calm the sudden pounding of her heart. She'd known this moment was coming. Cadillac was a small town and a meeting was inevitable. "For your information, this—" she fingered the lacey lingerie "—is for a friend of mine."

He gave her a knowing wink. "That's what they all say, hot stuff."

She narrowed her gaze. "What are you doing here? This party is for ladies only, and my name isn't hot stuff."

He gave her another wink. "Then I'm definitely at the right place, sugar lips."

Amen to that. Where the women were, Dallas Jericho was sure to be found. It was a reputation he'd earned at the young age of six when he'd crashed Karey Michaels's sleepover and refused to leave until he'd had pizza and Sprite *and* a kiss from Karey's big sister.

"If you're going for the red—" he reached around her and picked up a matching pair of crimson lace gloves "—you might want to add these with it."

"*I'm* not going for the red. It's not for me, and I see you're still butting into other people's business."

"Just yours."

"I don't need your advice."

"Really?" He leaned close, so close that she could feel the whisper of his warm breath at her temple. "Then what do you need?"

You. Me. *Naked.*

The answers rushed through her head and sent a wash of heat through her. "I think it's time for me to go home. I've got a stack of briefs to go over."

"Brief." He leaned back just enough to give her some breathing room. Thankfully. "Now there's the right notion." He reached past her to finger a purple pair of thong panties. His arm brushed hers and electricity shot through her body, the same way it always had whenever he'd touched her.

"Eden," she called out to the woman standing at the far end of the bar. "I'll see you for lunch tomorrow if I get out of court in time."

"Sure thing, sweetie." Eden waved her off and resumed filling the punch bowl.

Dallas arched an eyebrow as she gathered up her purse. "Still playing the Big Time Lawyer?"

*Unfortunately.* She forced the notion aside. Sure, the hours were long, the cases consuming. But being a partner in one of the most prestigious firms in Austin had its perks. She had her own parking

spot, a private secretary, and most of all, the satisfaction of knowing she was continuing the grand
Merriweather tradition. Like his father and grandfather before him, her father had been one of the
best criminal trial lawyers in the South. He'd had a
thriving practice in Austin, commuting to and fro
until a few years back. A heart attack had forced
him to slow down and he'd settled into life as a
judge in his hometown of Cadillac.

It was slow, but not slow enough. Marshall Merriweather had a mild heart attack just a few weeks
ago, which was why Laney had taken two weeks
of vacation time and come home. To see for herself
that her father took his doctor's advice and started
to relax. That, or retire. As stubborn as her father
was, Laney knew she couldn't force him. But she
could hire the best legal secretary available to help
with his caseload. She'd already contacted an employment agency in nearby Sharp County and had
a full day's worth of interviews set up for tomorrow.

She slid from the bar stool. Dallas's fingers
closed over her arm just as she was about to make
a quick getaway. "Don't forget your lingerie."

She ignored the tingling where his skin met hers

and concentrated on gathering up her purchase. "For the last time, it's not mine."

"Whatever you say."

"It's *not*." She wasn't sure why she felt so compelled to persuade him. Reputation, she told herself. She didn't want anyone getting the wrong idea. Even Dallas.

Especially Dallas.

"Red is definitely your color."

"I told you—"

"But I like purple myself. You ought to try these." He fingered the purple thong panties he'd singled out earlier. "Those old biddies down at the country club would ostracize you for sure if they got a glimpse of these. You'd definitely ruin that Miss Priss image you try so hard to maintain."

Laney narrowed her gaze. "Are you naturally this obnoxious, or do you have to practice at it?"

He shrugged. "What can I say? You bring out the best in me, darlin'."

She wanted to say something, but nothing snappy came to mind. Not with him standing so close and zapping her common sense. She shook her head and turned on her heel.

"Sweet dreams, Melanie Margaret..." His voice

followed her, a deep, husky sound that stirred the heat in her belly almost as much as her annoyance.

Almost.

But Laney had promised herself a long time ago that she would never, ever be a slave to her lust for Dallas Jericho.

Never again, that is.

She'd fallen victim once before, a moment of weakness that had nearly cost her everything. Her pride. Her self-respect. Her reputation.

It would never, *ever* happen again.

DALLAS JERICHO HAD NEVER considered himself a devout man, but as he watched Laney walk away from him, her head high and her back stiff, he knew without a doubt that a higher power existed.

Only a divine being could have created something as downright delicious as a woman. *This* particular woman.

Gray linen tugged and pulled against her hips, molding to Laney's bottom with each step, causing his groin to tighten. He'd always loved to watch her walk. They'd lived on opposites sides of town, but the route from the school, down the main strip through town had been the same. He could still see her headed home, her long, blond hair pulled back in a ponytail, her cheerleader skirt swishing with each step. He'd been so hot for her back then, which was why he'd done his best to convince her otherwise.

In the name of pride, of course.

He'd put himself on the line once, hoping against hope that a girl like Laney could actually like a guy like him. She'd turned him down for the eighth-grade homecoming dance, proving what everybody had been telling him since he'd been old enough to spell his last name. Namely that girls—nice, whole-some, *good* girls like Laney Merriweather—didn't waste their time on the son of the town drunk.

Bick Jericho had not only made a reputation for himself with his boozing and carousing, but he'd forever marked his three sons. The Jericho boys had been labeled "bad" well before any of them had ever thought of taking a drink. It was no wonder that Dallas and his two older brothers had started to live up to everyone's expectations. Dallas had been a hellion through middle and high school, and he'd been headed down the same road after grad-uation. Then Bick Jericho had wrapped his car around a telephone pole after a particularly heavy night of boozing.

Dallas had watched them lower his father into the ground and vowed to change his ways. But while he could work his way through school and get his degree, open his own construction business and put his own carousing ways behind him, he couldn't change the blood that flowed through his veins. He was Bick Jericho's son, and no matter that Dallas now lived a respectable life, for some people it just wasn't enough. People like Judge Marshall Merriweather, his sexy-as-anything daughter, and their hoity-toity friends down at the elite Cadillac Country Club.

Even so, he wanted her. He had way back then and, if the sudden thunder of his heart was any indication, the effect had only intensified.

"Penny for your thoughts." Eden Hallsey's voice pushed inside his head and drew him around. She took one look at his face, and said, "On second thought, my fire extinguisher's out back and I don't have enough water on tap to put out what's burning in those big green eyes of yours." Her gaze went to the doorway where Laney had just disappeared. "She looks good, doesn't she?"

He shrugged. "Older."

"Exactly. Older and more mature. More filled out and shape—"

"Do you have my order ready?" he cut in, eager to get off the subject of how well Laney filled out those slacks and that blouse and...

He shook away the vision and tried to ignore the growing hard-on making his jeans a mite tighter than was comfortable. "We're pulling a late shift over at the Dixon House and my crew is hungry."

His guys at Triple J Construction weren't the only ones with an appetite. Dallas himself wanted sustenance. A different sort than the six-foot submarine sandwiches Eden's bar had become famous for.

He had a hankering for a curvy blonde with deep blue eyes that glittered in the moonlight when he stroked the underside of her soft, round breasts...

Eden gave him a knowing wink. "Be right out."

He slid into the seat Laney had vacated and tried to ignore the scent of her perfume that lingered in the air. Of their own accord, his nostrils flared and he found himself drinking in the subtle aroma of warm woman and musky perfume that lingered in the air.

Christ, she even smelled the same. Worse, she affected him as intensely as ever. Just one whiff of her and he wanted another. And another.

*Crazy.* It had been ten friggin' years. Plenty of time for Dallas to have gotten over his damnable crush on her. A *crush*. That's all it had been. At least that's what he tried to convince himself whenever his memories got the best of him and he found himself thinking about her. Wanting her. Needing her.

Just as the thought hit him, his cell phone rang.

"Jericho, here."

"I've got one word for you—aqua."

"Mr. Dixon?"

"And not just a plain, ordinary aqua," the man rushed on, confirming Dallas's question. Claude Dixon was always more interested in what he himself had to say, rather than what came out of anyone else's mouth. He was one of a new breed migrating from the city into the surrounding hill country. A wannabe cowboy, as the locals liked to call them. Suit types who'd watched one too many Bonanza reruns and were eager to escape the stress of their busy lives by playing Hoss on the weekends. The problem was, Claude and all the yuppies like him brought the city with them. Rather than settling on a traditional spread and actually getting their hands dirty, they built oversize, posh houses with tennis courts and swimming pools, and called them ranches.

Not that Dallas was complaining. Thanks to the recent influx, he'd watched his business grow from a one trailer construction operation to a major company with development projects throughout the surrounding six counties.

"Alyssa Jackson has a similar shade of mauve in her country kitchen and her bunkhouse," Claude continued. "So it's out of the question for us to stick with that color. Why, we entertain the same group of friends. Whatever would they say?" Without waiting for a response, he rushed on. "Katherine wants the pale, summerset-blue aqua featured in last month's center layout in *Texas Elite*. So you have to change it. Now."

Dallas ignored the twinge of anger that rushed through him, along with the urge to tell Dixon what he could do with his new tile, his new house, his indecisive wife and the latest copy of his highfalutin' magazine. But whether Dallas liked it or not, he'd made a promise. Sure, the Dixons kept breaking their end of the agreement with constant changes. But that didn't mean Dallas had to break his. He'd given his word as a businessman that he would bring the project in on time and he intended to do just that. Satisfaction was his motto, even if Katherine Dixon decided on polka-dot tile.

"That's catalog number 9067892—"

"Wait a second," Dallas cut in. "Let me get something to write with." He fished in his pocket for a pen, then glanced around for a stray piece of paper, a cocktail napkin, *something*.

Seconds ticked by before his gaze finally lit on a wadded-up piece of paper sitting in a nearby ashtray. As he snatched up the trash and unfolded it, Laney's scent grew stronger and his nostrils flared again.

A crush, he told himself yet again. A crazy, friggin' crush that was best forgotten.

"Shoot," Dallas said, forcing his thoughts away from Laney and her scent and the unsated lust for her still pulsing through his veins, and concentrated on scribbling the number Dixon recited to him.

"Are you sure this time?" He asked the same question he'd asked the last time, and the time before that when Dixon had changed his mind.

"Positive. Alyssa Jackson is much too busy with her charity groups to read *Texas Elite*, though I'm sure she subscribes." A click sounded as Dixon hung up. Dallas took a deep breath, forced his fingers to loosen around the cell phone and dialed the number for his foreman at the Dixon site.

"Stop laying the tile," he told Charlie Peterson.

"But we're already done."

"Then start pulling it up. The Dixons changed their mind."

"Imagine that." A colorful curse erupted on the

other end of the line. "We've already put in three days laying this pink crap."

"It's mauve, and the customer is always right."

"Usually, unless the customer is a nutty, uppity fruitcake like Claude Dixon. He thinks that just because he has money, he can change his mind faster than that Madonna woman changes her hair color. Why, if it were me, I'd take a piece of this tile and shove it right where the sun don't shine."

But it wasn't Charlie. Nor was it his name nor his reputation at stake.

"Just pull up the tile," he said before hitting the off button.

He folded the paper and shoved it, along with his cell phone, into his pocket just as Eden walked up.

"Happy eating," she said as she handed him two large brown bags and took the money he offered her. "And don't be such a stranger."

"I don't mean to be, but I've got my hands full."

"I heard you're doing the new Dixon place. Lucky for them. Not so lucky for you. Claude's a butthead at times."

"Try all the time."

"But he's a butthead with a full pocket, so it makes him a little bearable."

The urge to argue hit him hard and fast, but he resisted. Eden was right and it was a smart man who recognized it. He'd fought the truth for a very long time. But he was older and wiser now. He wasn't a naive kid who thought a two-dollar corsage would be good enough for the town's golden girl, even if there had been a time when that girl hadn't been so different from him. When she'd known the same poverty. The same hopelessness.

She'd found a way out and left her past behind her, while Dallas had had to make do with his. Still, he'd always felt connected to her. So much so that he'd put his pride on the line for her.

A bitter smile twisted his lips as he remembered the wilting violet he'd bought at the market just an hour before he'd worked up the nerve to ask Laney to the homecoming dance. She'd said no, of course, and so the violet never made it out of the plastic bag. Instead she'd worn a two-violet corsage with ribbon and tiny gold things given to her by the captain of the junior high football team.

And damned if she hadn't looked so pretty his heart had actually flipped. A reaction that had sent a bolt of anger through him. And so, he'd dumped punch on her.

That one action had started the animosity that had continued throughout high school and kept them at each other's throat, right up until the night before Laney had left for college.

Things had been different that night. She'd been different. And for a few sweet moments, he'd come close to living out his ultimate fantasy—Laney Merriweather. Naked and panting and moaning and *his*.

All his, if only for a night.

## CHAPTER TWO

"THIS IS DEFINITELY the stuff fantasies are made of." Laney fingered the red bra she'd purchased and tried to ignore the burst of longing that shot through her.

Okay, it was pretty. But she wasn't the red bra type. Or the pink. Or the neon green. Or any of the other colors Karen had put on display.

Being a Merriweather was about pride and dignity and maintaining self-respect—and no self-respecting Merriweather would be caught dead wearing racy lingerie. While most mothers worried over the proverbial clean underwear, Laney's mother had been more concerned with her daughter being scraped off the pavement wearing something tasteful and befitting the daughter of the town's oldest family.

Laney fingered the lace once more, ignored the twinge of longing and folded the tissue paper back into place. This was not for her, no matter how much Dallas Jericho had insisted otherwise.

*Dallas.*

He'd been the most handsome boy at Cadillac High School—and the most irritating. She couldn't remember a day gone by where he hadn't been there taunting her, teasing her and driving her absolutely insane. He'd sat behind her in English class and pulled her hair. He'd sat in the front row at each and every football game and made catcalls while she'd cheered. He'd even shot a spit wad at her while she'd done her darndest to spell *proliferous* and continue the grand Merriweather tradition of never failing at anything.

He'd made her high school years miserable, and she'd lusted after him anyway.

*Then and now.*

Not that she was going to act on the attraction. She was going to keep her distance and her perspective and her reputation. In real life, that is.

As for her fantasies...

*Fantasy* being the key word, she reminded herself. She could dream all she wanted. After all, Dallas made one hell of a Tarzan. And a tall, dark and delicious cowboy. And an even more scrumptious pirate.

But remembering... That was something she wasn't about to do. No thinking about the one night when she'd thrown caution to the wind and discovered what it had felt like to be held and touched and kissed by Dallas Jericho.

She shook her head, freeing herself from the memories. No, remembering was definitely out.

"THAT'S RIGHT..." Dallas sat at his desk—and recited the catalog number for the new tile. "I need the shipment sent out first thing tomorrow. Same day service."

"Sure thing, but it'll cost you," the man on the other end of the phone told him.

"Just get it here."

After giving the necessary information for the order, Dallas hung up the phone, leaned back in his chair and wiped his tired eyes. It was late and he needed to turn in, but a big empty bed didn't hold much appeal.

Not after he'd crossed paths with Laney Merriweather for the first time in ten years.

It might well have been ten minutes. His reaction to her was as fierce as ever. As crazy. She was still way out of his league.

The moment the thought struck, he forced it

away. Maybe they weren't an exact match, but it had nothing to do with Laney being better than he was. Things had changed. Dallas wasn't the poor kid who lived in the run-down house with the gutter hanging from the porch eaves.

His gaze spanned the surrounding office and a sense of pride filled him. The room, like the rest of the sprawling ranch house that sat on several hundred acres just outside of town, boasted the best of everything, from the handwoven southwest rug covering the hardwood floor to the simple, but expensive brown leather sofa that sat against the far wall. It wasn't anything fancy like the houses over on Main Street, particularly the sprawling Victorian where Laney had grown up. This place was one hundred percent country—very big and tasteful and well-furnished. And more importantly, it was his.

No hanging porch gutter or peeling paint or leaking ceiling. He'd come a long way.

So why the hell did he feel like the same horny teenager with the battered leather jacket who'd lusted after her from afar?

He didn't get a chance to dwell on the question. A shrill ring nearly busted open his eardrums and he bolted to his feet. He reached the front door, opening it to an ancient-looking woman wearing a pink crocheted sweater and matching coral lipstick.

"Dadblame it, it's broken again," Eula Christian declared as she punched madly at the alarm system.

"It's not broken. You entered the wrong combination."

"Nonsense. I know this thing like the back of my hand. It's 6249712."

"That's 6248712."

"When did you change it?"

"I didn't change it. It's always been an 8."

"Nonsense. As the good Lord is my witness, I punched in a 9 yesterday and it worked."

"It couldn't have worked."

"Are you doubting the good Lord?"

"No, ma'am. It's just that—"

"Listen here, Dallas Zachariah Jericho." She pinned him with a scolding stare. "I don't take too kindly to folks blaspheming my creator, and doubt is blasphemy if I ever heard."

"Is that a new sweater you've got on?"

Her tirade stopped as she glanced down. "Why, this old thing? I've had it for ages."

"Well, it's awful pretty."

"It *is* my favorite." She smiled. "It's the color, you know. I just love coral."

"Coral is all you. Say," he glanced at his watch. "Aren't you missing *Walker, Texas Ranger*?"

Eula shoved her glasses up and peered at her own watch. "My, my you're right." She blew out an exasperated breath. "But I've still got to unload the dishwasher. And then there's the laundry in the dryer that needs folding."

"I hear Chuck Norris is going to fight without his white shirt tonight."

Her eyes widened behind the bifocals. "No shirt?"

"And no boots. Seems he gets interrupted by some art smuggler while he's in the shower."

"The shower?"

"And not one of those single stall jobs. This one's a double deluxe with sliding glass doors so he's got plenty of room to flex his muscles."

Excitement leaped into her eyes for a split second before her face fell. She fingered a fresh ink stain on his plaid work shirt. "You don't have any clean shirts for tomorrow. I've been meaning to get to that stack in the hamper all day today." The same way she'd meant to get to his pants yesterday. The same way she'd meant to dust the living room the day before that. And vacuum the day before that.

As a housekeeper, Eula Christian, with her arthritic knees and her poor eyesight and her bad memory, wouldn't come close to winning the Merry Maid Olympics held over in Kendall County every June. But as a person, she'd walked away with the gold more times than he could count.

He stared down at the woman who'd fed him on more than one occasion when his dad had been too drunk to see straight, much less work, and the cupboard had been bare. She hadn't had much, but what she had had, she'd graciously shared. She was a good woman with a good heart and he'd promised himself a long time ago that he would pay her back one day. And Dallas always kept his promises.

"I'll muddle through with what's in the closet. Besides, it's too late for decent folks to be slaving away doing laundry."

"It *is* well past quitting time." She cast one last glance at the now silent alarm before frowning. "The next time you change that code, make sure you tell me. I almost went deaf."

He opened his mouth to tell her for the umpteenth time that he hadn't changed anything, but all that came out was "Yes, ma'am."

Dallas watched Eula hobble toward the living room before he headed back to his office. Quitting time was for decent folks, not workaholic construction bosses. He still had to call his foreman and give him the new delivery information. Then he had to finish the expense sheets he'd just exceeded. Then... The list went on and on.

He drew in a deep breath and settled back down at his desk, determined to get his mind back on the job. *Just* the job. He wasn't going to think about Laney, or how sexy she'd looked tonight, or how he'd wanted to reach out and touch her and kiss her and—

*Wait a second.*

His thoughts skidded to a halt as his gaze snagged on the wrinkled paper he'd written Claude Dixon's new order on at the bar. The words *My ultimate fantasy* jumped out at him and stalled the air in his lungs.

Then again, it really wasn't the words, written in neat black ink with an efficient underline, that stopped him cold for a long, breathless moment. It was the triple *M* embossed on the top of the sheet of paper and the faint scent of warm, sexy woman that wafted through his nostrils. Before he could stop himself, he lifted the paper to his nose and took a deep breath. The aroma grew stronger, confirming the truth.

It was *her* notepaper.

*Her* words. *Her* fantasy. *Her* fantasy man.

Her *fantasy* man?

It couldn't be. Even as he read the description, he told himself it was just wishful thinking. Sure, he had a tattoo in that exact spot on his bicep—a souvenir from one wild night spent drinking in Austin over summer break—but it had to be coincidence. Laney couldn't stand him. Sure, she'd lusted after him. Once. While the night was still fresh in his mind, he'd been certain she hadn't given it a second thought. After all, she'd chickened out at the very end and left him with a massive hard-on.

While he still wanted her after all this time, no way did she want him.

Or did she?

The truth sank in as he read and reread the paper. She did. She really wanted him.

But even though she would allow herself the attraction in her most private thoughts, she wouldn't act on that attraction. Her hands-off attitude tonight confirmed that.

She was Judge Merriweather's daughter, and he was the youngest offspring of no-good, no-account Bick Jericho. There would be no happily ever afters between a woman like Laney Merriweather and a man like Dallas Jericho. But lust…

*Maybe. Maybe not.*

There was always the possibility that he was wrong, that someone else had written the words, that Laney despised him every bit now as she had way back when. That's why she'd stopped things before they'd gone all the way. Because she'd come to her senses and realized she didn't want to make love to him.

Or maybe she'd wanted it too much and that fact had scared her into putting on the brakes.

Maybe…

There was only one way to find out.

"THAT TAKES CARE OF THE Morgan review. Do you have the notes on the McCracken Estate? After that I've got those four small claims cases and then the Johnson cow dispute and—"

"Dad."

"—the Montgomery/Withers property dispute and—"

"*Dad.*"

Judge Marshall Merriweather glanced over the top of his black spectacles. "Yes, dear?"

"Slow down."

"I'm sorry if I was going too fast. Should I repeat the last—"

"*Slow down* as in take a deep breath. You're supposed to stay calm and relaxed."

"I intend to. I'll just pencil that in between the small claims cases and the property dispute."

She walked behind him and snatched the organizer from his hands. "There are no small claims cases. I handed those over to Cheryl Miller."

"Cheryl Miller?"

"Judge Walters's legal assistant. She's volunteered to help ease your caseload until I can hire an assistant for you. Dad," she appealed to him, her voice softer as she touched a tuft of his snow-white hair. "You have to take Dr. Willaby's advice to heart."

"I'm here, aren't I? Why, I could be trying cases with the best of them over in Austin if I had the notion, but the man said slow down, so I'm slowing. I sit and listen to small town problems, when I used to be arguing major cases in the city. Besides, a few land and cattle cases aren't that stressful." His eyes brightened with excitement. "A far cry from that capital murder trial your firm just took on. Have they decided who's going to lead the defense team?"

She averted her gaze and busied herself collecting case files from his littered desk. "Not quite."

"It'll be you, dear," her father said with confidence. "Why, do you know a Merriweather's been part of the legal team for every capital murder case this state has seen in the past twenty years? Everyone knows we Merriweathers make the best defense lawyers. They're sure to ask you."

They had asked, but Laney hadn't accepted. Yet. She would, of course, no matter how hopeless the case or the fact that the man was as guilty as a stray dog with a stolen steak hanging out of his mouth. Everyone, guilty or not guilty, deserved a good defense. Besides, Laney wasn't about to break a twenty-year tradition. She *was* a Merriweather, in all the ways that counted. Once she settled things here, found her father a good secretary and returned to Austin, she would take on the case and continue doing what she did best. Even if it did cause her a major headache.

She blinked her eyes against a sudden blinding shot of pain to her temples. The signs of her daily migraine. Oddly enough, she hadn't felt the all-too-familiar sensation in the three full days since she'd been home. Before she could dwell on the fact, her father's voice drew her attention.

"Where's the McGrath brief?"

"Being read by someone else."

"Who?"

"Me. I'll read, summarize and hand everything over to you later."

"What are you doing?" he asked as she grabbed the stack of files she'd gathered on his desk.

"Relieving you of some of these other cases."

"But those are mine," he said with all the possessiveness of a kid holding onto his last sucker. "They're priority." He tried to stop her, but she stepped out of his reach.

"Not anymore. This—" she retrieved a color brochure from her pocket "—is your only priority right now." She handed him a color brochure for Monty's Lake and another for Port Aransas. She might well have handed him a pair of eyebrow tweezers and a makeup mirror.

"What am I supposed to do with these?"

"Pick where you want to fish this weekend."

"Fish?"

"That's right. You love to fish." Or he used to. She could remember weekends spent fishing down on the pier at Monty's Lake. She would dangle her feet in the water while her father told her of those rare moments when he'd fished with his own father. When the man hadn't been arguing some groundbreaking case, that is. Those times had filled her with warmth and erased her earliest memories of the house over on Baker Street where she'd spent the first six years of her life, until Judge Marshall Merriweather and his wife had taken her in after her parents had abandoned her.

The judge and his wife hadn't been able to have their own children, so they'd adopted and Laney had been the lucky adoptee. One day she'd had nothing but the clothes on her back. The next, she'd had a real home.

She'd been forever grateful, and had vowed to make them proud. To make them and everyone else in town forget that she wasn't a real Merriweather, but the poor, unwanted child from the most run-down shack over on Baker Street.

She'd done just that. Throughout her childhood, she'd done everything in her power to put as much distance as possible between the girl she'd been and the lady she wanted to be. She'd spent her time studying, determined to be as smart, as educated as every other Merriweather before her. She'd watched her new mother diligently, learning the appropriate way to walk and talk and eat. She'd made friends with the elite of Cadillac and stayed away from any and everyone who reminded her of Baker Street.

Almost.

An image, of vivid green eyes, a killer smile and enough male heat to send her body into major meltdown rushed to the forefront of her mind.

*Dallas Jericho.*

She'd felt the attraction even as a child—the intoxication of his smile, the warmth of his eyes, the understanding, the *connection*.

Those six years she'd lived on Baker Street, Dallas had been her nearest neighbor and the only kid in her kindergarten class who hadn't made fun of her when she'd shown up wearing the same threadbare jumper day after day because she'd had nothing better. Her parents, both alcoholics, had blown what little money they'd had on drink. Dallas's own father had been addicted to the bottle, and so he'd sympathized.

Not that he'd ever said the words. He'd been too tough to say anything nice. But his actions had spoken much louder than any words of comfort he might have offered.

She could still remember sitting on the school steps, her stomach growling while she watched the other kids eat lunch. Her parents had been on a binge for the past week and the cupboard had been empty. She'd gone to school with nothing that day.

Dallas hadn't had much himself, just one banana and a soggy mayonnaise sandwich, but he'd shared both with her. She'd liked him from then on.

Even after she'd traded Baker Street for the nicest neighborhood in town, the *like* had continued, much to her dismay. She'd wanted to erase her past and pretend she'd never gone to bed hungry or cried herself to sleep because she'd been an outcast. Most of all, she'd wanted to forget how good that mayonnaise sandwich had tasted and how thankful and happy and protected she'd felt for those few moments as she'd sat next to Dallas on the schoolhouse steps.

She'd tried. She'd gone her own way, plunging into a new way of life and leaving behind the old. She wore the nicest clothes and walked the halls with the other "haves" while Dallas spent his time with the "have-nots." He'd been a rebel and an outcast with his shabby jeans and holey T-shirts and kiss-my-ass attitude. They'd been worlds apart back then, but every time he'd looked at her, the memory of the schoolhouse steps had bubbled up and she'd felt a consuming warmth. So consuming that when bad boy Dallas had crossed the line between the haves and the have-nots and actually asked her to the eighth-grade dance, she'd come so close to saying yes.

Too close.

Not wanting to risk her parents' disapproval, she'd turned him down. But it had been hard. *And* the best thing she'd ever done. Her rejection had been enough to anger Dallas and so he'd stopped being nice to her. That very night he'd dumped punch all over her and started the feud that proved her only saving grace throughout high school.

Her hormones had raged so fiercely back then and if he'd been nice... She would have given in to her lust for him long before the night of her going-away party.

She pushed the sudden image of Dallas hovering over her, his bright green eyes glittering down on her, to the farthest corner of her mind and tried to concentrate on what her father was saying.

"...don't know about this."

"Well, I do," she said, turning her full attention to the brochures. "This is just what the doctor ordered. Monty's Lake has some of the biggest freshwater bass in Texas. But if you want to do some saltwater fishing, Port Aransas is the place."

"They're each three hours away from here."

"And?"

He shook his head and removed his glasses. "I can't go that far away for the weekend."

"It's not a weekend. It's a full week. Next week."

"Next *week?*"

"Actually it starts this Friday."

He pinched the bridge of his nose, then shook his head. "That's out of the question. I've got work to do. I'm hearing two cases Monday morning. I've got mediation on Tuesday. I've got an arbitration hearing on Wednesday. I've got—"

"—me," she finished for him. "You've got me. A more than capable assistant until I find you someone permanent. I'll reschedule your hearings and reassign the mediation to someone else. I'll take care of things."

A smile tilted his lips as he reached up to push a strand of hair behind her ear. "You are more than capable, aren't you? How did your mother and I get so lucky?"

But Laney was the one who'd gotten lucky. They could have picked any child, but they'd chosen her, despite where she'd come from. Who she'd come from. For that she owed them. She always would.

She tapped the brochure. "So which one is it going to be?"

"Neither."

"That's not an option."

"Freshwater," he finally said after a scratch of his temple and another pinch at the bridge of his nose. "Your mother used to love grilled trout."

*Her mother.* That was a lot of her father's problem. He'd already been an overachiever, and once her mother had died, the drive had intensified. He'd picked up his pace the past few years, focusing on work rather than his grief.

"Mom wouldn't want you to push yourself so hard."

"Your mother knew what sort of man I was when she married me."

"Stubborn?"

"Goal-oriented."

"Why set goals if you won't be around to achieve them?" Her voice softened. "She wouldn't want you working so hard, and neither do I." She gathered up the brochures. "I'll make all the arrangements. You leave first thing Friday morning. In the meantime," she took the file folders from his hand. "You're officially relieved of duty until your one o'clock hearing about the Jackson's goat." At his blank look, she added, "Mr. and Mrs. Jackson are fighting over custody."

"Ah, yes." He smiled. "You know, you're liable to die of boredom before you get back to Austin."

"I think I'll survive. Besides, child custody cases have always fascinated me, even if the child in question has four legs. As for you, take a nap. Take a walk. *Relax.*"

"You're a slave driver, you know that?"

"It's called a chip off the old block, and I'm serious. I want you to take it easy. No sneaking any case files inside a *Field and Stream* magazine. Otherwise, I'll have to turn off 'Crazy'—" she indicated the CD that filled the room with soft lyrics in the far corner "—and bring in some of those relaxation tapes. There's nothing more soothing than the sound of dripping water."

He rolled his eyes. "Forget a heart attack. I'll surely die of boredom."

She winked. "Sweet dreams, Dad."

"LOOKS LIKE YOU OWE ME NOW, hot stuff."

The deep voice slithered into Laney's ears the minute she closed her father's office door. Her hand tightened on the doorknob as her body went on instant alert; the hair on her arms tingled, her hands trembled, her nipples pebbled. She forced her fingers to let go of the knob and fought for a nice, easy breath.

*Nice and easy.* That was the key where Dallas Jericho was concerned. She knew that, but damned if her body wanted to agree. The last thing she considered him, with his wicked good looks and his deep, bone melting voice, was *nice.* As for *easy...* Nothing about him was easy, especially her reaction to him.

She let out her breath slowly and turned, putting her back to her father's closed office door. "For the last time, my name's not *hot stuff,* and how do you figure I owe you?"

"I distinctly remember speaking those very same words to you last night." His green eyes twinkled as he grinned down at her. One tanned finger touched the collar of her blouse, just the barest whisper of flesh against soft silk, yet the sound echoed in her ears. Her heart pounded faster.

"You're passing on my words of wisdom, so I figure I ought to get a little kickback for coming up with them in the first place."

"I doubt you coined the phrase 'sweet dreams,' and the last I heard, you charged for Sheetrock and architectural plans, not words of wisdom."

He winked. "You get to be my first customer."

"Lucky me."

"You haven't gotten lucky yet, sugar lips, but I'm working on it."

His voice, so soft and teasing, slid into her ears and put every nerve in Laney's body on major alert.

*Soft and teasing?*

Dallas taunted and annoyed and stirred her anger even more than he stirred her hormones. Usually. But he was different now. He was soft and teasing and...*nice*.

Oh, no.

"You okay, sugar? You look a little—"

"—sick?" She nodded vigorously. "Yeah, suddenly I feel a little sick."

"Sorry to hear that, but I was thinking more that you looked a little hot."

"No." She ran a finger beneath the edge of her collar and tried to calm the panic rushing through her. "I'm fine. Really."

"No, you're not. Here, let me help." One strong, tanned hand went to the top button of her blouse.

## CHAPTER THREE

LANEY'S FIRST INSTINCT should have been to swat his hand away. He was touching her, of all things. More importantly, there were people nearby. She could hear laughter out in the hallway, voices, footsteps.

Surprisingly the sounds didn't stir the expected bolt of panic. They fed her excitement. Her heart thundered and her blood pumped faster as Dallas moved to the second button on her blouse.

"Yes, you surely do feel hot," he said, his fingertips brushing her skin again. "Don't you, Laney?"

Her lips parted, the truth poised on the tip of her tongue.

"...make sure that brief is here before next week. I'm leaving on Friday." Her father's voice drifted from behind his closed office door and zapped some common sense back into her.

"I...I'm fine with all my buttons in place," she finally said.

Okay, so he was being nice. She was a grown woman now. Not a young, naive teenage slave to her hormones. She could handle this.

She gathered her courage, forced a deep breath and rebuttoned her blouse beneath his watchful stare. "What are you doing here?" she asked, eager to divert his attention from the motion of her fingers.

"I had some building permits to pick up."

"That's on the other side of the courthouse. Why are you on this side?"

"There's two reasons for that."

"Which are?"

"The barbecue kickoff for the Car Cruise is Friday night. This year's proceeds are going to the Millers. Their daughter Sheila had a liver transplant last year and the medical bills are eating them up. I've got an extra ticket, so I thought I'd pass one on to you." He handed her the ticket.

"If I didn't know better, I'd say you were asking me out on a date."

Some unnameable something flashed in his eyes before they crinkled at the corners and he grinned. "The bigger the crowd, the more money raised."

She ignored a crazy twinge of disappointment. It wasn't as if she *wanted* him to ask her out. She wanted him to keep his distance so she could keep her sanity. She wasn't losing her head again the way she had the night she'd walked away from her going-away party, and straight into Dallas Jericho's strong arms.

"I forgot, you're not into the dating scene."

"And neither are you. At least not with me," he went on before sliding the ticket into her shirt pocket. "Except once, that is." His fingertips lingered just above the lace edge of her bra.

"That wasn't a date. That was just—"

"—lust," he finished for her. "You wanted me."

She wanted to refute his words, but that would be inviting trouble. Besides, he was right. She had wanted him. She'd wanted him her entire life and that one night, she'd indulged herself. For a little while, anyhow. Thankfully, she'd smartened up before they'd actually done *it*.

The thing was, standing there with him so close, so warm, so male, she didn't feel nearly as thankful as she should have. The only thing she felt was regret.

She shook away the notion and inhaled some

much-needed oxygen. "So," she managed to say after licking her lips and clearing her throat, "what's the second reason you're on my side of the building?" She expected him to mention the tax office next door or any number of other departments that ran the length of the massive marble hallway.

His smile widened and he shrugged. "What can I say? My curiosity got the best of me."

"What are you talking about?"

"Did you?"

"Did I what?"

"Have sweet dreams?" he murmured, his breath whispering over her mouth.

The question stirred a dozen images from the past. Bodies touching. Mouths tasting. Hands exploring...

She cleared her throat. "I, um, slept quite nicely, thank you very much."

"That's not what I'm talking about, darlin'. When you went home and slid into that slinky red bra and panties, did they inspire sweet dreams?"

"I told you. They weren't for me."

"But you at least thought about putting them on."

*How did he know?*

As if he read her mind, he grinned. "I didn't know. I took a guess and the flush creeping up your neck is answer enough."

"I really have to get back to work." Before she could pull away from him, he released her.

"So do I." He glanced at his watch before his gaze locked with hers once again. "I'll see you Friday." He hooked a strand of wayward hair behind her ear and the refusal stalled in her throat for several frantic heartbeats.

"Friday's no good," she finally said, once he'd turned to saunter toward the door. He really did have the sauntering thing down pat. Blue denim pushed and pulled at just the right places, accenting his muscular thighs and trim rear end. Only one word came to mind. *Yum.*

"...casual," he was saying. "You don't have to dress up."

She shook her head, eager to clear the lust and gather what little common sense she still had. "I'm not dressing at all."

He tossed a heated glance over his shoulder as he reached the door. "Fine by me, darlin'."

"N-no," she sputtered, wishing he couldn't render her senseless with just one look. "I mean I'm not dressing for the occasion because I'm not going.

I appreciate the ticket and everything, but I'm busy that night.''

He didn't say anything. He simply gave her a wink and reached for the door.

"I'm serious. I really am busy and I'm not—'' The sound of the door closing punctuated her refusal.

"—going,'' she finished despite the fact that she was alone in the room.

*Alone.* Yet she could still smell him. The scent of leather and sawdust filled her nostrils and kept her heart pounding long after the sound of his footsteps had disappeared.

*Pounding,* of all things, proof that the real Dallas was every bit as powerful as the one who lived and breathed in her fantasies. The one who touched and teased and made her forget everything except the feel of him.

*Everything.*

But Laney wasn't in the safety of her bedroom, lost in another delicious dream. *Just* a dream, with no repercussions. She was out in public for all to see. And she wasn't going to any barbecue cookoff on Friday night.

No matter how much she suddenly wanted to.

"Miss Merriweather?''

The question drew her attention away from the dangerous path of her thoughts. Her gaze shifted to the petite blonde standing in the outer office doorway.

The woman wore a simple yellow shift, the material slightly faded in spots from one too many washings. A tattered buttercup handbag hung from the crook of her arm. Her matching pumps, as old and worn as the bag, were scuffed around the toes. Her hair had been pulled back into a simple ponytail that would have looked chic except for the strands that had come loose to hang limply around her face. She was young, maybe mid-twenties, but her eyes held a telling maturity, as if she'd seen one too many hardships in her young life.

"I'm Brigette," she said. "Your nine o'clock appointment."

Laney glanced down at the application sitting on top of the stack. The most qualified applicant she'd come up with after carefully reviewing all the possibilities sent from the employment agency. "Brigette Summers?"

"That's me." The woman glanced at her watch. "I know I'm late, but my car picked this morning to die. Thankfully I live just a few blocks over, so I ran as fast as I could..." She paused for a deep breath. "Anyhow, I'm not usually late. I'm always early."

"It's okay. Have a seat and we'll talk."

"I know this doesn't make the best impression," the woman said, rushing on as she sank into a seat. "But truly, I'm always early. Even when the kids aren't cooperative, I manage to get out of the house in time."

"You have children?"

"No. I mean, yes. I mean, sort of. I live with my three younger brothers and sisters. Our mother's ill, so I'm taking care of them for her. But that won't interfere with anything. If you check my references, you'll see that I'm always on time and I haven't been sick in three years. I'm reliable. Trustworthy. And I can type ninety words per minute."

"That's very impressive. So have you ever worked in a legal office before?"

The woman's face fell. "Well, not exactly. I mainly worked retail for the past few years while I was going to Austin Community College, but I've got an Associates certificate in criminal law and I've taken every office procedure course there is. I can do this job."

She said it with such confidence that Laney couldn't help but believe her. This woman could do the job, all right. The trouble was, she didn't look the job. No three-piece pin-stripe suit with a tailored silk blouse. Her father, with his immaculate clothing and impeccable image, was having a hard enough time turning the reins over to his more than capable daughter. No way could Laney present this woman to him and tell him to have ultimate faith. Not with zero experience.

"You obviously have the necessary skills, but to be honest, I was looking for someone who would be more familiar with what this position entails."

"Of course," the young woman said, a thread of disappointment in her voice. "But I *can* do this job, Miss Merriweather. I graduated the top of my class."

"I'll keep that in mind." She smiled and extended her hand. "I'll get back to you." Even as the words left her mouth, she knew how unlikely it was. She knew it, and from the look in Brigette's eyes, the young woman knew as well.

Guilt rushed through her, but she pushed it away. She had to think of her father and his well-being. This woman wasn't the secretary for him.

Laney turned the application over and reached for the next one in the stack. If at first you don't succeed...

LANEY SAT BEHIND her desk a half hour later and watched her current prospect peck away on the computer keyboard across the room. *Peck, peck.* The tastefully dressed brunette glanced at the screen, then at the typing test, then back at the screen, then at her hands. *Peck, peck.*

"Regina, I hate to interrupt you, but have you ever actually worked as a legal secretary before?"

"Well, my title *was* secretary and I did work in a legal office. So I guess if you put the two together, you get legal secretary."

O-kay.

"So what were your duties?"

"I mainly answered the phones." She smiled. "And took all the lunch orders. *And* picked up all of Mr. Crawford's dry cleaning."

Disappointment rushed through Laney. "I'm afraid this job is a bit more challenging than that."

"You're telling me." She pecked a few more letters. "But challenge is exactly what I'm looking for. I haven't spent the past two years in school so I can go through life picking up white dress shirts with extra heavy starch."

"School?" She glanced down at the résumé and searched for the Education column. "You're a paralegal,'' Laney stated, hope blossoming. Maybe all was not lost.

The woman smiled proudly. ''Newly graduated from Fast Freddie's Mail Order Diplomas.''

Then again...

''I was going to take the Gourmet Cooking Course,'' Regina continued, ''because chefs make good money, too, and I really enjoyed taking all those food orders. But I figured that would be too tough on my manicure. It's one thing to pick up a phone and place an order for an asparagus sub with artichoke hearts and raspberry vinaigrette and quite another to actually make the darned thing.'' She stared down at her broken nail. Her forehead wrinkled. ''Jeez, I wonder if it's too late to sign up for the new semester?''

Laney smiled. ''I bet if you hurry, you can just make it.''

The interview with Regina set the stage for the rest of Laney's day and all fifteen of her prime candidates.

''Don't tell me,'' Laney told the last woman later that afternoon as she watched her peck on the computer. ''Fast Freddie's Mail Order Diplomas.''

''Darlene's Degrees by Mail.'' The young woman turned back to the keyboard and stared for several long seconds before plucking the next key. "The typing portion was extensive—an entire hour-long videotape—but I guess the real thing is a little more complicated than watching Darlene do it on TV."

Laney smiled and placed the woman's résumé in her fast-growing reject pile. "Have you ever thought of cooking?"

IT WAS HOPELESS.

Laney came to that conclusion over the next few days as she interviewed even more applicants, made preparations for her father's trip and his departure Friday morning, and did her best to ignore Dallas Jericho.

Impossible.

Every time she glanced over her shoulder, he was there. Having lunch at the diner where she ate her salad every day at noon. At the coffee shop where she picked up her double cappuccino every morning on her way to work. At the grocery store when she stopped off for an extra-large bag of Chips Ahoy— a girl had to get satisfaction one way or another.

Before she'd come home, her erotic thoughts had been enough to relieve the daily stress of her fast-paced, all-consuming job. But now that she'd seen

Dallas alive and in the flesh, no amount of fantasizing could relieve the frustration that built with each passing day. A different sort of frustration that didn't come with migraine headaches and a huge caseload.

The fantasies weren't enough anymore. She wanted the real man, even more than she'd wanted him way back when.

Laney stood in her kitchen Friday evening and did her best to ignore the thought. She grabbed a box of chocolate-covered cherries and an extra-large glass of chocolate milk and headed for the sofa.

While the cookies hadn't helped—too little chocolate and sugar she'd finally surmised—she had to keep trying. Otherwise...

She was *not* going to the barbecue cook-off.

Settling on the sofa, she flipped on the TV and channel-surfed for the next few minutes as she popped several candies into her mouth and tried to summon some excitement.

Her father had left that afternoon, after a lot of grumbling and several stiff lectures on why he should be allowed to take his cell phone and his portable fax machine. She'd managed to confiscate both, but only on the condition that he could take one case file of his choice to read in between high-pitched fishing moments.

The house was completely empty and she was alone with no one to worry about. She could actually concentrate tonight and focus totally and completely on the subject at hand—work.

Talk about an ideal Friday evening. Or it would have been if she hadn't worked so hard the past few days that she didn't have enough to keep her occupied more than an hour or so. More importantly, she'd had half a box of chocolate-covered cherries and still felt as hungry, as needy, as restless as ever.

She popped another cherry into her mouth and chewed. Okay, so maybe she would go. Just for a little while. After all, it was the Car Cruise barbecue kickoff. A tradition in Cadillac. Not to mention, the proceeds went for a good cause. It wasn't as if she'd be going just to see Dallas.

Why, she might not even see him at all. There would undoubtedly be a lot of people there. The entire town, most likely. Odds were that she could sit there an entire evening and not even catch a glimpse of him.

At least that's what Laney told herself. Now if she only believed it.

"FORGET THE AQUA-BLUE ceramic tile. Katherine wants pink and citrus now."

Dallas pulled the now tattered sheet of paper from his shirt pocket, X-ed off the shipment of aqua, penciled in the new colors, and ignored the urge to tell Claude Dixon what he could do with his new tile and his new house and his indecisive wife.

"Oh, and Katherine said to be absolutely sure that it's a light citrus, not the deep citrus. And the pink should be soft, more like shell rather than salmon. Salmon would clash terribly with the light citrus, and Genevive Worthington already has her cookhouse done in salmon."

Dallas didn't even want to imagine a salmon-colored cookhouse. *Giddyup! Here come the yuppie cowboys.*

"The cookhouse matches the barn," Claude continued. "They're both the same shade as the carpet in the tack room."

"*Carpet* in the tack room?"

"One hundred percent Berber. Nothing but the best for Genevive's prized Arabians, Coco and Chanelle."

Dallas swallowed the dozen or so sarcastic comments that rushed to the tip of his tongue and murmured, "No problem."

"Good." Claude rubbed his hands together. "I'll talk to you when the project is closer to completion. I'm off to Tahiti for the next few weeks, so it will have to be after that. Oh—" he glanced at his pocket planner "—then we're going to Italy with Katherine's family, so make that four weeks."

Four entire weeks with no changes?

A guy could only hope.

Speaking of hope…

Dallas glanced around the crowded VFW hall. The place was still brightly lit, the dance floor filled with clusters of people who stood around talking, waiting for the music to start. The band unloaded in the far corner, getting ready to play once everyone had finished eating.

*Everyone,* except a certain sexy blonde.

He glanced down at the paper where he'd scribbled the new tile colors, turned the sheet over and read the words again, the way he'd done each and every time he started to think that maybe he'd imagined the vivid description, the desperate longing, the *need.*

Then again, maybe he wasn't the man in the fantasy. Maybe Laney hadn't even written the damned thing. Maybe she wasn't even remotely attracted to him. Maybe he'd made a Grade A ass of himself by inviting her here.

That's what he was inclined to think. But he couldn't forget the dark, passionate look in her eyes when he'd cornered her at the courthouse. The way she'd licked her lips and flushed a bright red and trembled when he'd touched her just so...

So where the hell was she?

He wadded up the paper, shoved it into his jeans pocket and was about to turn when he heard her voice.

"My, but this is a phenomenal turnout."

A burst of warmth went through him and curved his lips into a smile before Dallas managed to tamp down the strange feeling. Hell's bells. He didn't want to feel *warm* when it came to Laney Merriweather. Just hot. Hard. Hungry. End of discussion. He'd worn his heart on his sleeve once before where Laney was concerned, and she'd stomped all over it. That was one mistake he was *never* making again. He might still have feelings for her after all this time—the first love sort of feelings, not the forever kind—but he had no intention of giving in to any of them save one. Lust. Pure, uncomplicated, tangle-the-sheets-and-burn-up-a-little-energy lust.

He summoned his best frown. "It's about time

you showed up," he said as he turned and deposited a box of cups into her arms. "We've got work to do."

SHE'D MEANT TO BE POLITE. That was it. A simple thank you that he'd given her the ticket and then her duty would be done. She couldn't exactly be rude, even if it was Dallas Jericho. Not in front of the entire town. But she never thought she'd get suckered into standing behind a counter, serving up Texas Twisters to a line of hungry townsfolk.

Not that she minded the work. The work she could handle. It was the working conditions that had her itching to jump the counter and run for cover.

Dallas Jericho was too handsome, too warm, too...*close*. Worse, he smelled even better than the warm, sweet funnel cake she was busy retrieving from the commercial deep fryer.

*Cooking*. She still couldn't believe it. Sure, she would be the first to lay money that Dallas Jericho had done more than his fair amount of cooking, but none in an actual kitchen.

A sudden vision of herself sitting up on the counter, Dallas in front of her, rushed at her. Heat flared in her cheeks.

"What color is it?"

His deep voice startled her, drawing her attention away from the strong grip of his hands to his smiling face. Her heart paused.

"What color is what?"

"My third eye. The way you're staring at me, I must have one right in the middle of my forehead."

She shrugged and forced the sensual image to the farthest corner of her mind. "You just don't strike me as the funnel cake type."

"Are you kidding? I can eat at least a dozen. Just ask Eula, over there. Hey, Eula," he called out. "Need some help?"

Laney turned to see the old woman who hobbled toward a nearby table, a plate of barbecue in her twisted hands. She shook her head, but Dallas wasn't put off. He rounded the counter and reached her in a few swift strides. Taking the plate, he guided her into a chair, reminding Laney of a young boy with tattered clothes who'd rushed to help pick up a sack of groceries her mother had dropped on her way out of the Piggly Wiggly.

Her new mother had tried to give him a dollar, and while he'd wanted to take it—Laney had seen the desperation in his eyes—he'd simply shaken his head and settled for a heartfelt thank you from both Laney and her mother.

"You're welcome." That's all he'd said, yet Laney had sensed a wealth of meaning in the phrase. Appreciation. Gratitude. *Kinship.*

She dismissed the last thought. While she'd been born to a less than savory family, things had changed. She'd grown up a Merriweather. As far removed from someone like Dallas as a person could get. She hadn't had to worry about food to eat or clothes to wear. She'd had everything. Thanks to her parents.

No, the last thing she felt for Dallas was kinship. Now admiration... She couldn't help the smile that creased her lips as she watched him retrieve a glass of iced tea from the beverage table and take it to Eula.

"Isn't that the lady who lives next door to the church?" she asked when he walked back to her.

"Nope. That's the lady who lives with me. She's my housekeeper."

"Housekeeper?" Her gaze shifted back to Eula who sat next to her walking cane, her hand trembling as she retrieved a bite of potato salad. "She actually keeps house for you?"

"She tries and that's good enough for me."

The admiration she felt for him blossomed even more, along with something else. Something softer. *A connection.*

She shook away the notion and focused on the funnel cakes.

"So how long have you been cooking Texas Twisters?"

"Since about six."

Her gaze shifted to him. "You've been cooking funnel cakes since you were six years old?"

His grin was slow and heart-stopping. "Since about six *o'clock,* darlin'. Janice May Alcott always runs this booth, but she has a stomach virus. Doc sent her home, so I stepped in to help out."

"You mean you've never done this before tonight?"

"I used to hang out and watch her when I was a kid." He pressed the button and batter poured into the sizzling grease. "And I'd eat all her leftovers. I also fixed this thing a couple of times whenever it got too temperamental. Janice isn't very mechanical." His gaze snagged on something just beyond her shoulder. "Neither is Mary Louise. She might make the meanest apple pie to ever arrive at a Sunday picnic, but when it comes to snow cones, she's plumb clueless."

They both glanced toward the woman across the aisle from them who stood beneath a sign advertising twenty cent snow blizzards. She stared quizzically at an ice machine before smacking her fist against the side.

"Trouble, Mary?" Dallas called out.

"Darned thing quit on me. One second it was grinding out ice and the next, nothing."

"Hold on and I'll take a look for you." He flipped off the switch on the funnel machine and wiped his hands. "I'll be right back."

*Dallas Jericho to the rescue again.*

Laney had just turned to dust sugar off the countertop when she heard a voice behind her.

"Two funnel cakes with extra cinna—Ohmigod! Laney. Laney Merriweather! Is that really you?"

Laney turned and came face-to-face with Cosmopolitan Barbie. Long, gleaming blond hair had been pulled back from a heart-shaped face. A generous helping of eye shadow and mascara accented wide, cornflower-blue eyes. A creamy silk blouse, no doubt Gucci, covered petite shoulders and an ample bosom. Tailored silk slacks molded to perfectly shaped hips and thighs.

*Perfect.*

That summed up Caroline Peterson in one word.

From her walk to her talk to her clothing. She was the product of good Texas breeding and old money, and Laney had idolized her back in high school.

"It *is* you," the woman declared. "It's me," the woman tapped her chest. "Caroline Peterson. Well, make that Caroline Peterson Montgomery now."

"You and Walter finally tied the knot?"

"What can I say? I'm hyphenated and loving every moment. We have two precious children. My, my—" she touched a perfectly manicured hand to her chest as if she couldn't quite believe her eyes "—you look exactly the way you did back in high school. Your hair is even the same."

Laney touched her conservative bun. "Old habits die hard." Especially when the habit had become a way of life. Her mother had worn the exact same style, just like every Merriweather woman for the past one hundred years.

Caroline peered closer. "You know, you still have the most incredible blue eyes. You really should liven them up. Maybe add some eyeliner. And those lips. I think a makeover is definitely in order. I'd be happy—"

"I'll pass. It's taken the last twelve years for my eyebrows to grow back after the last one."

*The last one* referred to the most memorable sleep-

over Laney had attended. It had been Senior Girls'
Night after a huge rival football game and a select
few lucky enough to call themselves Caroline's
friends had gathered at her house for an all-night
gab session and pizza fest.

One minute Laney had been munching a slice of
pizza and the next, she'd been Caroline's makeover
model. With so many eager eyes on her, she'd
agreed. She'd wanted to agree. To fit in. To feel
like all the other girls lucky enough to be invited
to one of Caroline's parties. To *be* like all the other
girls.

Caroline smiled at the memory. "It wasn't that
bad. Besides, your hair looked great. *Très* chic."
She turned and waved to a tall, good-looking man.
"Walter, come over here. Wait until you see who's
serving funnel cakes!"

Thirty seconds later, Laney was shaking hands
with Walter Montgomery. Walter, once a spoiled
eighteen-year-old, was now a stockbroker in Austin,
still carrying on the family tradition as a financial
wizard.

"Remember Laney? Why, she was the smartest
girl in our entire class," Caroline told her husband.
"Smart and conscientious and dependable, isn't
that right, Laney? We were always goofing off, but

Laney stayed on track. She didn't waste her time on boys. She was always focused, always rushing home after school to finish her work and—''

''Two funnel cakes coming up!'' Laney cut in. She had been focused. And dependable. And reliable. And she'd always been proud of herself because her father had been proud. But hearing Caroline recount her focused, dependable, reliable, boring past suddenly made her feel uncomfortable. Dissatisfied. Restless. Especially since she'd tried so hard for her friends to see her as an equal, as refined and proper as the rest of them. As if she'd been born to it like the rest of them.

She hadn't. She'd been poor Laney Boggs who'd come from the wrong side of town and lucked into a fortune. They all knew it. They'd known it then and they knew it now.

The truth echoed through her head and she pushed it away. She *was* one of them. Just as good, as deserving.

She turned toward the funnel machine and concentrated her efforts on working rather than thinking. She'd watched Dallas all evening. Turn the nozzle. Press the button. Swirl the dough. She could do this.

That's what she told herself, but ten heaving

breaths later, after dumping several blobs of dough that resembled Jaba the Hut more than a Texas Twister into the fryer, she realized she was way out of her league. She would just wait for—

The thought stalled as she tried to shut off the flow of dough. The knob wouldn't budge. If anything, the dough flowed faster, faster…

"Laney? Is everything okay?" Caroline asked.

"Everything's fine," she called out.

"Do you think it's broken?"

"No," she ground out as she struggled with the knob and her rising panic. "I think it's alive."

The deep chuckle stirred the hair on the back of her neck and sent tingles to her nipples. She realized in an instant that Dallas was right behind her.

"You're too nervous," his deep voice whispered into her ears. "You have to relax." He stepped even closer, until she felt the warmth of his chest at her back. His arms came around her. One hand settled over hers while the other slid around her waist. And, as easily as that, Laney found herself wrapped in Dallas Jericho's arms.

# CHAPTER FOUR

THE FINGERTIPS THAT HELD Laney's frantic grip on the fryer knob slid down until Dallas's thumb massaged the inside of her wrist.

"Relax," he murmured again, the word little more than a breathless whisper against the shell of her ear.

"But I'm making a mess," she protested as the dough continued to funnel into the hot grease at a steady rate. Even so, she didn't feel the same stir of anxiety she'd felt a moment ago. Now she felt the *heat*.

The heat from his body and the heat between them. The incredible, breath stealing, scramble-your-senses heat that she'd yet to feel with anyone except the man standing behind her, surrounding her.

"That's it," he murmured as her fingers loosened on the knob. His thumb slid from the inside of her wrist, up her palm, leaving a blazing trail that made her tingle from her head to her toes, and every point in between.

His fingers closed over hers and with an easy flick of his wrist, the knob turned and the dough stopped.

"That wasn't so hard, now was it?"

The word *hard* echoed through her head and she became instantly aware of her bottom nestled against his groin, his erection bulging beneath the material separating them.

"Poor choice of words," she murmured before she could stop herself.

His chuckle, raw and husky, did terrible things to her peace of mind.

Her mouth tingled and she had the insane urge to turn into the warm lips nuzzling her ear.

Nuzzling? Yes, he was definitely nuzzling. Licking. Making her tingle.

"Is everything okay now?"

Caroline's voice pulled Laney back to reality, to her scandalous position and the fact that Dallas Jericho was nuzzling her in full view of God and the good folks of Cadillac who might be of a mind to look.

"It's stuck," Dallas called over his shoulder.

"But we turned it off," she reminded him, her

voice breathless and soft and excited... Oh God, she *was* excited.

"We turned the knob off, but we're still turning you on, hot stuff." The hand around her waist crept an inch higher, his thumb rubbing a lazy circle against her naval. "Aren't we?"

Heat spiraled through her, making her lips part and her breath rush out.

When he touched the underside of her breast, she started. "Careful," he warned, "or someone's liable to know. Then again, maybe that's what you want. Maybe you want everyone to see what I'm doing to you. Is that it, Laney? Does it turn you on to think that somebody might see the effect I have on you? That everyone would know you aren't the prim and proper judge's daughter you're trying so hard to be?"

"You should stop."

"Do you want me to stop?"

Yes. No. Maybe. The answers rolled through her brain, mixing with the multitude of other things and making her even more confused. If only she could think. Focus. She couldn't, not with his thumb massaging her in such an intimate spot, his fingers burning into her rib cage.

"I...you need to."

"There are a lot of things I need, Laney. A lot of things I want. I can tell you right now that stopping doesn't qualify as either." He trailed his tongue along the shell of her ear. "You aren't, you know."

"What?" The word came out little more than a breathless whisper. Breathless? Oh, no, she *was* breathless, and she was definitely in trouble.

"So prim and proper. I knew it way back when and I know it now. You put up a good front, mind you, but it's not who you really are. You were made for kissing and touching and warming a man all night long. You were made for me. *Me.*"

His words echoed through her head, along with the sounds around them. The play of the band. The whir of the nearby snow cone machine. The crunch and slide of boots. The murmur of voices and the rise of laughter. It should have been enough to shatter the seductive web and pull her back to reality. But this was reality. Not a fantasy, but *real.*

The noises made her heart pound faster, along with the seductive words he whispered in her ear and the bold way he massaged the underside of her breast. It was luscious and decadent and downright shameful and for the space of a few heartbeats, she'd never felt quite so alive in her entire life. "Tell me you like this, baby."

"I..." She wanted to. The urge was so strong to tell him all the wicked things running through her mind. What she felt. What she liked. What she wanted. Right here, right now. Despite the crowd of people surrounding them.

*Her ultimate fantasy.*

As exciting as the realization was, it sent a wash of fear through her. She'd been hiding for so long, suppressing her true nature, that she didn't know how to stop. She didn't know if she *could* stop, no matter how much she suddenly wanted to.

"I... I—I think they're done," was all she finally managed to say.

"What?"

She swallowed. "The funnel cakes. They, um, look crispy."

She heard the draw of his breath, felt the tightening of his body, as if it took every ounce of strength he had to gather his composure.

"We're not done yet, you and I," he said before releasing her.

His words stayed with her for the next half hour as she kept her distance and tried to forget the man standing so close. An arm's length away if she'd been of a mind to reach out.

She wouldn't. She stayed on her side of the booth and left Dallas to his until the cook-off finally winded down and she managed to slip away while he talked with Drew Hayes about judging tomorrow night's Miss Cadillac pageant.

She could leave the man behind, but she wasn't nearly as successful escaping her fantasy man. He showed up much later when she crawled into bed. Oddly enough, she didn't welcome the erotic thoughts. Instead of satisfying her the way they usually did, they left her wanting more.

They left her wanting the real thing. *Dallas*.

"I CAN'T TELL YOU HOW MUCH we appreciate this!" Drew Hayes's excited voice drifted over the phone early the next morning when Laney answered.

She blinked against the onslaught of sunlight from her bedroom window and tried to focus on the alarm clock. What time was it?

"We need you at the grounds by six o'clock. That will give you time to check in at the judges table, get your name tag and find your seat."

"Name tag?"

"You're a real lifesaver. I didn't know what we were going to do. Every available person either has a relative in the pageant or already has their hands full with other duties. When Dallas said he knew you wouldn't mind filling in as the fourth judge, I can't tell you how relieved I was."

"But I didn't—"

"I should have known you'd be obliging. I mean, your father's been a sponsor of the pageant for the past twenty years. Why, just last year he donated an extra sum to add to the scholarship fund. So, I'm not surprised you're helping out. You're a chip off the old block."

*A chip off the old block.*

The comment pushed past her sleepy haze and drew her fully awake. She'd struggled her entire life to fit in, to make her parents proud, to *be* their daughter in every way possible. The fact that the townsfolk saw her as such sent a burst of pride through her and she found herself blurting, "What time did you say for me to be there?"

After all, it was just one night. The worst that could happen was that they would seat her next to Dallas.

Even so, she could handle the situation. She'd spent a lifetime ignoring her feelings for him. One more night was nothing, especially if it meant living up to the Merriweather name.

UGH. It was going to be the longest, most trying night of Laney's entire life.

She knew it the moment she slid into her seat at exactly eight o'clock and found herself sitting next to Dallas. He looked so handsome wearing creased Wranglers and a starched Western shirt. Worse, he looked so...*nice* with his easy grin and his twinkling eyes.

"If I were the sensitive sort, I'd be offended that you didn't say goodbye to me last night," he murmured as the lights flickered and the pageant kicked off with the mayor's wife singing an a cappella version of "You Light Up My Life."

"Then it's a stroke of luck that you've never been the sensitive sort."

"Maybe I've turned over a new leaf."

"And maybe Jennifer Monroe will actually leave the Aqua Net at home tonight."

Her knowing gaze shifted to the woman who sat in the fourth row. The women's beehive hairdo, already stiff with hair spray, reflected the whirl of stage lights as they searched and settled on the mayor's wife.

"And if I was *really* sensitive, I'd likely be offended that you're practically clinging to the other side of your chair. I don't bite, hot stuff." His grin widened. "Unless you ask me real nice and polite."

She searched for a smart-ass comeback. Something to stir his anger and turn him from this serious, perceptive, sexy-as-all-get-out man to the annoying, irritating boy who'd pulled her ponytail and hung Kick Me signs on the back of her blouse every morning at school. It had been so easy to keep her distance back then.

She cleared her throat. "I, um, think we'd better pay attention." The mayor's wife sang her last note and a round of applause echoed throughout the room.

As the pageant started and the contestants were introduced, Laney actually started to relax. It wasn't as if she had to talk to Dallas any more, what with all the noise and the music and the responsibilities that came with judging Miss Cadillac. She could just forget all about him and keep her eyes and her mind on the matter at hand.

He shifted in his seat and his blue-jean clad thigh brushed hers. Her heart started to pound. Her hands trembled. Heat rushed to her face. Worse, the subtle gesture made her go all soft and warm inside with anticipation.

It was a feeling she had to quell more than once throughout the rest of the evening. His thigh brushed hers. His arm slid against hers. His scent filled her breathing room. And more than once, Dallas himself filled her line of vision when her gaze, the traitorous thing, slid his way.

Finally, *finally,* the festivities drew to a close and Laney was able to make her escape. She jumped at the chance to leave the table to deliver the judge's decision to the emcee. The moment the envelope hit her palm, she bolted to her feet and nearly toppled the table. A strong hand on her arm steadied her, and left her breathless and shaken and wanting more. More of Dallas's strong warmth against her body, his hands sliding over her arms, her breasts, her…

Instead of finishing the thought, she retreated behind the stage. The next fifteen minutes passed in a blur as the winners were announced and a mob of well-wishers crowded backstage. Laney said her congratulations to the winners, then took refuge in the center of the mob, chatting with her father's friends and associates and doing her best to forget Dallas and the effect his nearness had had on her.

A half hour later, she slid off her shoes, sat down on the edge of the stage and stared out at the now-empty auditorium. The sound of fading voices drifted from the open doorway as the last of the pageant attendees headed to the cafeteria for punch and an assortment of cakes and pies—thanks to the ladies' auxiliary—and the chance to have their picture taken with the Cadillac High mascot.

Laney drew in a deep breath and frowned at the way her body still tingled from the three hours and fifteen minutes and thirty-six seconds sitting next to Dallas Jericho. She shouldn't be so affected. He was just a man.

*The* man.

The one who filled her past.

And her present, she realized when she glanced up to find him standing in the doorway, holding a piece of chocolate fudge marble cake and a glass of punch.

"I had to fight my way past Jim Mitchum and his eight kids for this," he said as he handed the punch and cake to her.

As the scent of chocolate filled her nostrils, her frustration peaked and she turned accusing eyes on him. "Why are you doing this to me?"

"Doing what, hot stuff?"

"You know what. You're being nice. *Nice,* when you don't even like me. You never liked me."

"Maybe this isn't about like. Maybe it's about finishing what we started. Aren't you tired of pretending?"

"I don't know what you're talking about."

"You know exactly what I'm talking about." He walked the few feet toward the sound booth. "You feel the pull. I know you do." He touched a button and one of the lights that surrounded them flicked off. "In your breasts." Another click and the room grew dimmer. "Between your legs."

"Don't." The word slid past her lips when he reached for the last button. She sat the cake plate and the punch aside and got to her feet. "Don't do this to me."

"I'm not going to do anything right now, darlin'." He clicked the last button and they were suddenly plunged into darkness. For several frantic heartbeats, she couldn't see anything. She could only feel. Her heart pounding. Her blood rushing. Her nipples tingling. "You are." A final click and the auditorium plunged into complete darkness save for the fiery red glow of a distant Exit sign.

She squinted and tried to adjust her eyes, but the blackness was too consuming. She could only hear his deep, even breaths and the raw, seductive rumble of his voice.

"Tell me what you feel, Laney," he murmured.

Laney wasn't sure what happened to her in those next few moments. Maybe it was the darkness that lent a surreal quality to the situation and made it seem more fantasy than reality. Maybe it was the fact that she'd longed for this moment so many times, for the chance to finish what they'd started that night so long ago. Maybe all the sugar she'd consumed in the past week trying to satisfy her craving for Dallas had finally started to rot her brain. Maybe all three.

She didn't know. She only knew that something broke inside her and suddenly she felt free. Uninhibited. *Hot.*

"Tell me," he appealed again.

And she did.

"M-my hands are shaking. My lips are tingling. My pulse is pounding."

"What else, Laney? What else do you feel?"

"My nipples..." She licked her lips and searched for a word to describe the electricity skimming through her body, zeroing in on the erogenous zones. "Hard," she finally murmured. "They're hard and tight and every time I breathe they rub against the lace of my bra and they get harder. They—'' she licked her lips again ''—they tingle.''

''What else?'' he pressed, as if he already knew what she felt. As if he felt it, too.

''I'm hot,'' she whispered. Her chest heaved as she tried for a deep, steadying breath. Her nipples rasped against her bra and electricity spiraled from the twin points, winding through her body in search of a more crucial area. ''Between my legs,'' she managed to say as the sensation grew stronger. ''I'm hot and...and wet.''

She heard his sharp intake of breath and her heart pounded. She expected to feel him at any moment, his strong hands on her, stroking up her arms, stirring her the way they had at the carnival.

''Now show me.'' The flick of a switch punctuated his command and the flood of a spotlight surrounded her. ''Show me how you feel.''

For a fraction of a second, she thought she saw the slight movement of his silhouette just beyond the bright light. The realization that he was there, waiting and watching, sent another zing of excitement through her already flushed body.

She licked her lips before touching a fingertip to her bottom lip. Flesh quivered against flesh as she traced her mouth before sliding the fingertip down her chin, her throat. Her touch paused at the frantic pounding of her pulse before moving on, *down.*

She slid a finger beneath the edge of her blouse, tracing the path where soft flesh met lace before moving to the first button. It slid free, then the next and the next, until finally her blouse parted. Cool air whispered over the exposed skin of her stomach. With a shrug of her shoulders, the silk slid over her shoulders, down her arms and puddled at her feet. Goose bumps followed, chasing up and down her bare flesh.

Her nipples pressed against the lace of her bra, eager to break free. She didn't oblige them. Not yet. Her fingertip circled a ripe, swollen crest that peeked through the lace and the air lodged in her lungs.

"Show me more, Laney."

With trembling fingers, she unhooked the front clasp of her bra. The cups parted and her breasts sprang free. She touched the undersides first, cupping the soft mounds, weighing them before anticipation got the best of her and she had to feel more. She skimmed her palms over her nipples and a shiver went through her. Heat skittered over her skin, chasing away the goose bumps and setting her ablaze.

*"More."* The one word, so raw and husky, urged her fingertips down. She slid her hand around her stomach, to the side zipper of her skirt. A loud *zzzzip!* and the teeth parted, the material sagged and the skirt slithered down her hips and pooled at her feet. She wore silk panty briefs, very tasteful and conservative, and for a split second, doubt crept into her passion-laden frame of mind. Her undies were a far cry from the red lingerie she'd purchased at the Wildchild party, or the purple thong Dallas had teased her with.

Then she heard his deep, guttural, *"Beautiful,"* and her hand seemed to move of its own accord. She trailed her fingertips over the satin of her panties. Her eyes closed as sensation rippled through her. In her mind's eye, it wasn't her own touch she felt, but Dallas's.

His hands stroking her through the fabric, his touch teasing the edge of elastic, his fingertips pushing inside to glide along the damp, swollen flesh between her legs, his finger sliding deep, deep inside the drenched flesh.

Her breath caught and she gasped at the incredible pressure that gripped her. Sweet. Intense. *Real.*

No matter how vivid the fantasy or how she'd touched herself in this exact same way many times before, it had never felt the way it did now as she stood bathed in the single spotlight with Dallas Jericho in front of her. *Watching.*

Another move of her fingers and her body swayed from the pleasure that rushed through her. She fought to keep her balance and her foot bumped something. Cold liquid seeped between her toes and her eyes fluttered open. She glanced down to see the foam cup lying on its side. Red punch stained the toe of her cream-colored shoe and a memory rushed at her.

She found herself remembering the punch creeping over the bodice of her white homecoming dress, the empty cup dangling from Dallas's hand.

"We can't do this." Trembling hands grappled for the forgotten skirt. "I can't do this." She yanked the material up and tugged at the zipper before reaching for her bra and blouse. "I won't." She'd just slid into her shirt when the overhead lights flicked on.

By the time she blinked and adjusted her eyes to the sudden change in brightness, he was gone.

Thank the Powers That Be.

She told herself that, but she didn't believe it.

She couldn't. She'd felt too alive a few moments ago and now she felt...

*Embarrassed. Ashamed. Mortified.*

That's what she should have felt, but the only emotion that closed around her and slithered inside was a fast-consuming loneliness.

*We're not done yet, you and I.*

His words echoed through her head, relentless as she gathered up her things and rushed outside to her car. As she slid behind the wheel, her heart still pounding and her body craving his touch, she couldn't help but remember that long-ago night.

It had been a grand party. Her family and friends had gathered to wish her well. She'd been headed off to college, her father's alma mater, and as exciting as the future had been, she'd been terrified, as well. She'd spent her childhood striving to fit in, to be the proper daughter and make her parents proud. And she'd succeeded.

But for how long?

The question had kept her tossing and turning into the night, until she'd finally given up trying to sleep. She'd crawled out of bed, slipped on her clothes and went for a walk.

And cried.

She'd been so overwhelmed by the future and

what waited for her. That's when she'd seen Dallas. He'd cruised by in his old Mustang and pulled alongside her.

Had she not been so upset, she could have turned up her nose and told him to take a hike. Instead, she'd crawled into his car.

They'd driven down to the river. He'd made her smile and forget all about her fear. And then he'd kissed her.

One thing had led to another and soon they'd been making out fast and furious, the lake glimmering in the far distance. When he'd tugged her panties down, she'd been so close to surrendering.

But her fear had stopped her, just as it had tonight, and she'd gone on to spend the next ten years thinking about him. Fantasizing. Wanting.

She didn't intend to put herself through another ten years of agony. The heat burned so fiercely between them because the fuse had been lit that night so long ago, and there was only one way to find relief. She had to let the fire run its course and burn itself out.

The sooner the better.

HE WAS THE DUMBEST MAN that ever lived.

Dallas came to that conclusion as he pulled into

his driveway a half hour after walking out on Laney Merriweather.

She'd wanted him. He'd seen the desire shining bright in her eyes. He'd heard the raw huskiness of her voice. He'd even smelled the heat coming off her. But more than anything, he'd felt her want, her *need* when she'd looked at him for that split second when he'd flicked on the spotlight and their eyes had met.

She'd wanted him, all right. But she didn't *want* to want him. While she'd let her defenses down for a few moments tonight, she was still fighting the attraction between them and battling the lust that burned in her soul.

It didn't matter. He could have taken her anyway. As turned on as she'd been, all he'd had to do was reach out. She would have melted in his arms at the first touch, powerless to resist the pull between them. It was too strong. Too overwhelming. Too damned intense.

The trouble was, he wanted her to want him. He wanted her to admit it. To him, and to herself.

And so he'd walked away.

He climbed from the truck cab. A twinge of pain pulsed from his still rock-hard erection and he damned himself a thousand times. What did it matter if she admitted it so long as they finished what they'd started? One wild night and he could work her out of his system once and for all. That's the way it had been with every other woman in his past.

The way it would have been with this woman if he'd done everything he'd been aching to do to her. If he'd kissed her lips and licked a path down her neck. If he'd sucked those incredible nipples into his mouth, first one then the other. If he'd slid her delicate fingers into his mouth and tasted her essence.

He punched in the security code and let himself into the dark, empty house. Christ, he was a jackass. She'd been right there. Ready and waiting and wet, for heaven's sake! She'd *wanted* him, physically anyway. That should have been enough.

Not this time. He wanted more.

While he admitted that much to himself, he wasn't yet prepared to think about why it mattered so much.

Instead he did his damnedest to force the image of her, naked and trembling and bathed in bright light, from his head as he stretched out on the sofa and loosened the button on his jeans.

His fingers grazed his throbbing length and want pulsed through him. He closed his eyes and tried to think of the Dixon House and the current tile color. Hopeless.

He tried to concentrate on the announcer's voice blaring from the TV. Instead he heard Laney. Her sexy voice. Her short, frantic breaths. Her shameless moan.

He'd wanted to touch her so badly, to pull her hand away from between her legs and replace it with his own, to feel her dripping over his finger, sucking it inside.

He'd wanted her to touch him, to slide open his fly and free his throbbing length, to stroke him from root to tip and back down again.

He mimicked the motion and as he pictured her in his mind's eye, he was no longer alone. Lonely. She was there with him, over him, her hands reaching for him.

She touched him, slow and easy at first before she grew more insistent, working him into a frenzy. His heart pounded. His ears rang.

His entire body ached for a release that wouldn't come. Not now. Not like this.

Not without her.

He opened his eyes to the dimly lit living room and realized after a few frantic breaths that the ring-ing wasn't just the blood pulsing to his brain. The doorbell sounded again, followed by a soft knock.

He drew in a shaky breath and climbed to his feet. No doubt Eula had decided not to risk the alarm. A swift tug and he managed to fasten his jeans enough for modesty's sake.

"For the last time, I didn't change the code—" His words stumbled to a halt as he pulled open the front door and found himself staring at Laney Merriweather.

Her face was flushed, her clothes rumpled. Her hair spilled down around her shoulders, her makeup faded from the sweat dotting her forehead.

"What are you doing here?" he asked.

"Isn't that obvious?"

His heart jumped at her words because he knew by the look on her face exactly what she wanted. He knew, but he wanted more. "Say it."

"We should..." She swallowed. "That is, I think..." She swallowed again. "I want this."

"Say it."

She looked ready to turn and run before she seemed to gather her courage. She straightened her shoulders, looked him square in the eyes and said the words Dallas Jericho had been praying to hear for most of his life. "I want you."

# CHAPTER FIVE

"I WANT YOU," LANEY SAID again, surprised at how easy the truth came despite a lifetime of denial.

She'd been terrified a few moments ago, *this* close to changing her mind. But then he'd hauled open the door wearing nothing but jeans. He'd looked so sexy, so hot that her fear had faded in the sudden longing that filled her. "You're sure you want this?"

"Just so long as we're both clear on what *this* actually is. I don't want either of us having any unrealistic expectations. I'm not looking for a boyfriend or a husband or a happily ever after." The only thing Laney expected from Dallas was a night of unforgettable passion. A night straight out of her most erotic fantasies. An ending to the story they'd started when she'd climbed into his Mustang that night and let him whisk her up to Cadillac Bluff for the most thrilling make-out session of her young life. "And I don't suspect you're looking for a wife, which is why this is perfect for both of us."

"This, as in?"

"Sex." She tried to sound as professional as possible, but her voice was breathless and husky and totally unprofessional, unless the profession in question involved five-inch stilettos, a black mini-skirt and a street corner in the red-light district. "Sex," she stated again, the word louder and clearer this time. She watched as his eyes narrowed, as if the possibility angered him almost as much as it fed the desire burning in his gaze. "Pure, uncomplicated sex."

"*This* is talking, darlin'," he said as he reached for her. Their bodies met and she felt the hard proof of his desire for a heart-stopping moment before he kissed her. "This," he said when he finally came up for air, "is the pure, uncomplicated sex part."

"Oh," was all she managed to get out before he kissed her again, slower and deeper this time, as if he'd spent his aggression from a few moments ago with the first kiss. This kiss was purely for arousal's sake, and every nerve in her body sprang to awareness.

He trailed her bottom lip with the tip of his tongue before sucking it into his mouth and nibbling. The sensation, both pleasure and pain, sent waves of heat spiraling from her head to her toes, bursting at every major pleasure point in between. Her pulse jumped. Her nipples tingled. Her belly quivered. Her thighs trembled. Her knees wobbled.

Her mouth parted and his tongue plunged inside, stroking and teasing and making her gasp for air. He didn't so much as pause, instead deepening the kiss, drugging her with his taste. His smell. His touch.

His hands trailed down her back, cupping her bare buttocks through the thin fabric of her skirt. When he realized she wasn't wearing any underclothes, he groaned. The sound, so raw and husky and male, vibrated into her mouth and made her heart pound even harder.

His fingers caught the hem of her skirt, bunching the material until bare skin met bare skin and his hand slipped beneath.

"You're so soft," he murmured against her lips when he finally came up for air. "So soft and wet," he added when his fingertips slipped between her legs.

In the distance, a car sounded. Lights skittered through the darkness.

"Tell me what you want."

"You," she breathed.

"Now? Right here? Where anyone could see us?"

"Yes." She was beyond caring. She ached for him and suddenly nothing else mattered. "Please."

At her entreaty, he quickly obliged. He slipped a finger inside. A sweet pressure gripped her and chased away any lingering doubts. Her heart pounded faster, her vision blurred and she forgot all about the beam of headlights that drew closer, brighter.

She hooked a leg over his hip, opening her legs wider, giving him deeper access. He plunged a second finger into her and she moved her bottom, increasing the sensation. The pressure heightened until she couldn't bear it. Her lips parted and a strangled gasp broke from her lips as the world exploded.

She arched, clutching at his shoulders, digging her nails into the hard muscle as wave upon wave of luscious ecstasy washed over her. She would have melted into a puddle if Dallas hadn't been there in front of her, surrounding her, *inside* her.

Her eyelids fluttered open and she found him staring down at her with an intense expression. Laney simply stood there, staring into his eyes, doing her best to understand what had just happened.

An orgasm. But not just any orgasm. This had been different. More exciting. More intense. More consuming. *Different.*

A zigzag of headlights cut through the dark night as another car turned onto the street. The sight jarred her from her crazy train of thought. She became acutely aware of her compromising position—her back pressed to the wall, her skirt up around her waist, his hard thigh bracing her legs apart—and the fact that Dallas's hand was still wedged between her legs, one finger still deep, deep inside.

A wave of embarrassment swept over her, quickly subsiding when Dallas picked her up into his arms, turned and carried her inside the house. The door slammed shut and his long legs made quick work of the darkly paneled hallway.

A few heartbeats later, Laney found herself in a large room dominated by a huge, four-poster bed. Oversize navy pillows and a matching goose-down comforter draped the mattress encased in blue-and-white pin-stripe sheets. Keys sat on the dresser along with a handful of change. A copy of *Field and Stream* magazine lay unopened on the nightstand. A pair of Wranglers was draped around one bedpost. It smelled of leather and sawdust and *him* and her nostrils flared, drinking in the scent the way her eyes drank in the sight.

"This is a big room."

"I like my space."

"That, or you're planning on a big family someday."

He shrugged. "Someday."

"Someday soon?" It wasn't that she cared if he had a significant other. She just wanted to make sure she wasn't about to do anything that would hurt someone else.

As if he read the thoughts racing through her head, he shook his head. "There's no one in my life right now." A grin creased his handsome face. "Just you." He pulled her to her feet slowly, sliding her down the hard length of his body, letting her feel every ripple of muscle, including the hard bulge stretching his jeans tight.

He sank down to the edge of the bed and fingered her blouse. "Take this off."

She shook her head. "It's my turn now." She pulled him to his feet and touched the open edge of his jeans before seating herself on the bed. "I want to know what you're feeling. Tell me."

He didn't say anything for a long moment, but then his lips parted and he murmured the one word that fed her desire even more than the sight of him. "Hot."

"Show me."

"But this is your fantasy."

Something about the statement bothered her, but then he reached for the partially undone zipper and her heart all but stopped beating.

The teeth parted with a slow, nerve-racking *zzzzzzip*. He watched her from beneath lowered lids as he shoved his jeans and briefs down and stood before her naked and beautiful and fully aroused.

While Laney didn't consider herself an expert when it came to naked men—she'd only slept with two and taken a quick peek at a *Playgirl* Eden had smuggled into the girls' locker room back in high school—she knew without a doubt that Dallas was a perfect specimen. He was all male. Tall, powerful, masculine. Dark hair dusted his long, muscular legs. The same silky down surrounded his flat brown nipples and sprinkled his powerful chest. A fine line of hair funneled down his rippled abdomen. Wisps of dark silk surrounded a large, thick erection that jutted toward her as if begging for her touch.

She had to oblige. He'd sent her over the top and

she wanted to do the same for him. She wanted to touch him.

Laney dropped to her knees in front of him. She cupped and caressed, stroked and stirred, with her hands, her mouth, her tongue.

"Stop," he groaned after several moments. He pulled her to her feet and crushed her against his chest.

"I want inside you," he murmured into her ear. "I need inside you. Now. Right *now.*"

His rhythm on the porch had been slow and controlled and Laney gasped at the sudden frantic change.

She liked it. She liked seeing the desperation in his hot, glittering eyes, hearing it in the raw huskiness of his voice, feeling it in his touch as he urged her down onto the bed. Reaching into the bedside table, he pulled out a condom, which he donned in record time before covering her with the length of his body. He was eager and out of control, as if he'd dreamed of this moment just the way she'd been fantasizing about him all these years.

As if.

Dallas was a passionate man because he'd had plenty of experience. He'd undoubtedly done this many times before with many different women.

There was nothing special about this moment. She could have been any woman.

Laney told herself that, she just couldn't make herself believe it. Not when he stared deep into her eyes and she saw the fierce longing that glittered in the fiery green depths.

With one swift thrust, he buried himself deep and she forgot everything save the intense pleasure that rolled over her and turned her inside out.

She wrapped her legs around his waist and rose to meet him as he thrust into her again. Deeper. Harder. She moved with him, slowly at first. The pressure built and he plunged faster, harder, until she couldn't stand it anymore. Her climax hit her like a giant wave, crashing over her, consuming her and sucking the oxygen from her body for a long, heart-stopping moment.

Dallas quickly followed. He plunged into her one final time. His muscles tightened, his body went taut and a deep groan rumbled from his chest.

Any woman, she told herself as he gathered her in his arms, their hearts hammering in perfect sync. *Any* woman.

She almost believed it, too. But then he touched his lips to her forehead in a gentle, warm kiss and whispered, "You're everything I've ever dreamed,'' and she knew without a doubt that what had just happened between them had gone beyond unfinished business.

The truth should have sent a burst of dread through her. Instead it filled her with pure, unadulterated happiness. Proof beyond a doubt that Laney Merriweather had just made the biggest mistake of her life.

She'd not only slept with Dallas Jericho. She'd fallen in love with him.

DALLAS STARED DOWN at Laney and watched the soft flare of her nostrils, the steady rise and fall of her beautiful breasts. Finally, after all these years, he knew. He'd spent so many sleepless nights wondering what it would have felt like to go all the way with her that night, to plunge inside her and fill her up. To possess her.

But he was the one possessed. He'd had her, yet he wanted more. He didn't just want inside her body. He wanted inside her head. Inside her heart.

And she wanted one night, or so he thought until she scrambled across the bed and threw her legs over the side.

''Where are you going?''

''It's late. I—I really have to go.''

"It's early, hot stuff, and the only thing that you have to do is crawl back over here—"

The loud blare of an alarm system cut off the rest of his words. Laney snatched up her clothes and started jerking them on while Dallas let out a heated curse and reached for his jeans.

"It's just me." A woman's voice carried down the hall, along with the steady tap of shoes.

"Hold on," Dallas called out. "I'll be right there."

"I'm really sorry." The voice moved closer. "I swear, you need to stop changing that code on me. How in the world is an old woman supposed to keep track of such things if you're always fiddling with—oh, my."

Laney clutched the edges of her blouse together just as Eula Christian appeared in the doorway.

The woman took one look at Laney and her face flushed a bright scarlet.

"I'm sorry... I didn't... That is... I had no idea you were entertaining. I mean, Dallas never... I'll just close this door behind me."

"I don't usually have women over," he said as he turned back to her. "You're the first. That's why Eula's so freaked out."

The first.

*And the last.* The thought rushed through her head and she forced it back out. She wasn't the last. She didn't want to be the last. She simply wanted out before she gave in to the urge to crawl back under the covers and stay there forever.

"I really have to go."

"Just wait." The loud ring of his cell phone punctuated his words. "We have to talk."

"There's nothing to talk about. This is over."

"It's just starting—" The cell phone rang again and he cursed as he snatched it up. "Just wait," he told her again. "Jericho," he barked as he punched the talk button."

"I can't." She started for the door, but he caught her arm, his fingers tight but not painful.

"We're going to talk." He shook his head as he shifted his attention to the phone call. "Not us," he said into the phone. "We've already talked and I can tell you that the citrus tile is this close to being installed. One more room and—" His words ground to a halt. His expression hardened and she knew who was on the phone even before he said the name. "Black cherry jubilee? But we're nearly finished, Mr. Dixon. My men are laying the last of it as we speak." He listened, his expression growing blacker by the moment. "No, I'm not saying that I won't do it. I'm just saying that it's not practical.'' Another heart-pounding moment of silence. ''I'm not saying that you're being impractical,'' he ground out. ''It's just a little late and we've changed colors four times already.'' Another moment of tense silence and he nodded. ''Fine. I'll stop the citrus and we'll order the black cherry. Give me the catalog number?'' He fished in his pocket and extracted a tattered square of paper. He unfolded the sheet, rummaged in the nightstand drawer for a pen and started to scribble. ''Got it. No, no,'' he growled, looking anything but pleased. ''It's no trouble. You're the customer.''

He punched the off button and tossed the paper onto the bed with a heated curse. Then he turned his full attention on her. ''We're going to talk. I want to know...''

His words faded as Laney's attention hooked on the paper. A *familiar* sheet of paper. She recognized the color, the monogram, the handwriting. Her own handwriting.

Her gaze shifted to his as she reached for the sheet of stationery. ''Where did you get this?''

''At Eden's bar. I needed something to write on and it was lying in an ashtray.'' He stared at her for a long moment. ''You're mad, aren't you?''

But that was the kicker. She wasn't mad. She was in love. *Love*.

She tossed the paper to the bed. "I have to get out of here." Away from him, from his scent, his touch and the penetrating light of his eyes.

He knew her deepest fantasies and if she stayed a moment more, he would know the truth. *Love*.

"You're not going anywhere."

"Yes, I am." She pulled her arm free of his grip and started for the door.

"When are you going to stop worrying about what people think?"

"Look who's talking." She turned on him. "You're so worried about what everybody else thinks that you've eaten a huge chunk of cash all because Claude Dixon can't make up his mind. You're still eating it."

His jaw hardened and he frowned. "That's different. It's business."

"Is it?" She focused her attention on him rather than the sinking feeling in the pit of her stomach that told her she was making an even bigger mistake by walking away from Dallas. She loved him. That's all that should matter.

That's all that would have mattered if she hadn't been a Merriweather and he hadn't been a Jericho.

"You know what I think?" She focused on her anger, eager to ignore the truth beating inside her with every beat of her heart. "I think you've spent the past ten years busting your butt to change everyone's mind about you and you're worried about slipping up. I think you're afraid that if you tell Claude where to get off, he'll tell people that you really haven't changed."

"Are you crazy? I *have* changed. I'm not some irresponsible badass."

"True, but you never were one. Not deep, down inside. A badass wouldn't have brought apples to old lady Carmichael every afternoon, or help Mrs. Walters do her grocery shopping at the Piggly Wiggly on Saturday mornings while the rest of the kids were watching cartoons or playing Little League."

"That was penance for all the crazy crap I did."

"Hardly. Everything you did, everything you pretended to be was just a front for a kind and good and decent kid who wanted everybody to like him."

"I never gave a shit—"

"You can deny it all you want, but you *did* care. I saw it in your eyes when I turned you down for the dance. I hurt you, but you covered it up by playing the hateful bully. You don't do that anymore—cover up who you really are. You finally let everyone see the real you, and they respect that. They like it. They like you.''

''Some do. Some couldn't care less.'' He shook his head. ''I'm not really concerned with everyone else. It's you I'm interested in. You I've always been interested in, since the first moment you smiled at me with your mouth full of mayonnaise sandwich.''

The memory fought its way into her head, but she was determined to keep it out, and even more determined to keep the conversation on him. ''The town likes you. You've found your acceptance and you know it. And now you're afraid of losing it by pissing off Claude Dixon. You're bending over backward to please him.''

''Like you bend over backward to please your father?''

''I owe him. He never treated me like I was adopted. He loved me like his own. He always has, despite where I came from.''

''And so you go out of your way to make him forget the fact that you aren't his flesh and blood.''

That's exactly what she'd done all these years, but there was just something about hearing the words out loud that sent a wash of shame through her. ''You just don't get it.''

"Oh, I get it, all right. It's not your father you're so eager to prove anything to. It's yourself. You've tried so hard to be a Merriweather because *you'd* rather forget where you came from."

"That's not it."

"I know, baby," he continued, his voice softer when he caught sight of the tears swimming in her eyes. "I spent most of my life trying to forget who my father was. The thing is, it doesn't matter who he was or what he did or whether we had a lot of money or a lot to eat."

The words cut too close to home and Laney shook her head. She'd been fighting her past for too long to admit the truth now. "All that matters is who I am right now," he told her. "I'm the man who loves you. The man who's always loved you."

His confession sent a burst of joy through her unlike anything she'd ever felt before. She wanted to laugh, to cry, to throw herself into his arms and confess her own feelings.

*Love.*

The truth pushed and pulled inside her, stirring a wealth of emotion—everything from elation to dread to full-blown fear. Because Laney Merriweather wasn't supposed to love Dallas Jericho.

And he wasn't supposed to love her. She didn't want him to love her.

No matter how good it felt.

She gathered her control and focused on the anger simmering inside her because Dallas was letting Claude Dixon get the best of him. "Who you are is a man who's losing a ton of money because he won't stand up to an impractical customer." And then she did what she should have done the moment Dallas opened his door that evening.

She walked away.

"THIS ISN'T THE BLACK cherry jubilee." Claude Dixon, back early from his trip, stood in the foyer early Sunday morning and stared down at the tiled floor.

"No, it's the citrus." Laney had been right last night. He *was* afraid of what people thought about him, just as she was.

How in the world could he expect her to ignore what everyone else thought when he, himself, was so wrapped up in one person's opinion that he'd sacrificed his own valuable time and money, not to mention his self-respect?

He couldn't. He had to practice what he preached, starting now.

"But I ordered the black cherry jubilee."

"You ordered this first."

"But we don't want this. Didn't I make myself clear?"

"Crystal. You want the black cherry jubilee."

"Exactly. You'll just have to pull this up and redo it."

"I'd be happy to, but it'll cost you."

"What are you talking about? Your contract promises full customer satisfaction."

"My contract also states that any changes will add additional charges and time."

"You're going to charge me?"

Dallas nodded and suddenly the fear that had been knotting his gut eased. "The price of this tile, plus the new tile and the added labor charges." He handed over the written estimate. "Just say the word, and the black cherry jubilee is yours."

Claude took one look at the estimate, saw the additional cost that Dallas had already incurred three times over and swallowed. His expression eased as he glanced down at the citrus tile once again. "Actually, this looks really good."

Dallas grinned. "At Triple J Construction, we aim to please."

"I DON'T MEAN TO BUG YOU, but I was in the building, so I thought I'd stop by and see if you've filled the position yet." The voice greeted Laney bright and early Monday morning as she walked into her father's outer office.

Brigette Summers stood just inside the doorway, her long hair pulled back in a neat bun. She wore another faded dress, this one a washed-out pink with flowers. The tiny white flowers had faded and a small safety pin peeked up at the neckline where the top button was missing.

A memory rushed at Laney and for a split second, she saw a small six-year-old girl wearing a threadbare orange dress, the waistband held together by a large safety pin as she sat on the schoolhouse steps and munched on a piece of banana and half of a mayonnaise sandwich.

"I'm not trying to be a pest or anything, it's just that this position is perfect for me. I live just four blocks over and can be here on a moment's notice, or I can stay late. I'm very dedicated. And I brought another résumé—" she held up a sheet of paper "—in case you misplaced mine."

"I'm afraid I still haven't made a decision yet, but I'll be sure to call—" Her words faded as the inside office door opened and her father's booming voice floated through.

"And this is me with a forty-pound trout." Judge Marshall Merriweather walked into the outer office followed by two ancient looking men who stared over his shoulder at the stack of pictures in his hands. "Hello, dear." He gave her a bright smile.

"Good morning, Dad, Judge Cyrus and Judge Dandridge." She nodded at the two men who spared her quick nods before turning their excited gazes back to the pictures.

"You say all the fish are this size?"

"That and bigger."

"What about trout? Why, they can't all be this big."

"Bigger," her father assured both men. "Just take a look at the rest of these over your morning coffee." He divided the stack of pictures and handed them over to the two men who quickly said their goodbyes.

"Pencil Cyrus and Dandridge in for lunch today and cancel the brief for the MacIntyre case. I can read it later tonight on my own time." He must have noticed her raised eyebrows, because a sheepish expression crept over his face. "You were right. I do need to take it easy and I'm realizing that."

"May I ask what brought about the change of heart?"

He winked. "Baby girl, there's nothing more exciting than reeling in a twenty-pound pike. I'd forgotten that in the past few years, but this weekend reminded me. Oh," he added as he glanced down at his planner, "give me three hours for today's lunch. We're thinking about going over to the country club for a little golf afterward."

"Golf? You? On a Monday?"

He didn't answer. He simply grinned and reached for the résumé in Brigette's hand. "Very impressive, young lady," he said before handing it over to Laney. "You look like exactly what the doctor ordered. I'm sure my daughter is anxious to talk to you."

"Actually I've still got a few prospects I need to look at before I make a decision," Laney said as her father turned to walk back into his office. He didn't so much as spare Brigette a moment's scrutiny, as if her appearance didn't mean a thing to him.

It didn't.

The realization hit her as she stood there and stared at the neatly typed résumé in her hands. For the first time, she really looked at Brigette. Not at what she wore or the quality of her clothes, but at her qualifications.

Dallas had been right. Laney hadn't been fighting so hard to convince her father that she was worthy of his name. She'd been trying to convince herself, anxious to forget that poor little girl in the hand-me-down orange dress, to forget the desperation she'd felt day after day when she'd gone to school with nothing and come home to nothing, to forget the hunger that had gnawed at her stomach and the tears that had burned her eyes and the loneliness she'd felt because she'd never been like the other kids. She'd never had a home or a family. She'd never truly belonged.

Even after Judge Merriweather had adopted her, she'd felt different. She'd been different. Not as cultured or as educated or as refined as everyone around her. Laney had been determined to turn things around, to fit in this time, to *be* a Merriweather so that she didn't ever have to feel like an outsider again.

Her father didn't see her as such. He was a man of principle who saw people for who they were. That's why he'd adopted her in the first place. He'd seen a needy little girl, not her dress or her mussed hair or her scuffed shoes or her pitiful background.

"I know you aren't ready to make a decision yet, but I'd appreciate it if you would keep me in mind." Brigette's voice drew Laney's attention and she glanced up at the young woman.

"Actually," Laney said with a smile, "you *are* just what the doctor ordered. When can you start?"

HER MIGRAINE WAS completely gone.

Laney stood on the corner of Main Street and Biloxi in the heart of downtown Cadillac the following Saturday morning and stared at the endless stream of classic cars cruising by in the parade. There were all shapes and sizes, from a '59 Edsel to a vintage '69 Corvette dragster. Her gaze touched each one, searching for the familiar black Mustang. And amazingly, her head didn't hurt anymore—not when she focused her eyes or concentrated or even worried.

And she was worried.

A full week had gone by and Dallas hadn't tried to contact her even once. She'd seen him at Eden's bar and the Piggly Wiggly and last night's Car Cruise carnival, but he hadn't once approached her. Much less taunted or teased her. Or tried to seduce her.

His retreat came as no surprise. The night they'd

slept together, he'd put himself on the line and declared his feelings, and she'd rejected him. Again.

She closed her eyes and fought against a swell of dread. What if she was too late this time? Sure, his love for her had endured all these years. It had even grown stronger, despite her first rejection. But they'd been kids back then. She'd been immature.

This time, however...

She'd still been immature, still living her life with the same mentality she'd had while growing up. Dallas had not only brought her most erotic fantasies to life, but he'd given her the freedom she'd only dreamed of having. Being with him had made her realize that being different was okay. Yet at the same time, she felt a strange sense of belonging. He made her feel excited and happy and complete.

She belonged with him, and so she'd given up her job in Austin and applied for a prosecutor's position right here in town. No longer was she going to kill herself doing a job she didn't enjoy only to drive herself toward an early heart condition like her father. She didn't want to wait until she was fifty-five to be happy.

Laney wanted her happiness now. She wanted Dallas.

She only hoped that he still wanted her.

Crossing the street, she worked her way through the crowd. Dozens said hello and Laney returned their greeting, but otherwise, she kept her eyes trained on the passing cars. Waiting… Hoping… *There*.

She spotted him a few cars from the corner. Her heart pounded as the vehicles rolled by. The moment Dallas reached the corner, she drew in a deep breath, said a silent prayer and stepped toward the car.

"Can you spare a ride?" Without waiting for an answer, she pulled open the door and slid in next to him.

"What are you doing?"

"Sitting."

"I mean, what are you doing in here? In my car? With me?"

"I told you. I need a ride." She twisted in the seat until she was facing him. "I need you."

His foot still sat on the brake and a burst of horns erupted behind them, but Dallas didn't budge. His full attention remained fixed on her as a dozen emotions chased across his face. Hope and fear and disbelief.

"What?"

"I need you. You were right about me. I was scared of standing up for myself, of standing out, of not fitting in. I wanted so much to belong, but I never did. It didn't matter what clothes I wore or who I hung out with or how many country club friends I had, I still didn't fit in. I've never fit in. Until you. You're the first person who's ever made me feel a true sense of belonging. *You.*"

A clamor of horns filled the air, followed by several calls from the onlooking crowd.

"Is everything all right?"

"You folks having car trouble?"

"Engine stalled?"

The voices drew his gaze and he glanced around before his attention fixed on her again. "People are looking at us."

"I know." She worked at the top few buttons of her blouse while he watched her with a puzzled expression.

"What are you doing?"

"Showing you my underwear." She pulled the top edges of the blouse aside and let him glimpse the red Wildchild lingerie she'd purchased her first night back in town. "It's not purple, but I called Eden and asked if she could put in a rush for a purple thong and a matching bra. In the meantime, this—'' she slid another button free ''—will have to do.''

*"But people are looking at us."*

''That's the point.''

He caught her hands midway down. ''You're confusing the hell out of me, woman,'' he growled, as he started sliding the buttons back into place. ''What's all this about?''

''I'm not afraid to be myself. I *like* racy lingerie.''

''I'm glad.''

''And I like you. I…'' She searched for her courage. ''I don't want you to be just my very own private fantasy. I want you to be my reality. I want—'' Her voice broke then. *Please don't let me be too late. Please.*

His hands stalled on her top button as he stared at her for a long moment, his expression unreadable. A breathless moment passed and then he smiled, and all the love he'd professed for her shone in the dark green depths. ''Tell me, darlin'. Tell me what you really want.''

''You,'' she murmured. ''I don't just like you. I love you. And I'll go you one better.''

For the first time in her life, Laney Merriweather didn't worry about who was looking over her shoulder or what they might think of what she was about to do. She cared only about the man in front of her. The man who fulfilled all of her fantasies and then some. The man she wanted to spend the rest of her life with. Starting right now. "I'll show you." And then her lips touched his.

\* \* \* \* \*

*Now that Laney Merriweather is…well, occupied with her cowboy, what is poor Eden Halsey to do when she needs someone to talk to? Little does she guess that her gorgeous guy is set to take Cadillac—and Eden—by storm!*
*Don't miss Eden's erotic adventures in*

*THE PLEASURE PRINCIPLE,*

*a Harlequin Blaze novel,*
*available in Sept. 2001.*

# HARLEQUIN Presents

**The world's bestselling romance series...**
**The series that brings you your favorite authors,**
**month after month:**

Helen Bianchin...Emma Darcy
Lynne Graham...Penny Jordan
Miranda Lee...Sandra Marton
Anne Mather...Carole Mortimer
Susan Napier...Michelle Reid

**and many more uniquely talented authors!**

Wealthy, powerful, gorgeous men...
Women who have feelings just like your own...
The stories you love, set in exotic, glamorous locations...

## HARLEQUIN Presents

**Seduction and passion guaranteed!**

HPDIR1

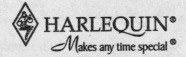

# Harlequin® Historical

From rugged lawmen and valiant knights to defiant heiresses and spirited frontierswomen, Harlequin Historicals will capture your imagination with their dramatic scope, passion and adventure.

Harlequin Historicals... they're too good to miss!

HHDIR1

# HARLEQUIN®
*Makes any time special* ®

**Upbeat, All-American Romances**

**Romantic Comedy**

**Historical, Romantic Adventure**

HARLEQUIN®
# INTRIGUE
**Romantic Suspense**

*Harlequin Romance* ®
**Capturing the World You Dream Of**

HARLEQUIN® *Presents*

Seduction and passion guaranteed

HARLEQUIN® *Super*ROMANCE®
**Emotional, Exciting, Unexpected**

HARLEQUIN® *Temptation*

**Sassy, Sexy, Seductive!**